The Souls of Quaking Pond

LLOYD GEORGE STULL

THE SOULS OF QUAKING POND.
Copyright © 2015   Lloyd George Stull

First Edition

Fulton Books, Inc.
Meadville, PA

First originally published by Fulton Books 2015

ISBN 978-1-63338-097-4 (paperback)
ISBN 978-1-63338-098-1 (digital)

1. Joe Miller family (Fictitious Characters)—Fiction.
2. U.S. History—Fiction.
3. Rural Indiana—Fiction.   I. Title.

Printed in the United States of America

To three cherished souls:
James, Wolfgang, and Barbara-Jean

Melanie;

Thanks for your Poems.

Contents

Quaking Pond Emerges

Westward Ho

The Ultimate Dodge

Fearful Choices

Manifest Secrets

Shake, Rattle, and Whoosh!

Perched on the eastern edge of Tornado Alley, Hoosiers are quite familiar with homes being buffeted by violent winds. Most, in fact, have personally experienced the devastating effects of a tornado touchdown. One central Indiana family discovers an unfamiliar shuddering can be as disastrous as monstrous wind.

Chapter 1

Miller Farm, resident home of Quaking Pond
Twenty miles southwest of Sugar Creek
Montgomery County, Indiana
April 18, 3:30 a.m., CST

The entire house shuddered as if a train had crashed into it, ripping Joe from his snoring. His wife, Kris, was already up on her feet, screaming, "Joe, the house is shaking...I think it's a tornado! Get the boys down to the basement."

As the floor swayed under his feet, Joe turned to Kris and soothed her. "Relax, hon. Can't be a tornado, there's no wind outside."

The china rattling in the dining room cabinet convinced Joe that something was happening. After clearing his head, he realized it was, of all things, an earthquake. He grabbed Kris, and together they raced toward the stairs where their sons were scrambling down two steps at a time, hollering "Mom" and "Dad" at the top of their lungs. Joe rushed the whole family through the front door, spilling them onto the porch. Trembling, it took the Millers a moment to realize the ground's shaking had stilled. All around them, the countryside echoed with the flapping and cawing of birds in flight.

Joe turned to his family and asked, "Everybody all right?" Three nervous heads bobbing in front of him answered that. Although frightened, his huddled family seemed fine. Sadie suddenly galloped around the front corner of the house. She leapt up on Joseph and Michael, nuzzling against them for assurance. Kris and her sons returned affectionate hugs with their beloved family golden retriever. The tense atmosphere of moments earlier relaxed. The Millers, like the birds, settled.

Eager to return to his bed, Joe did a hasty check of the outside of the house. He entered their home cautiously through the back-door, investigating the inside thoroughly. He found a few wall picture frames crashed on the floor and some knocked over stuff scattered in different rooms, overall nothing seriously damaged. Once satisfied there were no signs of weakness, he let the family go back in. They headed to the family room, switching on the TV news. The local station confirmed that the area had just had a magnitude 5.2 earthquake centered in southeastern Illinois, some two hundred miles away.

"Wow, if we felt that here, it must've really been shakin' down there," jabbered one of the boys.

While the rest of the family got something to nibble on, Joe left to check on the barn and animals. The cows were just calming down from a panicked run. Apparently, they had bolted at the beginning of the earthquake. Had it not been so early in the morning, the family might have noticed the cows acting strange before the tremor hit. Joe understood that animals seemed to be more sensitive than humans were to changes in nature. Whenever you saw the barnyard critters hike up their tails and run, you knew it was time to head for the hills yourself.

Joe made a quick check of the barn and gates. Relieved that no major damage had happened, he headed back to the house. Joe found his family having a yawn festival. Exhausted, the Millers made their way to bed.

The squawk of the alarm clock came entirely too soon, awakening the Millers barely in time to prepare for the school bus. Joe stood in the yard, waving to his sons as they boarded the school bus. With the kids off safely, he climbed on his John Deere ATV and sped off to check the farm grounds for quake damage. Earthquakes were not a common thing in these parts. In fact, he couldn't remember ever feeling a quake in Indiana.

Joe reckoned life went on in California and the rest of the West Coast with little attention paid to the earth having a little shake and rattle. It must be the same here in the Hoosier state. Kind of like an old bull scratching himself on a fence post then shaking afterward. Stirred up some dust, but didn't really hurt anything.

A quarter-mile south of the house, Joe coasted to a stop. He sat, straddling his ATV, carefully scanning the face of their old earthen dam. The farm pond had been around a long, long time. He sure hoped the dam hadn't sustained any damage. They didn't need the expense of repairing that during planting season.

Sitting there, Joe watched a big waterfall, swollen from recent spring rains, belch out of the pond spillway. After a moment, Joe continued on his quest, following the swift runoff to where it emptied into Offield Creek. Joe throttled back his ride as he neared the creek crossing. The concrete-slab bridge was swallowed by about four inches of rushing water. It looked like he was going to get a little wet this morning. He gunned the engine and splashed through the gushing water, shooting a four-foot rooster tail of water in his wake. Clearing the creek with just some soaked pant legs, he continued on. Kris would skin him alive, if she knew what he was doing. She was certain he was going to break his neck executing one of his ATV shenanigans.

His search of the property showed all the fences in good condition. The entire farm seemed to have survived the quake without damage. On his way back to the house, he kicked up another big rooster tail splash over the creek bridge. Perhaps, later this weekend, he would bring the boys out with him. Together, they would have some big fun racing across the bridge.

After lunch, Joe hitched a disc up to his Ford tractor, commencing the initial tilling of Kris's garden. A short time later, he made a final sweeping turn. He idled down the tractor and sat for a moment, appreciating his smooth even furrow marks covering the half-acre plot. Throughout the summer, Kris would proudly work the garden plot into a vegetable banquet. The sun was creeping slowly to the west, another fine spring day in April.

The pond's dam suddenly exploded in an impressive *whoosh!* "Well, I'll be damned!" Joe muttered. Perched atop his old Ford tractor, he stared at the massive tidal wave pouring out in all directions, launched through a narrow twelve-foot gap blown in the dam's middle. Had he not been gazing out over the pasture, he wouldn't have believed that much water could gush so quickly through such a narrow space. Joe leapt off his tractor, bolted to the house, and crashed through the backdoor, yelling for Kris to come quickly. Kris raced out the door, slamming it behind her with a loud clap. Joe grabbed her hand, towing her in his wake. Together, they raced up the small rise that overlooked the remains of their pond.

Kris could not believe her eyes. A slurry of raging water cascaded down the sloped valley west of the pond, uprooting small trees in its path. The water was so deep and moving so fast, she could not see the fence west of the pond. Uprooted debris rode the churning wall of muddy water, fanning out in an ever-widening spread across their recently planted cornfield downstream. Her heart sank, viewing the devastation the torrent was unleashing on all of her husband's hard work. The field would have to be completely resown, that is, after all the debris was hauled away. The whole endeavor would add a lot to the never-ending bills looming over them.

Kris gazed at the rapidly draining pond. What would they use to water the cattle this summer? Even more perplexing, how on earth could they afford to fix this mess? In a moment of sheer anguish, she burst into tears, wiping her eyes on the apron she still had tied around her waist. Joe encircled her shoulders with his strong arms, drawing her snuggly against his side. Huddled together, they stood motionless as the disaster churned by.

Joe turned to Kris and then bumped his hip gently against hers. "Shake, rattle, and whoosh, baby! We've had a helluva earthquake in Indiana." He chuckled. There was little that could be done until the pond emptied. Joe and Kris let their thoughts wander as they watched the water drain from the pond. They snapped back to their surroundings when they heard the noisy chatter of their boys, home from school, clambering off the school bus.

Turning their backs to the pond disaster, they strode arm in arm back toward the boys with Kris drying her tears on Joe's sleeve. The boys focused their attention on their mom's reddened eyes. Why was Mom crying? Joe and Kris pulled the boys into a huge hug, explaining about the pond eruption. Together, the Miller family walked back up the rise to survey the damage.

The boys' eyes bugged out at the brown raging river pouring out from the gaping hole in the pond's earthen dam. Water logged sludge tumbled from both sides of the broken dam. Huge chunks of earth from the dam's foundation were immediately engulfed in the swirling waters. The family watched in stunned silence, occasionally pointing out devastation caused by the massive flow of water and debris. As dusk darkened their view, the Millers headed in for supper. The disaster was best left till morning.

Early the next morning, the boys came crashing in through the back screen, slamming it as usual. Kris only put up a half-hearted complaint; it was obvious her concerns with the longevity of the door were completely ignored. Huffing from their race back to the house, the boys described an old mud covered sports car revealed by the pond's emptied water level. Kris encouraged the boys and their father to go investigate so she could peacefully finish preparing breakfast.

As the trio of excited Miller males crested the pasture rise, they were greeted by a nearly empty basin. The dam's center had finally sluiced out, leaving a wide-open passage for the remaining water to escape. Just as the boys had said, resting about twelve feet below the original south shoreline of the pond, sat an algae and mud covered Chevy Corvair.

The newly revealed cliff sides of the former pond space were slick with drying algae, giving it a mottled green-and-dark-brown appearance in contrast to the bright-green grasses ringing the pond's perimeter. Above all, it smelled. Whew! A rotted vegetation stench so strong, it left a repulsive taste in one's mouth. Years of decay had festered in the stagnant waters of the pond. It seemed they were all fighting to escape in one outrageous whiff. Flies buzzed everywhere, having a field day, skimming over all the enticing delights.

Joe's gaze drifted westward where fence posts had been sheared off. The woven cattle fencing was stretched to impossible lengths, mostly buried under several inches of reeking mud. The entire fence line would need to be cut out and patched in with a new fence, requiring several days' worth of work. Worse than the fence damage, though, was the field itself. Frustrated, Joe surveyed the swath of dirt and debris strewn across his recently planted cornfield. Cleaning it up was a hassle he didn't relish. The last thing to catch Joe's attention was of the completely washed out and busted up concrete-slab bridge to the backfields. He would have to rebuild it from scratch.

Joe's temples throbbed just thinking about all the extra work facing him right at planting time. Adding to his headache, the boys, still in school, would have limited time to help him. Joe insisted that his boys—Mike, seven, and Joseph, fourteen—study for good grades. His sons were going to have the grades that would afford them choices in whatever they wished to pursue.

No use crying over spilt water. It sure wasn't gonna clean itself up. Fixing the pond would have to wait till later in the year. For now, Joe would put up an electric fence to keep the cows out of the pond until he determined how safe the muddy pond scum was for the cattle or anyone else to be sloshing through. More importantly right now, he needed to get downwind from the stench blowing off the remains of the pond.

"Come on, boys, let's go back and figure out a plan for attacking this mess with your mother," he called to his sons.

The Miller's weekend morning breakfast was filled with lively chatter. Everyone randomly shouted out damage repair ideas. The family wrestled over the logistics of each solution. Naturally, the boys wanted to explore the emptied pond crater. Their dad swiftly nipped that in the bud in favor of more pressing work. In addition, there was the serious threat of dangerous stuff lurking in the murky afterbirth of the pond.

In the midst of the discussions, Mikey Miller shouted out, "We can call it the ol' quaking pond, Dad!"

"Hmm, that's not a bad idea, lil' chompers." Joe smiled, patting his youngest son on the head…neither of them knowing how accurately they had christened the pond. They were clueless that the recently vacated pond on their farm was not only ruined by the recent quake but had, in fact, been formed by a much larger quake decades earlier. In every sense of the name, it was a quaking pond.

Several weeks passed of extremely hard work, resulting in a replanted field, mended fences, and a sturdy new bridge crossing to the backfields. One of the worst projects had been picking up all the fish washed out with the pond water. The rotting fish stank horribly. In the days following the dam burst, they were a top priority on the cleanup list.

All that remained, now, was mending the empty pond crater. Keeping the boys safe from its lure had been a constant challenge for Joe. He had had to bark at the boys every time he caught them sneaking the pond floor in their tireless effort to reach muck covered things. In the end, the threat of a serious beating convinced the boys that their attentions were better spent on helping with the springtime planting chores. Despite the boys' resolve that they would never see the moment come, the day finally arrived when exploration of the pond remains was allowed.

* * *

May 30, 8:12 a.m., CST

Joe and the boys stood at the center of the ruined dam's opening. Dressed in mud boots and protective rubber-coated gloves, the trio advanced cautiously toward the mottled, uneven series of dried hillocks left in the drained pond's floor. A musky odor hovered over the entire area. A light breeze made the smell tolerable. The trio looked like space explorers standing at the portal to a muck covered alien surface.

They were all three eager to discovery what each of the protruding objects were. Joe turned to his sons and repeated the warnings he had instructed them earlier. "Walk very slowly over this ground. There could be hidden holes that might snap a bone, if you fall into one. Use your walking stick to keep stable and don't get too far away from me. Whatever you do, do not touch anything without your gloves on. The stuff left in this pond has been rotting down here for years. No telling, what germs and diseases it contains. It took me forever to get your mom convinced to let you walk around in here with me. She finds out you touched anything with your hands and we'll all three be skinned alive. You got it?"

Both of his sons nodded their agreement while fidgeting anxiously, more than ready to begin their adventure. Joe looked his sons in their eyes and issued one last warning. "There may be some old bones or carcasses of dead animals in here. Animals often wander into a pond and drown. Don't get freaked out, just call me over to take a look. And again, do not touch anything with your bare hands." Forewarned, Joe and his boys carefully stepped over the threshold of the drained pond. Their adventure leading them to the discovery of debris filled with history and mystery they would never fully grasp.

Harvesting Deeds

Be not deceived; God is not mocked: for whatsoever a man soweth, that shall he also reap.

—Gal. 6:7, KJV

Chapter 2

Miller Farm, resident home of Quaking Pond
Twenty miles southwest of Sugar Creek
Montgomery County, Indiana
May 30, 8:25 a.m., CST

Joseph, Joe's oldest son, quickly darted across the south side of the pond focused on an odd-shaped piece of metal sticking up from the mud. His feet pounded over the slick ground with the abandoned agility of teenage youth. That was, until he slipped on the edge of an unstable lump of aged mud and came crashing down on his chin. Joseph rose, covered in mud splashed across his front like the stains of a base stealing dive on a rain-soaked field. Mikey and his father clutched their sides in laughter at the slop-covered explorer.

"I told you to be cautious, didn't I? See what happens, Mr. Hotshot," Joe called to his son.

Ego deflated, Joseph continued forward more reasonably. As he clambered up the embankment, he slipped a couple more times before reaching the glistening object. Without hesitation, he reached out and grasped the object supported by a weathered stick. It curved inside his clutched hand as if it was made to fit perfectly. Joseph yanked what appeared to be a cane upward with a slight tug. It released with a soft snapping sound. Joseph held his prize aloft, swinging it about by its curved metal end like a sword. The rotted burlwood shaft crumbled into splintered shreds. Joseph was left holding a curved metal object in his uplifted hand.

As he whirled around, his dad arrived, asking, "What have you found, Joseph?"

Joseph held out his prize. "I have no idea, Dad."

Joe took the object from Joseph's outstretched hand. After turning it slowly in all directions, Joe looked up, beaming at his son. "Looks like you found the first treasure, my boy."

Joe explained that his son's discovery was an old walking stick grip. "This one is a beauty!" exclaimed Joe.

He motioned his sons to lean in closely to look at the object nestled in his palm. "See how the curved end comes to a gentle point like the nose of a dog?" Joe encouraged the attention of his sons. "This was the grip of a very expensive cane, made in the shape of a greyhound racing dog. Look here, you can see how its legs look like they are running across the handle. Here, at the back end, is a tiny wisp of a tail." Joe pointed at the delicate detail. The boys' eyes were glued to their dad's palm. They gently reached out and traced the lines of the tarnished old treasure. "We clean this up, and we'll find this is made of brass. It's green and black from aging down in this old pond," Joe continued. He and the boys speculated on how something this elaborate ended up on their farm. The connection between their rural farm pond and a notorious local bootlegger of the twenties was far from their suppositions.

Chapter 3

Rural West-Central Indiana
1926

Johnny and Maggie Magasono were in the midst of a much-too-fre-quent argument about Johnny letting people walk all over him.

Maggie shouted, "You need to show you've got a pair of brass balls and stand up to folks!"

Johnny explained, "It isn't in my nature to be nasty to people. My mother always taught me, 'Be good to others, and good will come back to you.'"

"Yeah, well there are a lot of other things your sainted mother taught you, which you've never paid any attention to. Why do you think you can hide behind this one? You gotta make those Thompson brothers pay up front, or you're never gonna see your money!" groused Maggie.

"They have always paid. And I know they will pay this time, too!" countered Johnny with an air of confidence.

"Awh, there is just no reasoning with you, you old git," resounded Maggie, harrumphing in disgust.

"The same could be said of you too, my dear." Johnny slyly hoped that hurricane Maggie was about out of steam.

"Whoever heard of a goodie-two-shoes bootlegger, anyway?" Maggie threw out with a flourished stance of her hands on her hips, her chin defiantly pointed at her husband.

"Darlin', just because I disagree with the government's choice to keep liquor restricted from everyone, doesn't mean I have to be a cantankerous person." Johnny soothed, hoping, yet again, that the silly battle was about out of grit.

"Yeah, well there is a whole nation of folks out there who would disagree with you on that! Seriously, Johnny, you need to toughen up and start telling people no. Just like when Jimmy had you show up at the train station in Whitesville, then plopped two stiffs on you to handle. You schlepped them off to that damn pond and dumped 'em in. Instead of telling him, you didn't want to get involved." Maggie continued in an effort to drive her point home.

"You know I owe Jimmy," replied Johnny. "He's the one who helped get us set up down here. We wouldn't have nuthin', and we'd still be dodgin' bullets from the coppers and Bugs Moran's thugs if we hadn't moved down here."

"True, but that doesn't mean we have to be Chicago's long distance morgue," Maggie conceded. One last barb just had to be flung. "You realize, if we get caught, we're the ones that'll take the heat for the deaths."

Exasperated, Johnny patiently responded, "Yes, yes, I know that. I don't think we'll hear from Jimmy again, anyway. He ran off to Sicily, after his brother Tony got wacked by Moran's boys."

"Oh, no? He has already dumped bodies on us, twice. I emphasize, bodies. You gotta say no to him, Johnny! I ain't goin' to jail, not for some two-bit loser from the South Side who can't control his trigger finger. You know as well as I do, he and his sleazy brothers will come sneakin' back to Chicago. They'll start up shooting rivals again, for revenge, if nothin' else." In one lengthy spew, Maggie blew out the last of her pent up spume.

Johnny shook his head and quipped, "I will tell him, no way in hell, if, he shows up again. He knows where the pond is now. He can dump 'em, himself."

"Yeah, like he could find his own arse, if it wasn't attached to his backside." Maggie chortled. "He shows up down here, and he'll be looking you up to help him find the damn pond. Next thing you know, he'll just dump the body on you and skedaddle. Then, Mr. Nice Guy will be handling another dead body, risking our necks for nothin'," Maggie continued to rage.

"Let's talk about this another time, darlin'. I'm trying to map out some new routes. The Feds have been sniffing around lately. I think they may be zeroing in on some of our drop points. I sure as hell don't want to get caught with a trunk full of hooch." Johnny coerced.

"I hear you. I will lay off, but please try to toughen up," Maggie finished. She turned and stomped into the kitchen to fix dinner.

Johnny shook his head, as his wife left his office. His Maggie sure could get wound up about things. He knew she meant well enough, but jeesh, sometimes he didn't think she would ever run out of steam. With the office to himself, Johnny stared down at the map of his current distribution routes. He considered possible new turns and zeroed in on a few new drop sites. The old Ford Jalopy, which kept dogging him on his routes, was sure to be the Feds.

Just like them to show up in some busted down wreck of a car, trying to make it look like they were some locals, driving around. Johnny might walk with a cane thanks to that bullet he took in the leg a few years ago, but his wits were as sharp as ever. Nobody was gonna sneak up on ol' Gimp Leg. He had the smarts all right. His wits had always served him well in avoiding situations. A big grin spread across his face, as he charted and schemed routes to throw off his tail.

Lafayette remained the choicest spot in Johnny's territory. For now, he held control over the speakeasies. His network of hoods kept the pool halls and shanty-bar peddlers supplied. He was continually amazed at how much sauce a few guys could go through, pouring out hooch a shot at a time. Some of the more aggressive of the bunch managed to sell off several whole bottles a week—prices varied dramatically from dive to dive. That they did, Johnny smiled to himself. They also varied in what he charged each of the dumb saps peddling his hooch.

The Sulli brothers had been expanding their influence southward from Hobart. As long as the Genna bosses were okay with it, Johnny had to be also. He would do well to scope out new territory, possibly down by Rockville and Greencastle. They weren't big towns but had proven thirsty grounds so far for his hooch. He ought to consider a new loading point too. For the past three years, he had picked up his juice from behind a barn, just outside Fowler.

If the Sulli brothers were moving toward Lafayette, a load point further south would be in Johnny's best interest. It was never beyond one of the working torpedoes, to raid a rival's supply. Attica might be a good spot. It was on the move. Once the Wabash and Erie Canal finished linking up to Attica, it might be a real happening place. That realization brought another big grin across ol' Gimp Leg's face. Attica was ripe for the picking.

Right now, he only had a few boys scattered out in that area. For a drop spot, it was straight down highway ten from Chicago's infamous South Side. That oughta make the bosses happy. They already shunted hooch made in eastern Kentucky down the Ohio River, then up to Chicago from Evansville, Indiana on highway ten. Heck, the Big Cheese might even cut him a swell price for saving him shipping costs.

Attica it was. Maggie would appreciate him using an area that was home to one of her favorite songwriters, Paul Dresser. She loved to belt out the chorus of *On the Banks of the Wabash, Far Away*. First thing tomorrow, he would find himself a safe, hidden location as a load zone. It had to be close to the main road, or else, he would catch hell for slowing the drivers down.

That settled, he poured his eyes over the map, looking for some temporary routes for his supply drops to give the slip to the Feds. Most of the times, he had found himself being followed along the route from Crawfordsville through Darlington and on over to Thorntown.

Thorntown, now there was a little spitfire of a town, nestled beside the convergence of Prairie and Sugar Creeks. A constant buzz of activity, the little berg had more bustle than the county seat, Lebanon. That hankering for life translated into a big thirst and good business for ol' Gimp Leg.

It was in Thorntown that one of Johnny's rag-a-muffins thought he could hustle ol' Gimp Leg out of money. The hoodlum rationalized that Johnny made an easy pushover; after all, Johnny did limp along on that gimp leg of his. That erroneous assumption was dismissed by a couple of solid bashes of Johnny's greyhound cane on the oaf's head. Johnny might be a gimp, but he was no piker. He still had a helluva swinging arm. After the misguided youth's thrashing, the boys in the area respected ol' Johnny Gimp Leg, unquestionably.

The melodic strains of Corelli's *Concerti Grossi* floated peacefully through the house, as Johnny's angel of music proved her mastery of the violin. Margaret Coughlin was an accomplished musician, and together, they enjoyed some of the world's finest music-Corelli and Mozart being their mutual favorites. His thoughts drifted as he absorbed the strains coming from the parlor.

Johnny mused about the raven-haired doll he had wooed into marrying him. Maggie was a cat's meow, rivaling any blue blood deb in both stunning looks and gracious poise. She had been the pick of the litter, for sure. He would never forget the beguiling smoky stare that blazed unabashedly from her shining onyx eyes. They were so dark that they showed almost no differentiation where her irises ended and her pupils began. A man could drift endlessly in those glassy mirrors, and indeed, Johnny had for twelve wonderful years. Her talents only began with her hotsy-totsy looks. A brilliant woman, Maggie's analysis of a situation resulted in the revelations of several positive solutions. She had foreseen many a tight moment, affording Johnny and she to squeeze by unscathed. She was definitely the beauty and the brains of their duo. Gawd, he was goofy over her.

Maggie finished the piece with an upward flourish of her bow. Twinkling like a diamond, she stood framed in Johnny's office doorway. She glowed elegantly, even now, in a simple print dress with her apron tied tightly about her slim curvaceous chassis.

Johnny snapped out of his daydream, quickened by the vision of her slender neck glistening with just a hint of perspired mist. Abruptly, he shoved his chair back and seized his beloved in his arms. He breathed in her fragrance, gently rubbing his nose against the nape of her neck. Maggie leaned ever so gently to her right, depositing the violin on the desk edge. As she brought her arm over to surrender the bow, they embraced in a passionate hug, locking their lips eagerly.

"I've got a roast in the oven," Maggie whispered.

"That'll give us a few hours." Johnny breathed hotly, lifting Maggie off her feet. They didn't bother with going upstairs. The parlor sofa would suffice. Spent from a rousing struggle buggy, the couple collapsed into a jumbled heap of panting and satisfaction.

Maggie nudged Johnny in the ribs. "Well, that surely took the tension outta ya." Maggie giggled. "I'd better check on supper."

"How long were we out?" Johnny queried.

"Oh, not that long, I don't think." As Maggie shrugged into her dress, she asked, "You don't think it might be Moran's thugs trailing you in that flivver, do you?"

"Nah, those flat tires are not going to bypass Al to come all the way down here. They have enough on their hands up in Chicago. Al has been cracking down on those palookas a lot lately. I wouldn't be surprised if there was some serious blood spilled soon. I really think it's the Fed bulls sniffin' up my arse. I'm gonna map out some new routes. See if I cain't catch 'em in the act." Johnny gloated.

"Make sure they don't catch your act, first," Maggie warned. Brushing her hair back with her hand, she sauntered into the kitchen to finish getting supper ready.

Johnny buttoned his shirt then shuffled into the office. Refreshed, he quickly spied a series of country roads that would make a perfect new path between C'ville and Thorntown. There were a couple of switchbacks he could use to make some drops along the way.

"We'll see just how smart you coppers—aren't." Johnny hooted. Satisfied with the new routes, he made his way into the kitchen.

"Hey darlin', you wanna head out to Smitty's over in New Ross after supper?" Johnny asked Maggie. "They have a new singer. Besides, I kinda like the feel of his roadhouse under the Odd Fellows hall."

"Sure, sheik, a little music would be nice."

"Great, that'll give your spineless husband a chance to collect the money Smitty owes him," Johnny said with a scurrilous grin.

"Oh, you know I love you, you silly fool. Let's hurry through supper, it's ready to set on the table," Maggie cooed.

They ate with gusto and cleared away the dishes, dashing off to get dressed. Johnny stood at the bottom banister as his enchanting wife descended in a shimmering, form-fitting, midnight blue mid-rise dress. Her lovely hair bouncing in marcel waves, set off by a cascade of sparkling beads spilling down both sides of her face, dangling from the tiara perched on her head.

"Wow, you look the berries in your glad rags!" Johnny crowed.

"Says you! You are looking quite dapper yourself, my lover."

From their fleet, they decided to take their shiny emerald-green Buick breezer. Maggie flung open the Buick convertible's driver's side door, and asked in a husky voice, "Mind if I drive?" Johnny nodded his agreement. Truth be told, she was a better driver than he was, as she had proven on several occasions flying into a bootlegger turn to avoid pursuit. Nobody would imagine a dame could handle the wheel like his Maggie.

Ah, the soft comfort of the leather seats enveloped his body, causing Johnny to sink back with a contented sigh. It was amazing to him, how the automobile had advanced so quickly. It was rapidly taking over the entire country. Oh sure, there were folks in the rural areas who still used horses to get around. In the cities, folks—who had any dough at all—were sitting pretty in a four-wheeled beaut like his smooth-riding Buick. His delivery ride was a Buick also. Its spacious trunk carried all the hooch he needed for each of his runs. Special heavy-duty springs supported the added weight. Finishing off his perfect delivery ride were good sturdy wheels, which helped getting around on some of the mud holes, passing themselves off as roads, out in the country.

Smitty's was hoppin' when they pulled up. A light rain had left a muddy patch to walk through. Johnny held tight to Maggie's arm, so she didn't slip. Both of them were wary of mud spoiling their good shoes. Johnny had on a pair of his favorite spats in soft butter-tan. Some of the birds teased him that his old man shoes were going out of style. Johnny was not about to give up one of his favorite things to wear. He argued that a good spat, covering a choice pair of two-tone wingtip shoes, was the cat's meow.

Two big galoots, brandishing their muscle bound chests, stood defiantly in front of Smitty's entrance. Of course, they recognized Johnny and his knockout of a wife—but rules was rules—nobody got in without the password. Johnny sidled up to the boys and then whispered, "Toot, Toot, Lulu!" The duo parted like the Red Sea, allowing Johnny and Maggie to descend into the den of iniquity. A glorious deep-throated voice rang out above the din. A sequined dream with flaxen hair shimmered in her beaded dress, belting out jazz favorites to the crowd's delight.

Johnny and Maggie were escorted to one of the choice tables where a vest-clad waiter took their order. Nothing shy of the best was brought to Smitty's crackerjack supplier. After a few songs, Johnny went in search of Smitty. He found him wrestling a wooden keg of beer onto a cross-shaped sawhorse meant to support it.

"You likin' that batch, Smitty?" Johnny asked, pointing to the keg cradled in Smitty's bulky arms.

"This here ale is the bee's knees, Johnny. I can't believe it's made just an hour or so from here. The Feds are left holding the bag with it practically under their damn noses." Smitty squawked, winking at his honored guest.

"Better keep that under your hat, you ol' ripper," Johnny warned. "Got my money, big guy?"

"Sure thing, Johnny, let me get it out of my hidey hole here in the back. Be right back." Smitty trailed off as he headed behind the stack of kegs lined up along the wall. He returned with a lump of cash stuffed in a leather pouch. He hurriedly handed it over to Johnny.

"This feels 'bout right. Don't need to count it, do I?"

"You know, I wouldn't hold out on you, Johnny. If not for you, I would be a struggling delivery driver. This blind pig is what makes me who I is today. It's all thanks to you. I'm not about to forget that." Smitty cowered by his opened keg.

Johnny hefted the pouch into his inner coat pocket, turned, and maneuvered back to his table. Flattery didn't mean much to Johnny. He had heard too many yes-men climbing over each other to out crow the next one to the big cheeses. Most times, they were waiting for the perfect time to stab the hood ahead of him, or even attempt to mow down the boss. Johnny's philosophy was: just pay me what you owe me, sell your hooch, and we'll all be happy.

His lovely bride sat mesmerized by the swooning songs wafting over the crowd. Maggie barely noticed her shining knight slide in beside her. Johnny tapped his breast pocket and grinned, giving her the clear signal that he had gotten his money. Now, he had to get after those Thompson brothers to calm his wife's scorn—about standing up to folks. They stayed for a few more tunes then decided to call it a night.

The drive home was pleasant, as a half-moon cast a comforting beam on the shiny metal hood stretching out in front of Johnny's view. Life was good. He was euphoric. Johnny had a new route laid out, as well as plans in the works for a new supply spot.

Chapter 4

Rural West-Central Indiana
Summer 1926

It was easier than Johnny had thought it would be to find a good supply spot south of Attica. A farm, nestled near the end of a country road that dumped into the woods, proved the perfect hidey-hole. Best of all, it was easy to get in and out of without a lot of prying eyes. The plan was to start deliveries there in about a month.

Happily, the boss man agreed to drop Johnny's cost. A kickback for saving the organization time and money. No longer would they have to haul hooch up to Chicago, and then, back down to central Indiana. Only concern for the boss was that the Feds might catch onto bigger trucks going in an outta that farm. For now, they would just drop off Johnny's portion from the main cargo headed up to Chicago. Eventually, there wouldn't be a need for a big truck when the Chicago operation started storing giggle water from the south in their new underground warehouse outside Terre Haute.

Johnny found himself a very happy bootlegger. The Attica farm drop was running perfectly like smooth butter. His new supply point was far enough south to keep the Sulli boys outta his hair. The drop location provided seamless delivery in his current territory.

Feeling a contented sense of real accomplishment, Johnny decided to take a shortcut down through New Richmond on his way to finish deliveries in Lizton and Crawfordsville. Johnny found it amusing that the upstanding folks of an itty-bitty town, like Lizton, were foolish enough to think there was nothing ill-gotten going on in their town. They obviously had not been out to Granger's barn on a Saturday night.

Johnny had just left Granger's farm when he noticed that rusted ol' Ford hay burner with its bumper hanging askew rounding the bend in the road. They drove past him, giving Johnny his first look at the tail he had had for months. They made no attempt to shy away, staring right at him. The driver was giving him a dark glare. The malice in that glance was foul enough to cause a chill to run down Johnny's spine. Ol' Gimp Leg decided it was time to skedaddle, double time. He mashed down on the gas pedal, fishtailing in the gravel. He sped, as if he was on the lam, toward his drop in Crawfordsville.

Finished with the day's run, Johnny pulled up to his back porch. He could see Maggie perched on a kitchen chair, chin in her delicate hand. Maggie had long ago stopped worrying or fussing over the delayed arrival of her husband. She knew he had to get his deliveries and pickups done before he got home. Sometimes that took a little longer. To have a spouse who was not upset and fritting about his whereabouts was yet another reason Johnny adored his wife. Supper was laid out like a small feast. Eagerly they both dove right in.

"Don't think that tail I've been seeing is the Bulls after all," Johnny announced, swallowing a gulp of delicious homemade bread.

Surprised, Maggie blurted, "Who do ya think it might be?"

"Well, I got a good look at the turkeys, today. They passed me on the road, up near Lizton. They look like a couple of yokels who just climbed out of a swamp. One of 'em gave me the evil eye," Johnny explained. "Sure never seen 'em before. Don' know what they're after. It's definitely the old Ford Jalopy that's been followin' me."

"What're ya gonna do about it?" Maggie asked, clutching her hand to her throat.

"Not much to do. No harm in somebody driving along on the same road. Figure, if they wanted somethin', they'd a forced me over today. It's probably just coincidence."

Coincidence my ass, Maggie thought but kept her tongue. She had promised to quit nagging Johnny about standing up to folks. Maybe it was just a pair of loony country folk out driving around.

"Hey, what say I take you down to Terre Haute with me?" Johnny asked with a puppy-dog look that could not be refused. "It would give you a chance to check out the doozy operations down there. They're a ripsnorter, and I know you're gonna go all sockdolager over 'em."

Maggie quickly replied, "Of course, I would be happy to accompany my swell hubby on such a humdinger of an adventure. When are we going?"

Three weeks from Friday seemed to be the perfect time. They could stay overnight and catch a performance at the Wabash Theater. Maggie loved the quaint city by the shores of the Wabash River. Downtown always had that delightful, freshly baked bread smell wafting over it from the Clabber Girl Baking Powder factory. Yummy!

* * *

On a Friday morning, Johnny rolled the Peerless out of the shed. With a leather shammy, he polished up a nice gloss sheen over the entire cream-and-magenta paint that covered his two-tone '26, Series 69. She truly was one of the "Three Ps of Motordom" with her elegant sleek beauty backed up by a throaty flat planed crankshaft that had won numerous world speed records. He and Maggie loved this car, better yet, they looked keen behind the wheel.

His stunning wife emerged from the house with a dual string of long pearls wisping between the open lapels of her sable fur car coat. Her soft cream-colored cloche hat, sporting a single brown-and-black feather tucked to the right side, completed her look as a vision of loveliness.

Johnny stood speechless, as she brushed by and tugged on his wide tie before dancing her fingertips along the brim of his charcoal Borsalino fedora. The engine growled to life, and they were off. They slowly drove down their narrow driveway to keep dust from kicking up on the car's shine.

An uneventful ride brought them to South Ninth Street in downtown Terre Haute. Maggie sniffed happily at the Clabber Girls' delightful freshly baked smell. She followed Johnny down a narrow alley to the backside of a building, whose moniker on the front read, "Lloyd Furniture and Upholstery." Johnny knocked on a simple wooden door with rusted metal hinges. In seconds, the door creaked open.

Tommy immediately ushered Johnny and that jewel of a wife of his into the tight vestibule. They followed, as Tommy led them to large double doors near the back loading area. He flung open the left side door and led them down a short flight of steps to a landing littered with fabric remnants and broken chair fixtures. With a big grin on his face, he twisted a wall sconce to his left. A large section of the wall behind them slid backwards and then rolled on greased wheels off to the right. The group walked forward.

Maggie's jaw hung open as she watched Tommy press a small button, barely visible, in the darkly painted wall. The floors beneath them gave a sudden jolt then began to lower slowly with a whir of grinding gears.

"Welcome to Terre Haute's grand brewery, my fine folks," Tommy announced while swinging his arm out and up in a gesture of sheer chivalry. "After you, my lady."

Maggie was stunned beyond words, gazing out over the well-lit city block filled by what had to be one of the nation's largest breweries—the Terre Haute Brewing Company. Johnny had told her on the drive down that the beer plant produced over forty-six million gallons of giggle water a year, employed hundreds of people, and served as the lifeblood of the town.

Still, she could not absorb all that she was seeing, and there was plenty more beyond her immediate view. Built in the 1880s before refrigeration, the brewery complex included four cavernous beer cellars. Each designed to store lager in eighteen and a half feet casks, enough to fill seventy-five wooden barrel tanks. The dimensions of the cellars were simply breathtaking. The ceilings were twenty feet tall and were a full twelve feet below the surface of the ground.

As Tommy guided them through the facility, Maggie found herself gasping regularly, repeating "phenomenal" and "what a lulu" over and over. At last they came to a tunnel aligning the complex's perimeter. Tommy explained that the perimeter tunnel gave workers access to the cellars and the beer pipeline. The pipeline, or lifeline as the bosses called it, fed not only the brewery tanks but also outlets to nearby local taverns turned speakeasies.

Maggie couldn't imagine that a structure and operation like this could exist with the Fed bulls crawling around all the time. "They didn't find this when they raided that big tiger blind back a few years ago?" Maggie inquired.

"Total bust for the Bulls, dear. All they got were a few old losers who couldn't crawl away from the bar fast enough," Johnny answered.

"The dusty old furniture store sittin' up top doesn't attract attention. Most of the beer ships out through the tunnel to a whole lot of loading points. So far, our little money maker along the Wabash is safe and sound. Gives a whole new meaning to *On the Banks of the Wabash* don't cha think?"

Johnny turned to Tommy and asked, "You have that load scheduled for next week?" A swift nod of Tommy's head told him all was in order. There wasn't much else to see down in the cellars. Johnny took his lady's elbow and escorted her back to the surface. As they came back out into the bakery-filled air, Maggie chattered like a caged bird. She gushed at Johnny for bringing her to see the operations. Hearing about them was not even close to what she had seen with her own eyes.

Johnny and Maggie relaxed comfortably in their upper floor hotel suite. Johnny stood at its large central window, gazing out at the shadows the descending sun cast on the Wabash River below. He found himself reflecting on what a lucky man he was.

Coming from humble beginnings, Johnny's great-grandparents had been among a small group of Quakers pioneering their way out to the Indiana Territories just a century or so ago. His great-granddad had been crushed under a wagon while wrestling a wheel back on the axle. The group had begged his Grams Williams to continue on with them.

They made it to the central western edge of the Indiana territory without serious incident or attacks from the savage two-legged beasts crouching in the woods along their journey. With land grants in hand, they formed their little community around a drafty log cabin sanctuary. Most of the savages in the area had finally signed a treaty with ol' Tippecanoe Harrison. The tribal remnants were carted off a few years later to outer territories, courtesy of former President Andrew Jackson's stern laws regarding tribal lands.

His momma, a third generation pioneer daughter, got swept away by an Italian carpetbagger. The renegade Magasono was sneaking back up to Chicago after swindling all the folks he could safely cheat down in the Deep South. It wasn't long after Johnny was born that his scoundrel father took off. His abandoned mom had to work several menial jobs to keep them fed and sheltered.

Johnny got the debonair good looks of his swindler father; however, he was brought up with the strict moral values of treating people well and kind, which his mother had learned at the feet of her Quaker mother. He may have become a law-breaking bootlegger and curse like a sailor; yet, he would never go sour on the promise he made to his momma—to always be good and fair to others.

Maggie brought him out of his wandering thoughts as she wrapped her arms around his waist and encouraged him to get dressed for dinner, as well as the theater he had promised her. After the concert, Johnny planned to take Maggie to a late Vaudeville performance by Ed Wynn in his newest act, which included a remarkably funny kid with wavy hair and expressive eyes named Red Skelton. He had heard it was a don't-miss act. He was certain Maggie would enjoy the break from their usual entertainment choices.

The concert and performance were corkers. After a peaceful sleep, the Magasanos awoke refreshed, ready for a sunny drive back home. On the stretch home, in addition to taking in the sounds and smells of rural Midwest cornfields, Johnny and Maggie discussed the impact Prohibition had had on society in America.

They concluded that instead of reducing crime, Prohibition had made criminals of ordinary citizens, as well as promoted the growth of sometimes violent organized crime. A situation they were all too familiar with from their days in Chicago's South Side. Rather than increasing health and safety, as the bleeding hearts contended, it had created widespread consumption of often toxic moonshine, which had sometimes caused paralysis, blindness, and even death. A truth they had seen with their own eyes, or heard from other rumrunners. President Hoover's "noble experiment" held little evidence of any nobility. They agreed the inexperienced stinker should spend more time and energy on the economy than sticking his righteous nose in people's personal choices. Johnny predicted, if Hoover kept grinding things the way they were, the country was gonna go bust.

Chapter 5

Rural West-Central Indiana
Fall 1926

Attica was buzzing along like a well-oiled machine. The Thompson boys had paid up their debts, as Johnny knew they would. Maggie was entertaining Johnny and a few guests, nearly every night, with her standout skills on the baby grand. His wife was a beautiful dream tickling the ivory behind a dilly of a polished box of strings and hammers. Who said gangsters had no culture?

As fall settled over the community, Johnny was feeling pip confident that he had thrown those boys in the old Ford hay burner off his trail. He found his new routes provided more scenery on his runs. As a result, he decided to keep using the back roads. After his visit with Maggie at the Terre Haute brewery, Johnny had worked out some improved bulk distribution plans with the bosses. Johnny could see some new dough coming his way. The extra moolah would serve to grease the wheels of his happy marriage. Guess being good to others wasn't the flaw Maggie had accused.

Long about mid-October, Johnny noticed that old Ford Jalopy barely held together by chicken wire on the road behind him. Damn, he thought he was rid of those flops. He sped up, putting some distance between the two vehicles. Around an upcoming curve, he veered sharp right then pulled in behind a farmhouse. He watched the Ford pass. Waiting until he felt sure they had gone on, he headed back out taking another country road to his house.

No further sightings of the Ford reassured him that once again he had given them the slip. *Wonder what those fatheads want,* he thought to himself. He told Maggie about the mystery Ford appearing again. She cautioned him to carry extra protection—no telling what the duds were after. Perhaps, they knew he was a runner, which meant he had wads of clams on him.

* * *

Not more than a week later, Johnny was startled out of a deep concentration. A loud rap at the front door could have woken the dead. As he got up to check out the front window, he caught a glimpse of Maggie's ashen face staring right at him in the kitchen doorway. Her hands were shaking with her elbows bent at the waist in front of her. Behind her, a scruffy looking lad, probably in his mid-twenties, held a pistol to her back. The front door burst open behind Johnny. In surged the wizened turkey who had glared him down up by Lizton. He aimed his shotgun right at Johnny's chest. The surprise jump left no room for negotiation. Johnny turned to the old chrome dome and demanded, "What's the meaning of bustin' into our home!"

The man ignored Johnny. He threw some cut lengths of quarter-inch rope at Maggie's feet and told her to pick them up. He instructed Johnny to sit on a straight-back chair. Maggie was shoved by the young turkey over toward her husband. Neither of the intruders was saying much of anything, just staring hard at Johnny and his wife.

"Sure dun well for yourself, legger," grunted the older man.

Pointing his shotgun at Johnny, the old hard-boiled man turned his attention to Maggie and barked, "Now git over there and tie your no-count husband's hands behind his back. Tie it tight, cause I'm gonna check." He belched.

Johnny went along with the act, not wanting any harm to come to Maggie by a trigger jumpy wise guy shooting out of fear. With his hands firmly tied, Johnny felt it was time to see what these two had to complain about.

"Is there somethin' I've done to upset you two?"

"Just hush up, you!" bellowed the old hard-boiled ruffian. "Boy, git over thar and tie up that moll," he barked at his accomplice. "We is gonna take a little ride. Friend a mine has a pond out back of his house, just east of har. Feel like goin' fer a swim, legger?"

"What the hell is this all about?" Johnny huffed.

"Aye don' feel like tellin' ya, yet, ya servant of the devil!" barked the assailant. "You and the peach walk on up the drive, nice and slow, in front of us. Got our car parked just down the lane a piece." The old geezer pulled a well-chewed cigar stub from his mouth and hawked a mucous mahogany-colored mass onto the ground near Johnny and Maggie's feet.

Johnny and Maggie were shoved into the cramped, filthy backseat of the beat up old Ford. The boy slouched into the ruptured upholstery of the front passenger seat and faced backwards, with the pistol aimed at Johnny's chest. Tears began to stream down Maggie's face. The wreck of a Ford's engine cranked up, and the car lurched forward.

Pleading with Johnny to think of something to do, Maggie realized their ride on the bootleg express was about to come to an abrupt end. Johnny kicked at some sheet-like rags at his feet. Staring down at the white rags on the floorboard, Johnny recognized a crudely stitched cross design with a tiny red teardrop shape in its center. At that moment, Johnny knew it was all over for him and Maggie. He began to thrash about, trying to free his hands.

"What are you doin', Johnny?" Maggie asked in a panic.

Johnny looked into her eyes and mouthed KKK. Color drained out of Maggie's face like liquid from an uncorked bottle. She was all too familiar with the Klan and their strict views on prohibition. A number of their friends had been beaten to a pulp by Klan enforcement bands. Some whiskey peddlers had even disappeared—most likely murdered.

The busted down fatheads, hiding behind masks, preached "100 Percent Americanism." They spouted the absolute purification of politics. They rallied in favor of strict morality, preserving it in an ironic twist of their own hate-filled methods of enforcement. Shrouded by hoods, they clamored behind the outcry of needed punishment for those who would defy the nation's prohibition laws. If God saw fit to have his duly elected officials ban the evil waters of alcohol polluting the souls of the innocent, then by golly, they reasoned, it was their God-given duty to avenge the transgressors.

For years they had roamed about the countryside, terrorizing Catholics, Jews, Blacks, and anyone else they deemed un-American. Their recent avenging targets were bootleggers and anyone who partook of the sinful concoctions they peddled. Never mind that many of their own Klansmen drank. Several even had moonshine stills squirreled away on their property.

Maggie knew with certainty, as did Johnny, that the gig was up. They grasped for each other's hands, clinging on for the last few desperate moments they would share together. Johnny found no plausible way to escape. Frustrated, he surrendered at last, savoring the touch of his dear wife's fingers. For their part, the two Klansmen just grunted and huffed as they drove indifferently toward the farmhouse with a pond out back.

Johnny knew where they were headed. His grandmother's old cabin and the now toppled Quaker meeting cabin were just around the bend on an old path that passed by the farm pond. A former road, it was now nothing more than a dirt path between fields.

As the weak headlights of the rattling old Ford illuminated the face of the earthen dam of the pond, Johnny turned to face Maggie.

"I could not have discovered a more perfect mate to have shared my life with," he professed to her in a quavering voice. "Please don't cry my beloved," he pleaded. He wanted the last image he had of his precious jewel to be her smiling face.

The Ford braked to a stop. The older Klansman clambered out of the front seat, dragging Johnny's greyhound cane out with him. Johnny didn't know the thug had stolen that from its resting spot in their umbrella stand. The old man stretched then opened the backdoor, yanking Johnny out by his bound hands. The overweight Klanner was deceptively strong through all his padding. He twisted Johnny around and shoved him to the ground near the pond's edge. He stepped on Johnny's back—satisfied with the heaving gust of air that sprang from the legger's crushed ribcage. Gazing up, Johnny saw the man raise his cane high in the air, then pummel it down with a beastly crunch against the back of his skull.

"You thought you was a big man, when you beat up my cuzzin's boy in Thorntown, didn' ya?" bellowed the Klansman. "Well, we has convinced him of the error of his evil drinkin' ways. We has accepted him back into the fold."

Stunned from the head blow, Johnny thought back to the young turkey who was convinced that he could pull a fast one over on Johnny. The deluded youth had tried to cheat him out of half-a-case worth of hooch. So these thugs were his kin. The lowbrow resemblance was now obvious. Johnny had only knocked the hotshot about a bit as a warning to the other boys not to mess with ol' Gimp Leg. Maybe Maggie was right, if he had killed the turkey, he wouldn't have ratted Johnny out to the Klan. Nah, being good and fair was how he preferred to go out of this world.

"You, mister, who thinks you are above the law, is the reason this country is dying under the drunken influence of the devil's own spit!" the Klanner blared, spraying spittle all over Johnny's face. "We're gonna show you the punishment you and your filthy lulu deserve. You has been corrupting all the fine folks of this har blessed state of the God-fearing UNITED STATES OF AMERICA!" he spat.

"Boy, bring that peach out har and throw her down on her back, right thar," he ordered his son, pointing to a spot clearly in Johnny's view. "Bring me that shotgun outta the front seat, too."

Maggie was thrown in a heap on the ground. She gazed over at her husband slumped on the ground near the pond. Maggie cringed as the Klanner landed another swinging smack on Johnny's head. This one left Johnny in a loopy haze. Bleary-eyed, Johnny could just make out Maggie's eyes staring back at him. Fighting to remain conscious, Johnny felt the cold barrel of a shotgun pressed against his skull.

"Sooo, thisss isss how it endsss?" he slurred.

"Oh, don' think you is gettin' off that easy," the Klansman snorted.

"My boy, over thar is a virgin. Workin' out his first time atop your missus sounds like a right good idea. Don'cha think?" he taunted Johnny. "Go on, boy, whatcha waitin' on?" he snapped at his youngin'.

Maggie screamed. Her hands dug into the soft grass, seeking purchase to scoot away. The young Klanner leaned over and slapped Maggie hard. The welt from the face slap burned, worsened by the salty tears pouring down her cheeks. Maggie flinched, as the Klanner dropped to a knee. Awkwardly, he started ripping her dress away from her legs. Johnny yawped in horror, witnessing his wife about to be violated. The last cane crack on his head had left him unable to speak. He felt himself drifting off into a fuzzy darkness.

The boy proved completely inept at the task before him. Out of frustration at his own inadequacy, he began kicking violently at Maggie's head and ribs. Several retorted sharp cracks bolstered his resolve. He pulled a knife from his back pocket, flipped open the blade, and brandished it like a sword over his hapless victim. Maggie begged for mercy as she shriveled, bleeding and sobbing beneath his outstretched legs.

Maggie resolved that she was not going to survive this. There was no further need for restraining her actions. She might be an accomplished musician, but she was also a stubborn ol' moll just the same. She shifted her weight onto one leg, unleashing a pounding blow to the boy's groin with her other foot. The thug gasped, doubled over, and clutched his injured manhood. Furious, he straightened up, growled menacingly, and began slashing Maggie with merciless abandon. The repeated blows drained her. A vicious stab hit home to her pulsing heart. After a few short jerks, her body sagged, seeping blood onto the pasture. Thankfully, Johnny had blacked out, amiably spared the gruesome scene.

Johnny jolted awake as he felt his head and shoulders being yanked up from a dunking in the pond's tepid water. "That didn't turn out like we planned," guffawed the elder Klansman. "Just so you know, she's dead as a doornail," he sniggered. "And now it's your turn, ol' Gimp Leg!"

With that, he rolled Johnny on his back, pressing him in place with his foot. He hefted Johnny's cane in the air, bringing it viciously down on Johnny's face, repeatedly, until it was an oozing, pulpy mass of bloodied flesh. Fading swiftly, Johnny remembered his Grandma's warning: You will reap what you sow. Looked like he was bringing in his harvest of years as a bootlegger. A final breath escaped Johnny Magasano's mouth, as he drifted off into blackness.

The Klanners dragged both bodies to the pond's edge. There they rolled them in with no more care than flinging slop over a fence to hungry hogs. As they walked back toward the Ford, the elder

Klansman saw Johnny's cane, glistening in the faint moonlight. He picked it up, snapped it over his knee, and flung it into the pond.

They got in their old beat up barouche, proud of their righteous vindication against one of the devil's own. They didn't worry about cleaning up after themselves. The farmer, who owned the farm, was just another of the more than a hundred and sixty thousand Klansmen scattered all across the Great State of Indiana.

Shifting the old Ford into gear, the Klanner's thoughts wandered to a recent Klan rally speech where the local Exalted Cyclops admonished his fellow Klansmen: The Klan's duty is to protect our Great Nation from Catholics, Jews, Darkies, and any other foreigners who try to sneak up on our shores. Political corruption, immorality, and defiance of prohibition must not be tolerated. Grinning lopsidedly, the Klanner reveled in the satisfaction that he had done his duty that very evening. Joyous in his righteous deeds on behalf of his fellow Klansmen, he hummed spiritual refrains from favored hymns all the way back home.

Ghostly White Paleness

Goth is a subculture and a genre of music with a rich history and interesting people. Many goths meet people first then discover the music later. The people aspect is very important to the community. They gravitate readily to like-minded people. They believe that—good and evil—beauty and destruction—light and dark—can't exist without each other.

Chapter 6

Miller Farm, resident home of Quaking Pond
Twenty miles southwest of Sugar Creek
Montgomery County, Indiana
June 2, 9:44 a.m., CST

Now into day four of their pond exploration, Joe and the boys were growing impatient with their discovery of mostly indistinguishable bits of stuff. The time frame of the things in the pond was limitless. They started the day by pulling the old Corvair up onto level ground. Sadly, most of it was not salvageable. Years of soaking in pond water had rotted out the upholstery and other inside components. There might be some hope of cleaning up the body frame and engine parts to salable condition, but not without a lot of elbow grease.

Eager to explore, rather than salvage, they traipsed down into the basin leaving the car for another day. The quantity of bone fragments found in the muck was staggering; most were deteriorated to the point of obscurity. They had not found any human skulls, yet. They had, however, stumbled across a couple of cow skulls and what appeared to be a fox or some other kind of small dog skull. The scattered bone bits looked like picked over remains from a Thanksgiving turkey feast.

The pond had emptied most of its aquatic residents along the torrent path. The day after the deluge, they had quickly set about collecting the rotting fish and turtle carcasses to prevent the attraction of scavengers. The stench had been atrocious the moment the sun hit the carrion. Even now, days later, Joe and the boys found a few decaying fish remains putrefying in the mud.

Joe knew every day he piddled around picking up tidbits of worthless junk meant he wasn't getting his pond repaired. They had discovered at least a couple of natural springs in the former pond basin. Once the dam was back in place, their flow would help to refill it. That was gonna be a slow process, though, probably wouldn't be enough water in it to service the cattle until at least late next spring. He wasn't at all pleased with the prospect of spending a year running the pump in the well house for the cattle.

Joe looked across the pond to see Mikey waving frantically from a pile of moss covered logs at the trackside base of the pond. As Joe sloshed his way over, his son freed a small silvery amulet strung on a brittle strand of leather. It had been caught, dangling from a splintered stick of wood protruding from one of the logs. It's slipping out with the rushing water arrested by the sliver.

"What is it, Dad?" Mikey asked excitedly, hoping he had found a treasure.

His father turned it over in his hand and declared, "It's an Eye of Horus pendant."

"Eye of who? Why would anyone want to wear someone's eye?" Mikey blurted.

"It's the Eye of Horus or Ra," Joe explained. "It's not an actual eye. It was a symbol of protection that the pharaohs and Egyptians wore to remind them of their protector. Kind of like the cross Mommy wears. It makes her feel safer and reminds her of God. Ra was one of the Egyptians' gods. This one is not very old. It's probably just somebody's necklace lost in the pond."

Chapter 7

Central Indiana
High School in session
1981

"Freakin' Freaks!" the taunters blared, as they passed Matthew and his friends in the courtyard. Matthew continued his comments after a brief shake of his head. Being ridiculed by others was a normal day for the cluster of goth-clad youngsters.

"I realize that nature requires balance, and that those poor bastards represent the bad yang to our good yin, but must they always be so vocal about it?" queried Matthew.

He let the smoke from a long drag of cloves drift out of his lungs then Matthew waxed on about the need for balance in the earth's energy forces. For his argument, he drew from the lecture he'd just heard in Mr. Grayson's physics lab. Matthew intoned to his friends the gist of the lecture where Mr. Grayson spoke of the required opposing forces for every force in nature. He finished off by recanting Newton's third law, which states that all forces exist in pairs, to every action, there is always an equal and opposite reaction. Matthew thought to himself, *I really am an intellectual badass.*

Looking up, he saw a muscle-bound hulk approaching their way. Andy, one of the school jocks, leaned in close to Matthew and belched, "Nice nails, queer boy."

Matt simply turned to his friends and stated, "Another fine example of nature's need for balance. With his malodorous breath, his exceptional athletic ability is the only hope he has of propagating his genes. Well, my fellow companions, as much as I would love to continue reviewing samples of nature's forces at work, I must head off to history class." With that, Matt unfolded his thin stork-like legs and lifted his skeletal body from his perch on the retaining wall. Matthew stumbled off toward his next class with the haltering gait of an uncoordinated, rail-thin teenager. The bounce in his step brought on by the new sense of belonging just recently achieved by his inclusion in his goth circle of friends.

The students were classmates at the prestigious Tudor private school on Indianapolis' northeast side. Tudor's laid back emphasis on tolerance and general acceptance of each individual lent to a relatively safe environment for Matthew. He and his fellow goth friends were able to thrive there academically while incurring a minimum of harassment.

This was not to say that the wraith-thin, pale group of androgynous goth did not get continually starred at. Frequently, they were slurred with contemptuous barbs. Different is rarely accepted by the mainstream; the Goths' unique attire and outward appearance were ripe for ridicule. To further compound their mysterious appearance, the Goths were often ensconced by a faint bluish cloud of clove scented cigarette smoke.

Tudor, like many schools in the early '80s, was no stranger to teenage drug usage. The school's wealthier parent population proliferated substance abuse through cash-enabled children. Alcohol and pot were the standard drugs of choice, tame by comparison to other parts of the country. Although officially banned, smoking on campus did happen in the open courtyard and bathrooms, at least, until the perpetrator was caught. For the goths, a stolen drag on a clove cigarette set their day right.

*　*　*

Matthew Henderson, unlike many of the überwealthy students attending Tudor, came from more humble origins. His father, Michael, was an emergency room nurse at St. Vincent's in North Indianapolis. Michael had worked very hard to gain his degree and subsequent position. He sent his son, Matthew, to Tudor to ensure the next generation of Henderson's had a better opportunity in life. Michael and his second wife, Allison, lived in a modest bungalow in the quaint Broad Ripple neighborhood of Indianapolis with Matthew and his two younger half-brothers.

Matthew adored his siblings, having cared for them since birth. He was so grateful to have brothers. Before his father married Allison, Matthew felt destined to be an only child. He had no idea that he was already a stepbrother to hellions his estranged birthmother had spawned.

Basically a shy and gentle soul, Matthew read voraciously. He rarely left the shade of his house, which contributed significantly to his already pallid complexion. He had straight mousy brown hair that hung limply down the sides of his face. Matthew was clumsy and gangly thin. His parents figured what he lacked in physical prowess, he would compensate for with his mental strength. Matthew demonstrated an innate intelligence through his exceptional grades. His father and stepmother were most encouraging of his interest in studies and bragged *ad nauseum* about his stellar grades. Matthew was whisper quiet, so much so that his parents rarely even noticed he was in the house. It wasn't an intentional oversight on their part. Matthew was simply a very low-maintenance child.

His early years in school proved reinforcing to his perception of the world as a dismal miasma of death and darkness. The kids made fun of his sallow skin, maliciously haranguing him about his awkward physical inabilities. Friends were few for Matthew growing up, as none wanted to be seen with the emaciated bookworm. He found himself on most days in a lonely corner of the lunchroom, waiting for the class bell to ring. With reclusion forced upon him, Matthew buried himself in books. He discovered a fond kinship with the maudlin writings of the Victorian period.

As he transitioned into high school, his teachers praised his obvious intellect. That encouragement caused him to hold his stature a little more aloof. He became more aware of the other students around him; he particularly noticed his increasing interest in girls. His eyes fell longingly on Griffin, a slender brunette who had dyed a streak of magenta along the right side of her hair.

He noticed that she read similar novels to him. After weeks of quiet observation, he summoned the courage to chat with her. She smiled up at him, her teeth gleaming through the deep magenta lipstick she wore. Her grey eyes lost in the smoky shroud of dark mascara lining her eyes. They began an earnest discussion of favorite novels. Griffin and Matthew quickly fell into a friendship of mutual interests. They sat for hours talking about favorite authors and their fondness of the Victorian era. It was an exhilarating time for Matthew. The loner had found someone he could comfortably relate to on several levels. Griffin even appreciated his wanness and rakish-thin body. She encouraged him by telling him that he blended in perfectly with her goth friends. Eager to include her new friend, Griffin invited Matthew to meet some of her friends at a local coffee shop.

Matthew joined her at the Abbey, a popular Gothic haunt. He was initially surprised at Griffin's entrance. She wore white foundation, which contrasted sharply with her deep black lipstick. Silver chains, festooned with several crosses, dangled from her neck. To complete the shock effect, she wore fishnet stockings under a prim-cut black frock.

Seeing the stunned look on his face, Griffin smiled, and said, "Come on, ghost boy." Matthew followed her into the coffeehouse.

They ordered a coffee each then plopped down in the comfy, overstuffed sofas serving as the establishment's seating. Crushed deep tones of velvet covered all the upholstered furniture, paired with scarred low coffee tables randomly flung about the space. Augmenting the funeral-parlor slash vampire's den look, the entire shop was entombed by heavy, dark-colored velvet curtains. A light mist of clove smoke lingered in the dimly lit confines.

Griffin's friends were equally clad in classic goth attire. The boys were all spectral like himself. Several sported dark eyeliner. From their leather-wreathed wrists protruded sharp silver studs. Each male seemed to have some religious emblem dangling from either a slim leather strap or a silver chain around his neck. The girls were white faced with contrasting red or magenta lipstick and deeply outlined eyes. Most wore patterned stockings and dark-period skirts with tight-fitting jackets. So tight, in fact, that it seemed to project their heaving breasts from purposely unbuttoned tops.

Griffin's group of friends greeted Matthew, complimenting him on his delightfully pasty skin. They readily engaged him in their witty conversations, making him feel included for the first time in his life. It was great to be accepted for who he was without a soupçon of disdainful judgment on the side.

Wow! So this is what it is like to be a part of a group, he beamed deep inside his soul.

The coffee and conversation flowed for several hours. The group explained the religious symbols they sported. Several enlightened him on their individual interests in the complexities of the varying cultural concepts of the afterlife. Matthew sat gazing at the myriad emblems of eternal existence on display. Respective of their individual choices, some wore crosses, others Egyptian ankhs, and others proudly displayed emblems of the Eye of Horus. A few sported pentagrams, admittedly worn to freak out the predominately Christian community. Matthew found himself fully engrossed in the group. He was genuinely sad when it was time to head home.

Over the coming weeks, Matthew regularly accompanied Griffin on visits to the Abbey and other dark ethereal haunts in the city. It wasn't long before he was convinced into dying his hair jet-black and wearing a thin line of eyeliner. He found the signature outward swoop he flared on the outer edge of his eye contrasted sharply with his lurid skin.

As he read more extensively on Egyptian mythology, he became fascinated with the Eye of Horus—an ancient Egyptian symbol of protection, royal power, and good health. Further intriguing to his scientific mind were the implied mathematical theories associated with the symbol. It seemed a perfect representation of his life. He purchased and began wearing a silvery Eye of Horus emblem strung on a leather string. Matthew's choice in clothing evolved as well. He began wearing mostly tight black pants with absurdly tapered pant legs tailored to cling closely to his narrow frame. He found a couple of billowy white-ruffled open-front shirts at a vintage store in Broad Ripple. These he proudly wore on his coffee jaunts with his fellow goths.

His parents had noticed the attire their son wore to go out. They figured it must be the new fad with his age group, anticipating it ending soon. They were both extremely tolerant and open-minded, not inclined to discourage their intensely private son from gaining a social life. The eyeliner was a bit much they thought, but it was okay with them as long as he was happy. His rakish body and delicate hands, combined with his current goth look, convinced most that he preferred boys. He seemed genuinely interested in Griffin, so his parents discounted that misperception. Not that his sexual orientation mattered one way or the other to them—they loved him regardless. They hoped he felt comfortable enough to tell them forthright, eventually.

Matthew's forays into the world of Gothic culture evolved into a close clutch of friends, several of whom attended school with him. Emboldened by their comradery, they all became more comfortable at school—strength in numbers. Eventually, the goths began wearing their coffeehouse attire to school. Even the boys dared to use eyeliner, a few went so far as to apply dark lipstick. Most of them sported fresh coats of black nail polish. At lunch, clustered around an outdoor space, enshrouded by a haze of clove smoke, the goths soon acquired a look and smell that defined them as a campus subgroup.

Entirely non-threatening, despite their appearance of impending doom and death, the goths mostly engaged in philosophical discussions on life's true meaning, death, and the afterlife—heavily influenced by the writings of Poe and other tragic romantic writers. The recently published vampirism writings of Anne Rice attracted the goths like moths to a flame. Engorged with the messages told through the stories they read and the music they enjoyed, the goths rapidly developed a common identity. The goths had arrived as a new defiant clique on campus.

Matthew was finally enjoying a cherished moment of belonging in his life. Blissfully unaware that peace was about to be interrupted by his estranged birthmother, who had recently drifted back into Indiana. Peggy, Matt's birthmother, had left him and his father to run off for the excitement as a groupie some eight years earlier.

Having reestablished herself in Indiana, it dawned on Peggy she should at least make an effort to reunite with her estranged teenage son. It had been years since she and Matthew had talked; chances were he would want nothing to do with his old used up mom. She resolved to contact him, regardless.

Matthew surprised his mother by not outright rejecting her pitiful attempts at reconciliation. He had, after all, been raised by his father and stepmother to be tolerant and accepting of others. A principle his parents illustrated daily with their treatment of him.

Michael accompanied his son on his first visit with his estranged mother. Not thrilled to speak with his ex-wife, Michael was not about to let his fragile son be traumatized by a woman he knew had no real concern for anyone other than herself. Peggy had left her little ones in the care of Bobby so she could enjoy her time with her estranged family. Over lunch at the Redwood Inn restaurant in Crawfordsville, Peggy recanted her wanderings over the past several years.

Far from the glamorous life Peggy had envisioned, Matt's mom had found out the hard way—life on the road was no picnic. Peggy explained that over eight years of barely succeeding at scraping enough together to make ends meet, she finally hopped off the bus in Nashville. With no support from her no-count boyfriend, Peggy found herself a cheap rent apartment for her and her two toddlers, Trevor and Jake. She cleaned herself up, slowly recovering from her abusive relationship that had included frequent beer-enhanced beatings from her boyfriend and numerous whacked-out trips on various cheap drugs.

Food stamps and a part-time deli-counter job helped her survive. Progress was slow. Truth be told, Peggy admitted that she missed the action and drugs from her former run. Depressed and desperate to make some changes, Peggy bragged about having saved up enough for bus fare for her and the kids to return to where she had grown up near Ladoga, Indiana. Her parents were gone, but a childhood cousin said she could stay with their family until she got her feet back on the ground.

Integrating into a Christian principles household was a major challenge. Peggy whispered feigned interest in the Lord and turning her life around, solely to gain a toehold back in the community. It was great, she conceded, to have someone to watch the toddlers, allowing her to get a full-time job. The constant supervision of her whereabouts proved a major disappointment for both Peggy and her cousin. The imposed curfew provided absolutely no entertainment in Peggy's life. She craved some excitement beyond work, returning home to care for the toddlers and helping out with household chores.

Peggy revealed how, after a couple of months, she convinced her cousin to let her go out to see a movie. "Movie my sweet ass!" Peggy excitedly spoke her inner thoughts at the time. Instead of going to a movie, she hopped in her cousin's beat up ol' Chevy Nova and sped to the nearest bar in the sleepy old town. It was there, she met Bobby Mertz. She spotted his fine wrangler-butt leaned over a pool table. Seductively, she had sidled up to him, after the crack of his cue slamming the seven ball into a corner pocket.

"Hey there, you tall drink of water," she mimicked in the purring cat's voice she used on Bobby.

"A couple rounds of drinks passed and next thing you know," she told Michael and Matthew, "we were laughing and hanging all over each other." She paused. "You know how guys just fawn over me," she drawled. Michael and Matt sat silently, stunned listening to the woman carry on oblivious to anyone else's feeling but her own. Peggy continued, "Anyway, we exchanged numbers and so began my new romance.

Peggy continued her story telling how returned to her cousin's house late, stinking of beer and cigarette smoke. An explosion of raised voices and shouted threats erupted, resulting in the resolution that Peggy needed to find her own place. Thankfully she had met Bobby. She nudged that relationship forward as quickly as possible. In less than a week, she had dumped her desperate need for a place to stay on her new beau's doorstep.

Bobby wasn't sure he wanted a woman and her two young kids moving in with him. After some serious heavy physical persuasion on her part, Bobby agreed that having someone to cook and clean, as well as a decent piece of ass readily available, might not be so bad after all. Peggy further convinced Bobby by adding that she wasn't talking marriage, just moving in. The next week, Peggy and her young'uns moved in with Bobby in his rented farmhouse just outside of Crawfordsville, a very spacious house nestled on a quiet farm property.

Not finished whining about her circumstances, Peggy complained bitterly about the hardest thing she had to get used to: the rumbling shake and haunting blare of the shrill whistle of the freight trains, as they sped down the tracks late every night and again early in the morning. The old farmhouse was situated just a couple thousand yards from the Monon rail line that ran between Lafayette and Wallace Junction. After a few weeks, her system had finally adjusted to the noise, light, and shaking.

Peggy went on to boast that Bobby, unlike her previous boyfriend, provided well for her and the boys. He was prone to slapping her around after a few beers, but nothing she hadn't lived with already. After ten months together, it looked like she might have found a spot to roost. Downside was there was no one to watch the kids. She lamented with a sorrowful face that she never got to accompany Bobby out on the town. Instead, she spent her days watching the kids, cooking, and cleaning. She kept to herself her true thoughts: If she had wanted a boring life like that, she could have stayed with Michael in Indy.

As she wound her life summary to an end, the bill arrived. Peggy purposefully ignored it then gushed her thanks as Michael pulled his credit card out to pay. The lunch ended with Peggy begging Michael and Matthew to allow her to see her son again to rebuild broken ties.

And hopefully get Matt to watch my young'uns, she mused to herself. Actually the only real reason she had initiated this little reunion in the first place.

* * *

As Peggy drove home, she ranted aloud, "What kind of a freak has Michael allowed my son to become? What is it with the black hair and wearing a necklace? If not a sissy boy, he has to be some stoned pot smoker." Not that she was one to talk, but something had to be seriously wrong with that boy. Matthew visiting her was going to go over like a lead balloon with Bobby. Why didn't she just leave well enough alone and not call the kid? When she arrived home, she told Bobby of her meeting with her firstborn. A good slap up side her head emphasized the point that Bobby made—no more kids moving into his place. Amidst tears, Peggy pleaded that there was no intention of that. She just wanted to see Matthew on occasion. "Perhaps, he could even help watch the kids some," she chirped enticingly. It would give her a break and provide them some time to spend out on the town together.

Michael and Matthew's drive back to Indy was filled with bitter disappointment on Michael's part, regretting that he had ever thought that woman could be a mother to his precious child. In typical Peggy fashion, she had made the insufferably long lunch all about her. Never once asking how Matthew had fared over the past eight years of her absence. He groused to Matthew his apologies for having made the mistake of getting that woman pregnant. He was joyous Matthew resulted from the union, but regretted any association with Peggy. Matthew assured his dad that he had great parents in him and Allison. Matt continued to explain that he fully understood—birthmothers were not always caregivers to their offspring. His dad lamented that was probably why Matt was so morbid, wearing black all the time. Matt chuckled to himself, knowing that his fascination with morbidity and mysticism had nothing to do with a mother he really didn't know. He was attracted to the Gothic lifestyle, because it fit his personal mood and offered him a bevy of friends who shared his interests.

As finals approached and the school year neared completion, a frenzied atmosphere of intensive studying and anxiousness pervaded on campus. Matthew was looking forward to the summer vacation, now that he had a group of friends with which to share. He was not surprised that he heard nothing from his mother after their lunch. She hadn't made any contact with him for years, so there was no deep bond from which to feel violated. With summer on the horizon, he focused his energies toward a great summer break.

Chapter 8

Central Indiana
Summer 1981

Matt's fellow goth classmates had set up plans to get together at area coffeehouses a couple times a week. After school let out, Griffin and a few other friends actually hung out at Matthew's house on a regular basis. They compared ideas and mostly sat up in his room, chatting about the world, life's ultimate meanings, and their attraction to the mysterious afterlife. Matthew continued to delve into venerable Egyptian mystics, eagerly reading many scholarly as well as fictional works on the life and deaths of the pharaohs and priests of the ancient Nile valley. He relished fondling his Eye of Horus as he read.

Matt's parents were tolerant, yet confused about the whole thing. His friends were actually polite and respectful, despite their bizarre appearance. Their younger children, to the goths' credit, seemed to simply adore Matthew and his friends. Whispered discussions were frequent between Michael and Allison as to why the group of youth were so ghostly white and always clad in shades of black. Answers proved challenging, beyond saying that Matt and his friends were a little different. But then, Matt had always been different. Matthew was soft spoken, philosophical, intelligent, tolerant, and respectful of others. What more could parents expect from their son? The morbid funky style of him and his friends, his parents could live with.

The summer progressed pretty much like any other summer in the Midwest. The corn grew, and the whole region brimmed with heat and humidity. Matthew and his newfound friends mostly hung out and chatted. What should have been an exciting goth outing at a Cincinnati amusement park ended early after a series of disappointing encounters with unleashed redneck patrons.

Back home early, Matthew explained to his parents about the excessive abuse they had endured while at the park. He resolved that he had no further interest in going where he was definitely not wanted. He explained that New York seemed more open-minded and suited to him. Maybe he would start looking into colleges in the metropolis where he was more likely to blend in with the diversity of peoples bustling along the busy streets. His parents weren't sure that a Midwest boy, even from a moderate-sized city like Indy, was prepared for the rigors of a city of millions. It was probably just a phase for their son—the idea would be gone in a week or so.

Over the course of the summer, Matt was introduced to a few drags on a joint. None of his friends were heavy users, as they enjoyed deep discussions that required a certain level of cognition to conduct. There were times, though, that drifting off into a cloud of haziness enhanced their somber mood. Matt and his friends preferred smoking clove cigarettes as a source of relaxation, and for setting a smoke-filled ambience for some totally bitchin' discussions. There was no denying, however, that the demons of Poe and the edgy haunting of the vampire world conjured by Anne Rice were heightened by the swirl of a cannabis buzz. His parents were blissfully unaware of his foray into hemp exploration. He never participated to a level that produced the distinctive glaze in his eyes or the common reddening, which would have contrasted sharply against his outlined eyes. His parents were well aware of his clothes smelling like those wretched cloves. If that were the worst their son was into, they considered themselves lucky.

Late in July, Matt's birthmother phoned him on a Saturday, begging him to visit her in Crawfordsville to watch the toddlers. It was her anniversary, she whined. She wanted to spend the evening with Bobby. Whoever said his mother was unreliable? She could always be counted on to come asking for something she needed. She promised to pay him for his time. What the hell, he decided. He liked the toddlers, and he had no real plans for the weekend. After checking with his parents, he agreed to drive over by noon.

On arriving, his mother hustled him about the house, showing him the location of food and things for the kids. Finishing with how to operate the TV, she bolted out the door to get her hair done.

Bobby actually arrived back at the house before his mother returned. He left nothing to the imagination, as he threatened to beat the crap out of the freak that had invaded his home. The toddlers were screaming at him to leave Matty alone. Bobby finally backed off, pacing and grousing about the house, complaining about the circus-show offspring his girlfriend had spawned. At the height of one particular rant, Peggy burst in through the backdoor. Frightened, she explained amidst a flurry of cringing gestures that Matthew was her son.

Taken aback by the unusual cleaned-up appearance of his girlfriend, Bobby relented his raging. He was glad to have someone watching the little brats for once. He and Peggy could actually have a night out on the town like adults. They would be able to leisurely enjoy a meal, in lieu of gulping food down at some fast-food joint. Better yet, no frantic greasy sex afterward at home. The pair scurried off, clueless as to where they might end up.

Matthew settled the toddlers in for supper. He found it quite challenging to keep food on their forks, rather than sprayed all over the kitchen. The old farmhouse was quite nice with high ceilings and tall cabinets in the warm old country kitchen. The living room sported a large fireplace. The staircase leading up to the second level could have come from a fine hotel's lobby. French doors and white cornice work added ambience to a wraparound porch that overhung big multipaned windows, offering vistas of the rolling fields surrounding the house. The structure of the house belied the filthy condition in which the house was kept.

His mother and siblings were, quite simply, pigs. Clothes of all sizes were strewn about, interspersed between empty cartons, discarded magazines, newspapers, and food wrappers. The toddler's toys were dirty and flung everywhere. There were tight little paths between the mounds of clutter. Not a single chair or sofa in the house provided an unlittered space.

Matt finished feeding Trevor and Jake. He became repulsed by the pile of dirty dishes and glassware overflowing out of the sink, sprawling across the ample countertops. It seemed there was no dishwasher in this house, neither electric nor the two-handed kind. He attempted to clean up some of the mess, but the kids insisted on him watching TV with them. Compared with the overwhelming challenge of cleaning the filthy house, the toddlers' needs easily won out. Matthew's parents would scream if they saw the chaotic mess in which Peggy lived. Matt was grateful it wasn't his home situation.

Matt wrangled the kids to bed around nine o'clock. Having settled them, he fell into the sagging couch and drifted off to sleep. He was jolted from his slumber by a shaking rumble and jarring whistle of a passing freight train. Surprisingly, the absolute stillness of the rural setting settled quickly back over the house. Matthew once again drifted off.

Early in the morning, his mother and Bobby stumbled noisily into the house, swaying off of each other, stinking of cheap beer and cigarettes. A large belch from Bobby brought their slurred serenade to an end. They stared bleary-eyed at Matt then grunted that he might as well stay the night. It was entirely too late to be driving home, they muttered. Propping each other up, the wrecked pair staggered into their bedroom at the front of the house.

Matt found a blanket lying over a chair in the living room, which seemed to have the least amount of food stains covering it. He sunk back into the trough of the couch, supporting his head on a couple of extra cushions. Before nodding off, he pulled the soiled blanket over himself. He turned the volume up on his Walkman to drown out the rutting sounds coming from the front of the house. Thankfully, Bobby and Peggy's sexual stamina matched their cleaning energy. The house swiftly fell silent, pierced only by a few gentle snores.

At daybreak on Sunday morning, the toddlers came bounding down the stairs to be loudly shooed away by their mother. They then came charging into the family room to find Matthew sprawled on his stomach across their couch. Gently, Trevor lifted a cushion to reveal an eyeball staring back at him with smudged charcoal beneath it.

"Arugh!" Jake screamed. The pair of toddlers then raucously dashed into the kitchen to make their own cereal, as they did every morning. Matthew stumbled into the bathroom, wiping the liner off his face. He joined the kids in the kitchen and poured himself a bowl of cereal. They sat munching, as his mother wobbled in through the kitchen doorway, clutching at the robe she had thrown on—her appearance the makings of a nightmare.

"Morning," she belched, smacking her lips repeatedly until she ran out of spittle. "Thank you for watching the kids, Matty," she burbled with strained sincerity.

She turned suddenly and disappeared into the family room where she rooted around in the refuse, littering the table by the back-door. Retrieving her purse, at last, she tottered back to the kitchen with a ten-dollar bill outstretched toward her son.

"Sorry, it couldn't 'a' been more," she slurred. Grasping her head, she shambled off toward the front of the house, mumbling, "You're welcome to stay longer, if you want." Matt wisely took the cue to get going while the going was good. He waved good-bye to his toddler stepbrothers from the car and headed home.

* * *

Matthew and his goth cronies had recently read Anne Rice's *Interview with the Vampire*. Filled with giddy excitement, the group was convinced that it mirrored their own lives. They spoke for hours on end about their desire to stalk the nights in New Orleans, surrounded by the whispering drapes of hanging Spanish moss and the clatter of horse hooves on the cobbled streets. Nearly every coffeehouse gathering wound up with a lengthy discussion of the early American French town. They fantasized that the present day New Orleans was, surely, just as mysterious and dark as it was in the time of Lestat. So great was their interest in the discovery of the southern port's charms, they spoke at length about potential road trips to the fabled city of decadence and mystery. They were sure the book would be made into a movie.

About three weeks after her anniversary, Peggy found herself pacing the house like a caged lioness desperate to escape. After her recent dip in the rural nightlife, she needed another fix, soon. She called her son to plead her need of his rescue from agonizing boredom. As a tantalizing tidbit to encourage his babysitting her hellions, she added the offer for him to bring some of his friends. Matthew acquiesced to her pleas and invited Nate and Connor to join him.

His friends were not keen on the drive to some backwoods country location, but they didn't want Matthew to sit over there bored on his own. At least, they could debate ideas under the maple trees on the hill. Besides that, Matthew had told them how dark and spooky the spot was with no lights for miles and wind rustling through the leaves of the big drooping trees. Sounded like a perfect place to while away a few hours.

After arriving at Matt's birthmother's place, he and the boys scattered under a front maple tree, watching the toddlers stumble about playing with their toys in the yard. Disturbing their tranquility, Bobby pulled into the drive, yanked open the truck door, leaned over the hood, and yelled, "Come on, woman. We ain't got all night!" Peggy flew out of the house, fastening buttons on her blouse as she leapt into the pickup.

"I see your freak brought little playmates this time. Aren't you worried to have those queer-baits hanging out with your young'uns?"

"They are harmless, hon. They just look weird," Peggy countered.

Having wrestled the toddlers to bed, Matt and his friends decided to check out the ominous barn behind the house. The goth boys were not disappointed by the pitch darkness in the country. In fact, none of them had experienced such an empty feeling of utter void. In the barn, they discovered the lights only worked on the lower level. Without lights to show the way, the boys gingerly crept up the worn, uneven steps. They guardedly ascended into the deep, dark cavern of the hayloft. The faint blush of light, filtering up the staircase opening, cast speckled shadows on the hay mound beams. A summer breeze gently swayed loose shafts of straw across the piles of past harvests. The contents had been dried for so long that the odor was not so much mown grass, as it was musty dust with a hint of mildew. Overhead, hanging tendrils of dirt cascaded down from webs strung in large dangling loops all around them. The boys marveled at having found the perfect gothic alcove.

Snuggled in the soft bedding of the hay mound's mass of time-worn hay, the boys continued their discussions of vampires and the siren's call of New Orleans. At length, Connor pulled a joint from his pocket and lit it up. Warnings of caution erupted from Matt and Nate. They all agreed that the barn was a tinderbox waiting to ignite. The joint was passed, carefully, from hand to hand. Soon the chambered upper tier of the barn had a floating bluish haze to add to the mystique of the somber setting. Conversation waned, as the boys relaxed in the afterglow of a mild buzz. They were startled back to consciousness by the eerie trill of a whistle and rattling shake of a passing train.

"Damn, what a rush!" Connor yelled above the din of the passing train. Unhallowed silence settled over them within a few heartbeats, interrupted only by a light breeze, whistling through some slats in the barn's weather worn siding.

The calm was shattered when Nate shrieked piercingly. He frantically pointed to his right where a deep-orange ember crinkled in an ever-widening circle from the lit joint at its center. Shaken by the passing train, he had dropped the burning torch into the hay at his feet. Blue-and-orange flames leapt from the glowing spread of reddening fibers. In the darkness, the boys stamped frenziedly at the flames with their feet, desperate to crush the life out of the fire before it grew. The stamping served to scatter smoldering embers in a wide random spray. Straight away, they found themselves surrounded by rivers of flame blazing through suffocating smoke. Panicked, they ran for the stairs to escape the ensuing consumption.

Matthew raced to the house to call the fire department, as his two companions twisted an outdoor faucet to life. The sickly trickle of water was useless against the raging inferno. Matthew woke the toddlers, carrying them a safe distance from the barn. The entire structure popped, spewing red-hot glowing sparks into the air. Filled with decades of dust and combustible material, the burn was fast and furious. The roof and supporting beams collapsed in a whirl of fiery ash, chasing itself in cyclone swirls of updraft. There was nothing the boys could do. They clutched the toddlers and each other, hoping against all hope that the house did not go up in flames as well.

The first rural firefighters arrived in a surprising twenty minutes. By then, the heap of glowing red-hot remains of the barn was far beyond salvation. Their only option now was to spray down the garage and house in an effort to contain the fire to a single structure. The leftover embers of the barn were still glowing amid rising plume clouds of dense black smoke, when Bobby and Peggy screeched the pickup to a stop in the driveway in front of their rented home.

"What the hell have those freaks done?" Bobby fumed.

All the kids were huddled, frightened and in shock, behind a protective band of paramedics and firefighters. Bobby ripped himself out of the driver's seat. In his haste, he managed to trip and tumble face first onto the gravel drive. This served to compound his murderous level of fury. He stampeded toward Matt and his friends with his arms flaying wildly. Venom-filled curses rapidly fired from his spitting lips, as he lunged at Matt. To his surprise, he was caught midway by a considerably bulkier volunteer firefighter. Holding Bobby at bay, the firefighter delayed him long enough for Peggy to rush forward. She demanded to know what had happened. Bobby swore and struggled to break free of a pair of firefighters restraining him. The arrival of the sheriff was not a moment too soon to calm the entire situation down several notches.

The boys related the same story they had told the firemen. A spark from a busted bulb, in the lower level, set off the uncontrollable blaze that, in turn, destroyed the barn. Covered with soot and smelling of charred wood, not a trace of pot smell remained on the boys. Bobby doubted the line of bullshit they were shoveling. On the other hand, the old wiring in the barn was several decades old. It certainly could have set off the blaze. Inquiries of why they were even in the barn, resounded in a unanimous account of intrigue by curious young men checking out the old structure.

Bobby called the owner to explain the mishap. The retired owner arrived at the farm a couple hours later to assess the damage. The barn had not been in use for several years with the cattle all moved to another property. Nearly everything had been consumed by the intense heat. Only the partially melted skeletons of an old International Harvester tractor and what had been a Chevy Apache pickup truck remained recognizable among the ashes. The torched barn was a tragic loss of a treasured old vestige of the county's agrarian past; however, there was little that could be done with the scorched remains. Bulldozing them away and returning the ground to a tillable state seemed the logical course of action.

Bobby ranted for a full hour after the owner left. Threatening what he would do to the boys and Peggy if he had to pay for any of the mess. "And God help you all if I get evicted!" Bobby raged. Pacing erratically, Peggy's bellicose boyfriend popped the cap off his third beer in less than twenty minutes. Bobby continued drinking steadily; the house became a hornet's nest of fury. He was having a royal conniption fit, pounding his fist into walls while picking up dining chairs and slamming them forcibly back in place. He had the entire group cowering in fear. Swinging at Peggy's head, the seething bully bellowed, "I want this milquetoast gaggle of pansies out of my house. If you don't agree, you can just go with them."

Trying to dodge intended blows from Bobby, Peggy tearfully begged, "Please, gather your stuff boys. You better get out before Bobby does something foolish."

Foolish, the boys thought. The raging, drunken lunatic was totally beyond foolish. The boys escaped as soon as they could dodge past the drunken raging bull. The ponderous drive home was filled with banter about the blaze, the terrifying ranting of Bobby, and above all, the trauma of the barn burning. Matt had no intention of nearing Bobby or his worthless mother ever again. Tonight had been the final straw for him. The boys remained animated, as Matt dropped his friends off at his respective home. Exhausted and distressed, Matthew pulled into his driveway and made his way into the kitchen.

He took a couple of halting steps toward the sink for a drink of water. Suddenly, the lights flicked on, bathing the kitchen in blinding brightness. His parents stood shocked by the odor of burnt char on their son. Seeing smudges of ash all over his face and arms, Michael and Allison enveloped him in a huge embrace. Releasing to his parents cradling, Matthew shuddered and freely wept. Tears streaming down Matt's sallow cheeks, he explained in graphic detail the events of the harrowing evening.

His parents asked him to not return to his mother's house in Crawfordsville. The nonchalant attitude of his mother combined with the remote setting of a country farmhouse was simply too dangerous. Beyond that, the volatile temper Bobby displayed could easily become a life-threatening situation for their son. Matthew readily agreed. It was not like his mother actually spent time with him while he was over there. He was just a convenient, inexpensive babysitter for her.

The summer continued with Matt and his friends recounting the death-defying blaze they had survived. They regaled their fellow goths with the isolated solitude and pitch darkness of their country adventure. The more they talked about it, the more this cryptic setting became a favored fantasy for the group to recreate. Nate and Connor were soon clamoring for Matthew to take them back out to the farm. The forest behind the house sat enticingly in their minds as a potentially more ominous setting than the barn had been. They affectionately christened the unexplored woods, the dark forest. His protests of parental discord kept his friends content until school started back up.

Chapter 9

Central Indiana
Early Fall 1981

The first few weeks of the fall term passed in a frenzy of the usual adjustments for the new and returning students. The goths quickly resurrected from their summer absence, forging an even tighter-knit group. The newly defined faction stood firmly against the assailant of daily slurs slung their way. Life settled comfortably for everyone amidst the turning leaves of fall.

Still convinced that the dark forest would be the perfect lair, Matthew's closest friends continued to pressure him to return to the farm. They were not deterred by the facts that it was an hour drive away and not easily accessed. The novelty and challenge of reaching their secret lair in the dark forest added immeasurably to the overwhelming desire of the youths to explore it.

At home, Matthew remained his quiet self; however, he did venture out more frequently. His parents attributed his somber mood at home to the conclusive blowup from which he and his birthmother had parted each other's company. He was a typical seventeen-year old, pushing parental boundaries to stake out his place in life. He remained so ethereally quiet, his parents rarely knew whether he was home or out with his friends.

In a brazen attempt to convince Matthew to accompany them to the dark forest lair, his friends vowed they would use one of their parent's cars for the trip. That way, Matt's mother and raging boyfriend would not recognize the vehicle. They would make the trip on a late afternoon weekend, park on a stretch of country road past the farmhouse, then sneak down the railroad tracks under cover of the long growing shadows of sunset. They would all carry flashlights to light their way, ideally arriving at the dark forest lair shortly before dark. At last, Matt relented, and the boys set a date.

The boys met up at a coffeehouse on the appointed day. From there, they eagerly piled into the chosen car. On the drive over to the country, Connor proudly pulled a baggie from his pocket, displaying its dried, wrinkled contents of withered fungi. Connor's cousin had brought some Mexican shrooms up with him while visiting from Arizona. A new experience for the boys, they decided it was a worthy christening treat for their newly discovered philosophers den of the dark forest.

They arrived at a safe pull-off point on the rarely travelled country road where Matt's mother lived. It was late afternoon; the fall sun still cast a fading light. Stealthily, they walked down to the railroad crossing, creeping past the house unnoticed. The mile or so walk down the tracks to the start of the woods was uneventful. The tracks brought them to a railroad trestle bridge that towered some ten feet above the dark forest valley.

Upon reaching the summit of the bridge, they were rewarded with an unexpected bonus, an expansive vista of the forest below. As they scanned the sights from their new vantage point, they all spotted the same intriguing clump of moss covered, blackened with age stones, off to their left. A cemetery! Could the adventure possibly get any better? Their lengthy conjectures about New Orleans and the radical enticement of its ancient cemeteries had suddenly taken on a very tangible reality. Below them, a choice graveyard awaited their exploration.

The entire ditch, beyond the graveled rail tracks, was obstructed by a tangled forest of thistles. As the sun moved into its lowest station for the day, the boys fought the unkempt brambles to reach the hallowed ground. After negotiating around them, the boys confronted an old trackside barbed-fence. Most of the tension had long ago sprung from the strands of languorous wire; however, the wire had uniformly clung to the rotting old fence posts whose rusted staples were meant to last. Hand holding the dangling wires apart, each youth squirmed through. Their slim physiques proved invaluable for clearing the pulled space between the rusty unbending strands. Nevertheless, none of them escaped a barb or two impaling append-ages. Bleeding and agitated, the boys relentlessly plowed forward. They triumphed into a warren of weathered ancient grave markers. Their crusted, lichen–and–mold covered surfaces etched with hand-carved names and descriptions of the deceased.

Resting on fallen logs, the boys surveyed the overgrown plots, marked solely by their crumbling fungal splattered stones. Darkness around them deepened into blackness, broken only by the startling whiteness of their own ashy skin. Eventually, the boys broke out the bag of shrooms and began nibbling on them. It was a new experience. The boys wisely chewed sparingly, anxious about an unfamiliar trip. Bantam hot flashes caused a mild sweat to break out on their brows. The darkness suddenly swirled with bands of colors crashing into each other, then mixing and swirling apart before their eyes. Small chirps of crickets became deafening crescendos of noise. The boys became disoriented, and their speech came slowly and disjointed. Rather than speak, they each leaned back and chose to ride their journeys in meditative silence.

The small nibbles they had consumed diminished after a cou-ple of hours. Still, it had been a totally tubular experience. The boys sat, describing each of their varied trips. Chatter about various top-ics soon turned to the perceived similarities between the dark forest cemetery and the fabled lore of vampiric old New Orleans. Satisfied that the dark forest cemetery lair was worthy of repeat visits, the goths ignited their flashlights and fought their way back through the brambles and fence wire to the tracks.

Suddenly, the ground began to tremble. A distant pinpoint of light pierced the night in front of them. The train! The nine o'clock freight train bore down on them. The beam of light from the train's headlamp radiated out to cover both sides of the tree canyon, between which the tracks traversed. Scooting down to the fence line, the boys watched wide-eyed as the train clacked past them in a whoosh of wind. Startled to alertness by the passing train, they climbed up the embankment and set a rapid pace up the tracks toward their parked car. They had been in their shroom-induced trances for a much more radical time than they had realized. They were going to have to make waves to get home to Indy, pronto, before anyone noticed they were gone. To avoid detection, they used the faint moonlight peeking through the cloud cover to negotiate their way. A couple of near tumbles on the protruding rail ties weren't serious enough to slow their progress.

That was, until Matt toe-stubbed into a full-on face plunge onto a non-budging corner of an I-beam rail. In the fall, he carved a massive laceration across the left side of his skull. The impact was so severe; it immediately threw him into a convulsion. His skull droned repeatedly against the rail, creating a sound similar to the faint twang of a dinner fork drummed on a thick cut of steak. Foam began oozing from between his rattling teeth, dripping down his cheeks in a small rivulet of frothy white bubbles. Without apogee the seizure ended with a final arch of Matthew's spine. The intensity of the involuntary muscle contractions lifted his body over six-inches above the stone-covered track bed. A gush of air wheezed from Matthew's mouth, as his body rag-dolled into a limp heap, eyes staring upward at the dark night sky.

Hysterical, the boys shook Matthew repeatedly while feeling his chest and neckline for any faint hope of a pulsing beat. Lightly buzzed from their dark forest adventure, the boys fretted about what actions to take. Matthew was clearly dead. His mother and the knuckle-dragger, Bobby, had no clue that they were out on the tracks. From what they had witnessed during their visit with the pair, they were confident that neither of the dull adults would prove helpful nor even concerned about their situation. The reality was, no one knew where the boys were.

After some quick debate, it was decided to pitch Matthew's supine body into the pond just below the tracks where they stood. If his body were found, no one would know how he ended up in a pond. They would tell anyone who inquired that they had not seen Matthew after he left a coffeehouse in Indy. Frightened and uncertain, the boys made a pact to keep Matthew's death and the discovery of their secret lair guarded secrets. Sobbing and quavering, the boys easily hefted the gaunt figure of their cherished friend. Nate and Connor launched him in an expansive arc into the pond. The morose splash signaled the finality of their treasured friend. Clutching each other's shoulders, Nate and Connor made their way back to the car.

They wept and commiserated their agonizing loss the entire return journey to Indy.

Matthew's slim body floated for a time. His Eye of Horus necklace hovered above his chest, eventually drifting free of his neck. Freed it floated delicately before being drawn downward by the weighty drag on the metal emblem attached to the leather strand. It clunked with a faint *thwunk* against a sunken log. The leather strand floated in the under current, swaying about like a pendulous underwater seaweed strand. On one swaying loop, it snagged on a protruding splinter of wood where it would remain until found several years later. Matthew's body drifted toward the tall reeds lining the western edge of the pond. Mired there, his body was never discovered. It decomposed through parasitic invasion and nibbling by the aquatic and airborne scavengers of the pond.

Matthew's parents franticly searched the house for their son, who hadn't slept in his bed the night before. Where could he possibly be? They called the police to report him missing. They became dispirited immediately at the first question the detective asked. Does Matthew have any friends? Yes, they knew he had friends but sadly they had never thought to gather their names or any contact information about them.

Inquiries at several local goth haunts proved fruitless. A vague lead of Matthew's possible whereabouts was his expressed interest of venturing to New Orleans. An investigation at Matthew's school yielded further elusive leads.

Michael's call to Peggy resulted in a tirade of ridicule on his parenting abilities. Not surprisingly, no further communication ever occurred between the estranged exes. The conclusion of the police investigation was that Matthew had run off to New Orleans to fulfill some youthful fantasies. A posting of his photo and description was sent to the NOPD, who pitched the file into a burgeoning heap already filling their understaffed coffers. After several months of no response, Matthew was assumed gone forever—his existence merely a whisper of ghostly white paleness.

Vanishing Veterans

"Battle Hymn of the Republic"

Mine eyes have seen the glory of the coming
of the Lord:
He is trampling out the vintage where
the grapes of wrath are stored;
He hath loosed the fateful lightning of His
terrible swift sword:
His truth is marching on.

—Julia Ward Howe, 1862

Boogie-Woogie

Boogie-woogie is an African American style of piano-based blues that became popular in the late 1930s and early 1940s, but originated much earlier. While the blues traditionally depicts a variety of emotions, boogie-woogie is mainly associated with dancing.

Swing bands of the 1940s incorporated the boogie-woogie beat into some of their music. The Andrews Sisters sang some boogies, after which the floodgates were flung wide open. It was expected that every big band should have one or two boogie numbers in their repertoire to accommodate the dancers learning the Jitterbug and the Lindy Hop dances, which required the boogie beat.

Chapter 10

Miller Farm, resident home of Quaking Pond
Twenty miles southwest of Sugar Creek
Montgomery County, Indiana
June 2, 10:20 a.m., CST

Joe finished explaining to Mikey about the Eye of Horus. Surprisingly, Mikey had actually listened to the explanation without squirming. Explanation received, he was ready to slosh through more mud to find something else. Joe fell in behind his youngest son, as Mikey eagerly trudged toward another gooey hillock.

Movement in the oozing residue of the pond's floor was really quite difficult, even for an adult. The Millers had to frequently pull a foot free with their hands to dislodge it from the clinging mud. Each and every time, the freed foot was accompanied by a satisfying *schwuck* sound and a splatter of mud droplets. Although Joe would never admit it to the boys, he also found it fun as they mucked about in the mud and slime.

The boy's mother, Kris, did not find their mud-splattered clothes fun at all. After the previous day's exploration, she had banned them completely from anywhere near the house. Kris immediately established detailed clean-room procedures for the house. Unless it was followed completely, there would be no supper for the explorers. She reminded them constantly, "I'm not going to have filth from that stinking pond in my house. You hear me?" The thought brought a smile to Joe's face, picturing her with her hands on her hips, shaking just a little, as she laid down the law to the men in her household. She might be little, but she could wield a powerful punch with just her words. All three of the Miller males knew better than to cross her.

With a frown etched on his face, Mikey called out, "Dad, I'm losin' m' boot! Help!" Joe turned, reached down to his son's boot top, and pulled it free. None of them wanted to accidentally set their sock-clad foot in the muck. Heck, Joe figured if it happened, they would just have to burn both the boots and socks.

"There Mikey, you're free. You feel like I can let go of you?"

"Sure, Dad, I got it now." Mikey steadied himself. "Whew! That was a close one. I almost lost m' boot!"

"That would've been a nasty shame, little one. I'd've had to carry you back to the barn. And then, go buy you a whole new pair of boots before we could get back to exploring."

"I'll be more careful, Daddy. I don't wanna stop exploring. I'm having too much fun!" Mikey squealed and cast about for the next discovery.

"Hey, Joseph! You finding anything over there?" Joe hollered. He could see Joseph about twelve feet away with this head bent over peering into the murky goo. As Joe started toward his eldest, his boot snagged, causing him to stumble.

"Whoa, Dad, you almost fell over!" Mikey exclaimed. "Whad'ya trip on?"

"My boot has caught on something," Joe said, as he reached down into the mud with his gloved hand. His fingers clamped around an object mired in the gunk. Prying it loose, he could make out a pair of round disks attached to a strap. Freed, an unmistakable shape beneath the dripping ooze revealed itself. "Well, I'll be, Mikey! This looks like an old pair of motorcycle goggles."

"Looks like dirty alien glasses to me, Dad!" Mikey giggled.

"Nah, when we get these cleaned up, you'll see that it's a pair of goggles motorcycle riders wore to protect their eyes," Joe explained. "This must be from way back during World War II."

"When was that, Dad?"

"Back in the 1940s, Mikey, over sixty years ago." Joe held up the dripping pair of goggles and called out to Joseph, "Look at this pair of old goggles we found, Joseph!"

"That's cool, Dad!" Joseph shouted. "I think I found something too. It's sorta shiny! May even be gold!"

"You keep finding all the shiny stuff!" Joe cheered. "Hang on, Mikey and I will come over to you. We'll take a look at it together."

When Mikey and Joe got to Joseph, he was in the process of vigorously rubbing a tiny little object in his hand on his jeans to dislodge the caked-on mud.

"Look at this, Dad!" Joseph exclaimed, holding aloft a button-sized disk. "It's got a spread eagle design on it!" he whooped in excitement, proudly dumping it into his dad's extended palm.

"How do you keep finding all the treasures, Joseph?" Joe asked with a brimming smile. "This looks like a Union soldier's button. We'll have to get it cleaned up to be certain. Did you just find one?"

"So far, Dad, I was looking around for more."

"The way the water flew out of this pond, if there were others, they could be anywhere," Joe snorted. "Maybe we'll find some more. 'Cause if it came off a uniform, there'd've been several." The three Millers scanned the immediate area, stirring through the mud, finding zilch.

"Let's slosh in and clean up boys?" Joe urged. "It's about time for lunch. By the time we get finished washin' up, your mom will have lunch ready under the shade trees. Sure will surprise her, if we're sittin' near the backdoor when she comes out."

The boys agreed it was a grand idea, at which point, the trio began the arduous task of treading through the slime back to the house. While they were cleaning themselves up, they hosed down their found treasures. The cleaned items unveiled a tarnished brass button, plus a leather-strapped pair of well-worn motorcycle goggles. The Miller men were pleased as punch with their morning haul.

Kris was indeed surprised when she popped out the backdoor to call her men for lunch. She found them grinning up at her from their perch under a big ol' maple tree in the backyard. "Well, look what the pond monster dragged in," she chided her hungry family. "I'm surprised you all are sitting here, knowing there is *so* much more to explore."

"We're hungry, Mom!" Mikey burst out, giggling.

"You got that right, little one. What you got to feed us, woman?" Joe jokingly quipped at his wife.

"Keep talking like that, mister, and all you'll get is slapped upside the head," Kris retorted. Laughing at her family's antics, Kris turned back into the house. She returned with a tray filled with sandwiches, chips, cold canned drinks, and some packaged desserts.

"Just what we needed, hon." Joe beamed. They all sat around munching while filling Kris in on the morning's finds.

Chapter 11

Montgomery County, Indiana
Tuesday, May 2, 1865

Corporal Thomas Wheeler sat wearily staring at the flames dancing about the fire in his parent's fireplace. The tiny four-room house was all that was left of them. A harsh winter two years ago had stolen both of them from him. The doctors identified their killer as smallpox. Thomas had been deep in the battlefield, when a letter sent from his sister finally reached him. There was nothing he could have done had he been at home; nevertheless, he would have liked to have comforted his parents and bade them farewell. He had seen many people suffering from the disease, on and off the battlefield.

The pain his parents had to have endured saddened him deeply. He knew, from witnessing it firsthand, the anguishing manifestations plaguing those who contracted the disease. Before finally succumbing to death, the victim's body suffered itching red rashes all over their skin, high fevers, the shakes, diarrhea, and vomiting. His parents were elderly, their bodies already weakened by the scarcity of food during the war. The only comforting thing his sister had written him was that they did not last long in their miserable condition. They essentially died of starvation and thirst, not being able to get any nourishment past their swollen mouths and throats.

It was hardly a comfort to them, or him. Thomas still shuddered at the pain they suffered. Not that he was any stranger to suffering. Three years in the Union forces at the forefront of the fighting, in the second corps of the Army of the Potomac, had provided all the suffering a man should ever have to withstand. So much bloodshed, so many mutilated corpses, and all for what, to free a group of people that weren't even sure what freedom really meant. No, that wasn't fair. The emancipated slaves did indeed know what it meant to be free of the harsh treatment of their masters. They did not know, yet, what it was to be a free citizen of the United States. That would come with time perhaps, but not right now.

Thomas rocked gently in the rocking chair his momma had rocked him in as an infant. His mind wandered to the various battles he had participated in during the course of the war: the Second Battle of Bull Run, the Battle of Antietam, the Fredericksburg, and Gettysburg Campaigns. He had been standing guard among the crowds, listening to President Lincoln deliver his memorial dedication speech at Gettysburg. His stature and compassion towering over those gathered on the blood-soaked field.

Under General Meade, they had routed the Southern scourge in Richmond and had sent their yellow-bellied hides a running for the hills. Thomas smiled as he recalled the crestfallen look on Robert Lee's face as he left McLean's House at Appomattox. The Confederate General was dressed in an immaculate uniform with shined boots and a polished dress sword. Grant showed up in his usual rumpled uniform and half-drunken state—an embarrassment to the troops. Thomas remembered, as Lee rode off, a chorus of raucous cheers arose. Grant rightfully put an end to their celebration. He remonstrated that the defeated Confederates were once again our countrymen, and we should not exult over their downfall. Thomas brooded to himself that that kindness was truly one of the noblest statements out of Grant's mouth.

Little good all the fighting and bloodshed had done, evil still reigned supreme in the nation, divided or not. Thomas had galloped his way home from Appomattox. His time in the army was at an end. He needed to get home to mourn his parents properly. He rode into Indianapolis, ready for the final fifty miles left in his journey to his boyhood home. He had heard rumors that something had happened to Abraham Lincoln, but no one seemed to know for sure. Thomas's arrival preceded the arrival of the funeral train of the president by just two days. It was true, he discovered, Lincoln had been assassinated by an actor named John Wilkes Booth. How could such a great man be struck down by such a cowardly deed? There was truly no justice in the world.

Thomas had stayed with a cousin in nearby Brownsburg so he could view his fallen commander while his body lay in state at the Indiana Statehouse. Thomas sorrowfully stood in the long line of mourners honoring the president's body. He, like the nation, was in shock and great sorrow at the loss of their beloved president.

Thomas saw no reason to continue on with his life. His parents were gone. Betsy, the neighbor girl he had been sweet on before he marched off to war, was gone. She had married a guy from over the Stateline. Staring at the flickering flames in the fireplace, he was reminded of the auburn-haired maiden with blue eyes, the color of deep summer skies. She had a natural fragrance that drew him in like a moth to a flame. He was building up the courage to court her when instead he rode off to defend the nation he loved. Love, a shattered concept for Thomas. Everyone he had ever loved was gone from his life. In their place, nightmares jolted Thomas from his sleep each and every night. They repeated in vivid detail the violent atrocities he had witnessed as graphic as the day he saw each recurring massacre happen. Rocking ever more slowly, his thoughts confirmed that life had lasted long enough for him. As the embers burned to ashes in the fireplace, Thomas drifted off to sleep.

Thomas woke with a start and shivered in the chill morning air that filled the house. Today would be his last, he resolved. He dressed himself in his war-tattered uniform, straightening it as best he could. Shining his mud-splattered boots, he realized he had no parting obligations. His sister had moved to Illinois, some sixty miles away, to be with her husband's family. She had taken what few livestock had been left after his parent's passing. No one, Thomas lamented, would know that he had passed. Might as well get it over with today. He mounted his trusty horse and began riding across muddy fields and greening pastures. About seven miles from his parent's house was a large pond that he remembered from his youth—it would become his final resting place.

A spring shower with mildly blowing wind soaked him and his horse to the bone, a fitting state to his somber mood. Drenched and fully depressed, Thomas reached the pond. As he anticipated, not a soul was around. The rain had driven the farmers in for the afternoon, at least, until the showers ended. Thomas dismounted and slapped his horse on the rump, sending him trotting away. He knew someone would find his healthy mount and care for him.

Standing tall with resignation, he began marching toward the southeastern shore of the pond. He marched forward until his body rose and began to float. His body's buoyancy naturally upended him into a prone position. Thomas lay perfectly still on the surface of the pond. His navy woolen uniform still adorned with a few Union brass buttons soaked up water like a dry sponge, dragging him downward. The combined weight of his boots and uniform pulled him further toward the underside—closer and closer to the thin edge of the pond surface. Soon, his head began bobbing, dipping under the water, and ever so slowly drifting back up. He didn't struggle to stay afloat. With each dip under, he gulped in as much water as he could. His body fought to prevent its drowning; however, Thomas's will of self-destruction was stronger than his body's natural defenses. In no time, the lapping water covered his nose and mouth.

Thomas opened his mouth, allowing the pond to envelope him completely. As he drifted down on the nether side, his eyes captured the fading light from the surface. His thoughts centered on soon meeting his parents and his fallen comrades in arms. He might even get to see his beloved president, again. As the last light faded from his vision, he found the peace that he had fought so valiantly to preserve for all his countrymen.

Chapter 12

Montgomery County, Indiana
December 1946

It sure felt good to be home again in Indiana. Eddie Hall needed plenty of home cooking and some serious relaxation time. The last three years had been sheer hell. He had witnessed endless violence and death. If it weren't for his good buddies fighting right beside him, he wasn't sure how he would have survived. In fact, it really was a miracle he had survived; so many of the boys never made it back. Damn, it gave him shivers down his spine just thinking about all the gruesome, misshapen bodies strewn across the battlefields of Africa and Europe. All because some crazy Nazi Jerry thought he had to rule the world. Well, they fried his ass. He would rot in the depths of hell for all eternity.

Eddie stretched on the motorcycle seat and cracked his back. Guess it was always going to give him trouble, thanks to that shrapnel he took from a mortar blast in Fédala. "Favor of God," it meant in Arabic. Heck, the only favor he found there was not dying from one of the Jerry's bullets whistling over his head. Now, other parts of Morocco were gorgeous, not that they had had any time to sightsee. General Patton, launching Operation Torch, kept their butts a movin', chasing right after the ol' Jerries straight over the top of Africa. And what a slaughter it had been, on both sides, for three years straight.

Dismounting his humdinger of a ride, Eddie popped a handkerchief from his pocket. He gingerly wiped the dust off the Chief logo on his shiny new Indian Chief motorcycle. He was dang proud of his beaut. A two-tone, cream and cornflower blue, body with fenders set off by decorative leather fringe around the base of the comfy seat. Leather saddlebags hanging from the rear wheel well finished off the look. It was, in every way, a Dillinger worthy ride with guttural horsepower. With one last twist of his back, Eddie strode into the lobby bar of the famed Crawford Hotel. He stripped his driving goggles off his head as he cleared the front door.

Some of his war buddies were joining him that afternoon for a few mugs of swell Schlitz beer raised to the end of the war. Eddie hoped to stay the night with his pal and fellow veteran, Charlie Groves, at his parent's farm just east of Crawfordsville. Charlie had ended up with a gimp leg courtesy of a knee-shattering bullet in the Palermo skirmishes. Eddie couldn't believe Patton made them storm the coast of Italy with no armor backup. A few bullets couldn't stop the ol' Cottonbalers, though; they were, and always would be the toughest bunch of bastards in the war. After the big guns got there, they had the Eyetalians and Nazis on a real run for their lives. Ah, the good ol' days of the war. There were so many sharecroppers with gorgeous gams and tight waists, lining up like eager beavers to thank a soldier the way he wanted to be thanked. Better not let Patton or any of the officers catch you going at it. Everyone sweet-talked the dames, especially sharecroppers who passed themselves from guy to guy with reckless abandon. Without argument, they were a good way to catch disease. Knock on wood, he hadn't caught anything.

Eddie was early and chilled after his ride, so he seated himself away from the breezy front lobby. Content to wait for his friends to arrive, Eddie might as well get some grub. With a flourish, he hailed the waiter, snatching his white cloth napkin off the table then tucking it under his chin. He ordered up some chow. The blue-plate special arrived much quicker than he expected; his meatloaf and three veggies were served piping hot in front of him. He dove right into the drab food. Army rations and occasional roadside fruit had been his diet for way too long. He eagerly ravaged a basket full of freshly baked bread, with which he finished up the gravy-soaked deliciousness of his meal. Ah, life was good back in the Midwest. Just as he was sopping up the very last drippings left on his plate, in walked Charlie with Jimmy, another fellow veteran, right behind him.

"What's buzzin', cousins?" Eddie greeted the pair.

"Here to see what delusional women you have bamboozled into thinking you're the cat's meow, ol' boogie-woggie Hall!" Jimmy jabbed at Eddie.

"I can't help it, if the dames are khaki-wacky over my ducky shincracker moves!" Eddie quipped, with a few shuffles of his stompers to prove his point. "Besides if you weren't such a dead hoofer, you'd have more dolls hanging off your arm. Never saw anyone dance as bad as you do, Jimmy. Really how can a guy be so darn handsome, and yet, not dance worth a hoot?"

"Ahw, Eddie, we weren't all gifted as a rug-cutter, like you," Jimmy joked, as a big smile spread across his face. "Guess I got the good looks, and you got the magic feet."

"That's enough out of the both of you." Charlie groused. "Thanks to that Eyetalian's bullet, I can't dance at all. I have to rely on my brilliant wit to attract the dames."

"Wit, eh? That would explain you not having a honey, Charlie." Jimmy chuckled as he explained. "'Cause you ain't got any wit, ya nit wit!"

Roaring at Jimmy's humor, all three men embraced each other in a group bear hug. "Sure good to be here with you guys. This is gonna be a gas!" Eddie added.

"Hey, Eddie, Charlie tells me that Fifth Avenue gas-horse out front is yours," Jimmy egged his friend on.

"Ain't she just in the groove!" Eddie glowed. "Blue, the color of a gorgeous woman's eyes!" "If you behave, I may take you on a ride later."

"You mean I can take her for a drive?" Jimmy asked excitedly.

"Oh, hell no, remember, I saw you driving around in Italy," Eddie snorted with a defiant shake of his head. "I wouldn't let you alone with my babe for anything. You'll have to ride back of me, if you want to try her out."

"Sit down, boys. The grub's good here. We should order some chow. The rest of the boys are driving in from Lafayette and Danville, could be a while yet. Whatcha say?" Eddie asked, raising his right eyebrow.

They all sat and ordered up some dinner and drinks. The night had all the makings of a big ol' whoopee. When dinner arrived, the trio attacked their plates. They all had a huge appreciation for home-cooked food after months of army rations and many a skipped meal.

"So tell me, Eddie, are there any virgins left between here and New York?" Charlie asked his friend. "Actually, are there any between here and Berlin?" He finished with a huge grin swept across his face.

"Oh, Charlie, I left a couple in Ohio for you. There is one old ugly one, missing some teeth, over in Indianapolis." Eddie teased. Eddie couldn't help it that he had such a reputation with the ladies. His debonair looks, muscles, and fancy dance steps made him the center of attention for all the dames. Charlie and most of the guys were just jealous, and who could blame them.

On his way home after discharge, Eddie had managed to sleep his way through the dames and sharecroppers all the way from New York to Hobart, Indiana. Eddie was encouraged by the sheer number of lonely women deprived of male companionship during the war. Eddie was only too happy to brighten their day, and their night.

The dining area began to fill up with dinner guests. Before long, everyone in the place was transfixed by the trio of veterans' war stories. The notoriety of the Seventh Infantry Regiment was known to everyone in the States. The crowd from rural Indiana was thrilled to have some real live heroes in their midst. They clamored to buy the boys a drink of thanks. The stories and raucous noise got even louder as Tommy, Dick, and Billy showed up. The crowd roared with their antics, applauding their stories of conquest all across the African cap. The shouts of thanks rang even louder when the boys detailed their capture of Hitler's retreat at Berchtesgaden back in April.

What an incredible evening. The boys were already giddy to be safely back home. To receive such warm heartfelt thanks was just icing on the cake. The veterans were royally ossified after the endless congratulatory drinks. They stood swaying on the sidewalk, trying to prop each other up. As patrons exited the hotel, they slapped them merrily on their backs. Suddenly, the hotel manager appeared, insisting that the boys stay the night in his hotel, his treat. They had brought so much unexpected business in with their war tales; it was the least he could do. None of them, he pointed out, was in any shape to drive. He would be honored to house some of America's finest heroes. Reluctant to accept a free night's rooming, the former soldiers acquiesced on the side of reason and followed the manager back into the hotel to waiting beds.

Late the next morning, the groggy group descended to the dining room for a much-needed breakfast and gallons of coffee. They laughed about their reveling from the previous evening. Again, they marveled at how thankful their fellow countrymen were for all the pain and punishment they had endured—to ensure freedom for all Americans. They all agreed that warm reception and heartfelt passion had pervaded throughout the country. They knew they were damn lucky to have survived. The retired warriors were extremely grateful for a grateful nation.

Eddie, in his typical over-the-top fashion, began to regale the boys with stories of his shenanigans since leaving New York. How, they wondered, could a kid from such a small country town in rural Indiana be such a grandstander? He assured them it wasn't his small town background, but rather, Hobart's proximity to Chicago's active South Side gin-joints that had helped him acquire his boogie-woogie reputation. He bragged about getting togged to the bricks, looking real spiffy, to go romping from one ritzy joint to the next. Eddie played a mean trumpet and a wicked saxophone, another reason they called him Boogie-Woogie Hall back in the ranks. He would often jump up on stage in Chicago, just to show the crowd gathered that he was very in the groove.

After his arrival back from the war, Eddie had continued his passion for dolls, drinking, and having a great time all across the country. He snagged his spiffy Indian Chief in Cleveland. He was not about to arrive back home on the bus like some poor ol' chump. He loved that motorcycle, almost as much as he loved getting into trouble. He raced about like a daredevil. On several occasions, he had come close to tipping it over.

The boys sat and chewed the fat for a couple of hours over some strong black coffee. They actually had more in the hotel than they would have had at home. Rationing was still in force, and coffee was like gold out on the streets. They inquired about each other's plans for the future. Most of the group was going to help their parent's out on their farms, like Charlie. Eddie exclaimed he wasn't ready to settle down, quite yet. No surprise there, the boys agreed. Eddie said he planned to spend Christmas with his parents up in Hobart. That way he could still drag a hoof at the frolic pads on Chicago's South Side. Otherwise, there was no way he could handle the boredom of Hobart at night.

He ran the idea of starting his own service garage past the group. Thought he would start up out in California. Catch him some new scenery and give the West Coast dames a chance to enjoy his handsome mug. They all breathed a sigh of relief. There might be a few women left in the region for them, if, Eddie moved out West. They all agreed that big money was to be had in service work. Given Eddie's skilled hands, the boys championed his decision to open an independent garage.

Eddie thanked them for their vote of confidence. Turning to Charlie, he asked if he could hang out at the Groves's farm for the night. Charlie was happy to have his war buddy around another day. The plan was for Eddie to stay the night, return to Hobart the next day, and then head out on his great western adventure after Christmas. That settled, the group made plans for having a reunion of the boys the next year. Eddie was sure he would be able to make his way back out to Indiana.

The group said their farewells amid parting hugs, heading off toward their separate destinations. Eddie hopped on his Chief and followed Charlie out to his parent's farm. Charlie's parents were over-joyed to have the gregarious Eddie stay the night, inviting him to stay even longer. Eddie graciously declined, determined to begin his trip back up to Hobart the next morning.

Charlie and Eddie chatted in the warm country kitchen for several hours, making future plans and promises they were unlikely to keep. The euphoria of having survived the brutal realities of the European and African campaigns was tempered by the relative uncertainty of their futures. Eddie continued to brag about his potential conquests. He just couldn't help being a lounge lizard. There were just too many women, and not nearly enough time.

As early afternoon passed on with a sigh of silence, Eddie began to get antsy for some action. Knowing that none of the bars in the area would be of interest to Eddie, Charlie suggested he go for a ride. Eddie took his advice, pulled a wool cap over his goggles, and hopped on his Chief. A good high-speed romp on some country roads would burn off some of the excess energy he had buzzing.

He raced down country road after country road. At one point he, swallowed a bug. "Where the heck did that motorized freckle come from this time of year?" He rent the air, spitting the little giblets of the critter off his tongue. Up and down the muddy roads he roared. It wasn't much, but at least it was something to do. He was glad he had decided to head back up north the next morning. The slumbering boondocks of Crawfordsville was no more hotsy-totsy than his home town of Hobart. At least up there he could scoot into Chicago to have a ball. He drove through downtown C'ville and found the sidewalks already rolled up for the evening. Yowzah, how was he going to even survive the night in this place?

He decided to race out the serpentine Ladoga Road south of town for one last run before the daylight ran out. The wind whipped into him, pressing his thick wool jacket tight against his muscular chest. He barreled into curves and leapt over little hills on the road, causing his stomach to do a little jump before landing each time. He had gone out about six miles out when decided it was time to head back. On his way back, he turned down a side road that looked particularly hilly.

"Soitenly, should be a dandy ride over these little bumps," he chortled aloud. Down the road he tore, revving the engine on each tiny peak. As he climbed yet another hill, he came upon a railroad crossing. He bumped over the poorly laid crossing. Midway across, he caught a glimpse of the tracks extending toward the distant horizon. He slammed on his brakes and did a one-eighty back onto the tracks. Applesauce! This was going to be darb fun, he just knew it. A light dusting of snow belied the true roughness of the ties between the rails.

What the heck, this could be a real barn burner, Eddie thought. He eased his Chief down into the tie bed between the rails. Lined up, he coaxed the ol' girl with a little gas. He was off, bouncing down the track with his teeth rattling. His vision leaping up and down like a wobbling chicken pecking at feed on the ground. Despite the jarring, it was the cat's meow. He goosed the speed up, just a notch, having grown accustomed to the slippery wiggle of his tires on the icy, wooden ties. He would occasionally hit an offset tie that would bump his butt into the air.

Fully enjoying himself, he was cruising along at a comfortable clip. He had passed a farmhouse and buildings next to the track. Up ahead, he could see a big pond off to his right. He was staring at it, not paying attention to the tracks, when his front tire snagged on a loose rail baseplate. The slick metal plate slid across the snow slickened wood of the rail tie, unexpectedly wrenching the front tire of the Chief to the right. Fighting to gain control, Eddie could not avoid slamming the front tire into the rail. The motorcycle's momentum tipped the rear tire upward at an angle that launched Eddie ass over teakettle over the handlebars. His plummeting arc pitched him toward the pond nestled below the track bed.

Plunging toward its chilly depths, he shouted, "Horse feathers, this ain't gonna be good!" Despite all his warring accomplishments, Eddie couldn't swim. In fact, he knew from the few attempts that he had made, he sank like a stone the minute he hit water. This was not going to end well. His vision of a garage in California was about to become nothing more than a dream.

His body slammed into the freezing pond water in a spectacular belly flop. The force of the impact knocked his goggles off. His forward thrust carried him some ten feet from the shore. A distance from which, he knew, he would never make back to shore. His heavy wool coat quickly absorbed massive amount of water, serving as a deadweight to lower his struggling limbs below the water's edge. He tried to inhale one last gulp of air; instead, he sucked in a lungful of water. His heroic return to the Midwest marked only by a few bubbles cresting on the wavering pond surface.

Later, after darkness had fallen, the evening freight train came roaring down the slope from the north. The engineer was behind schedule. This stretch of track, with no towns around, was a great spot to catch up some lost time. Barreling down the tracks, the engineer never saw the motorcycle lying on its side against the right rail. The engine plowed into it with full force, obliterating the machine into hundreds of shrapnel-like shards, which rained down on the underbrush lining the sides of the railroad bed. Later, curious people would marvel at the unrecognizable bits and pieces of rubber, metal, and leather, wondering what they could have been. The diminutive debris would surrender no clues about the loss of life they represented.

Quaking Pond Emerges

Native American Indian Removal Act

My friends, circumstances render it impossible that you can flourish in the midst of a civilized community. You have but one remedy within your reach, and that is to remove to the west. And the sooner you do this, the sooner you will commence your career of improvement and prosperity.

—Andrew Jackson

1811–1812
New Madrid Fault Earthquakes

The sequence of earthquakes that began early on the morning of December 16, 1811, in present day Northeast Arkansas and Southeast Missouri, remain the most significant recorded seismic event to have occurred in eastern central North America.

Chapter 13

Miller Farm, Resident Home of Quaking Pond
Twenty Miles Southwest of Sugar Creek
Montgomery County, Indiana
June 2, 6:50 p.m., CST

Joe Miller and the boys had been sloshing through pond muck for hours. As dusk descended, the trio labored through the sticky hillocks toward home. Perhaps tomorrow, they would give it a look over for any more treasures the pond might reveal. They could see several large objects poking above the sludge. The day had been long, and they were all ready for supper.

Clearing the busted dam gap, Joe and the boys still had to footslog their way over the mud and debris strewn in front of them. When the dam had burst open, rocks and pieces of detritus had flown outward in a hail of hurled matter. The plummeting chunks of earth had left craters in the ground on impact. Many of the clumps had exploded, sending little shards skittering across the ground. Walking through the field, Joe was reminded of the blasted war fields he had experienced during his tour in Afghanistan.

Joe was startled out of drifting down that unpleasant train of thought, when his youngest son tugged on his sleeve and asked, "Daddy, why does this big rock have a dip in it?"

Joe looked down at the rock Mike was pointing to and hefted the two-pound chunk of granite. "Mikey, my boy, you have found yourself a Native American grinding stone." In his hands, Joe held a worn oval piece of granite with a hollowed concave surface on top. He smiled brightly at the object and detailed the rock's origins. "This was made by the first peoples who used to live in this area. No telling how old it is."

"What's it do, Dad?" Mikey asked. "It looks like a smooth rock to me."

Joe held the rock out for Joseph and Mikey to look at. He explained that the original peoples in the area were farmers, just as they were. A grinding stone was formed from a hard piece of rock. By chipping away at the top of the rock, the Natives would nick away gravelly bits until they had made an oval or circular indentation. They would then put dried corn grains in the dip. Using another smooth river stone, they would rotate the river stone against the top of the grinding stone. This crude grinder would crush the grains of corn into meal. When the grains were ground into a course powder, a squaw would brush the powder into a nearby container. The meal could then be used to make bread, or something similar to Mom's pancakes.

Joe grasped his son's little hand and gently rotated Mikey's fingertips over the craggy surface of the stone. "See how rough this is?" he asked Mikey. "This bumpy surface would have helped grind the grain more easily. This granite grinding stone would have been a great one to use."

"Wow, Dad it's really cool that this old rock could do all of that," Mikey chirped.

"You've got a great find there, Mikey. Let's take that up to the house and show your mom." Joe patted his son on the head and then added with a wink, "We can tell her we brought her a new kitchen appliance."

"Dad, she won't think that's funny," Mikey chided. Joe hefted the weighty stone into the crook of his arm to carry, as he and the boys headed toward the water hoses at the barn. Striding across the pasture, Joe pondered what the Native American population around these parts must have been like.

Chapter 14

Shawnee Village of Black Wolf,
Twenty Miles Southwest of Sugar Creek
Montgomery County, Indiana
Fall 1811

Blue Feather stopped for a moment to stretch the muscles in her back. She had been grinding corn under the shade of a young black locust tree on the indented oval rock of granite for a couple of hours. Dried seed pods shed from locust trees littered the ground around her. She now had enough cornmeal for a week's worth of cooking. The corn harvest had been exceptionally good this year. They even had enough grain to use for trade. She smiled as she thought of some of the tools, baskets, and cloth she might ask Black Wolf to barter for. He would complain, of course, then "surprise" her with her desires as gifts a few weeks later. Naturally, her mate would take credit for his generous consideration of her needs. He was a strong man with a tough exterior but a warm heart. She knew those qualities made him a great warrior, a generous provider, and an incredible lover. He was that. She grinned to herself at the thought.

Blue Feather's toddler son, Black Fish, scampered about in front of her chasing butterflies and splashing through the shallow brook that gently wound its way between the homes comprising their village. What a peaceful spot Black Wolf had found here in this valley between two rolling hills. The spring-fed brook was surrounded on all sides by a healthy growth of sapling poplar and black locust trees.

To the north and south of the brook stood dense forest of sturdy poplar and maple trees. The abundance of Grandmother Earth's hooved children had kept their village well fed and clothed over the many moons they had lived in the valley. The heady fragrance of late summer peony blooms filled the air with a delightful scent. Such a wonderful day. Blue Feather leaned back a bit and allowed the sun's rays to warm her smiling face.

Blue Feather's daydreams were broken by her middle son's return from drawing water. Pausing for a break, she and Dancing Moon comfortably drank some of the cool brook water he had just carried over. Refreshed, Blue Feather suggested she and Dancing Moon should walk into the woods and gather some of the ripe paw-paw fruit for their evening meal. A sizeable grove grew in the woods a short walk south of the village. Blue Feather and Dancing Moon comfortably strolled under the shade of the pawpaw grove's broad, drooping leaves, gathering a basket full of the fleshy sweet fruit. The fruit was ripe from now until winter's first breath chilled the land.

With a breeze blowing pleasantly beneath the shade of the grove, the pair settled for a brief rest from the morning sun while munching on the delicious fruit. Dancing Moon rarely had a leisurely moment alone with his mother. Eager to learn his family's history, Dancing Moon recognized a perfect time to ask.

"Why have we traveled so far away from our former hunting grounds?"

Blue Feather's simple answer was, "It was best and safest that we fled the wave of palefaces invading our sacred hunting grounds."

Dancing Moon knew the Shawnee were fierce warriors. They were among the most feared and respected of all nations in the Great Miami River valley. Aware of their great victory over the equally fearsome Iroquois nation, he asked, "Nie-kea, why did we flee the white man instead of defeating him in battle?" As he shifted to look up at his mother, dried leaves crackled and rustled beneath him.

Blue Feather decided to answer her son with stories of the family's migration to their small valley settlement—one full moon's walking from their original tribal village along the Miami River. Patiently, Blue Feather took a deep breath and proudly detailed an account to her son.

"Many moons past, frightening numbers of white men poured over the mountains into our Miami River Valley. They were preceded by their warriors, armed with fire sticks and swift horses. Their fire sticks and thunder makers could kill our warriors from a distance before we even got close to the paleface. The white devils massacred hundreds of our nation with their metal stones of death and steel knives. Worse, they infected our peoples with great illness, causing hundreds more from our noble tribes to die painfully. There was nothing that could be done for them. We survivors had to watch them fade into the great hunting grounds of the heavens."

Shuddering and sighing heavily, Blue Feather continued. "We Shawnee together with the Miami nation battled heavily against the white man's expansion into our lands. At the same time, our battles stormed. The white men violently fought among themselves. The British, the French, and the newly formed tribe called the Colonists all intended to seize our lands that they called the Northwest Territories. Sometimes they fought together against us, at other times they just fought each other. During this time of unrest, our great leaders like Little Turtle and Blue Jacket would make peace with one group of white men, only to stave off another advancing group of palefaces. It was so confusing for everyone. No one could be trusted. Fighting seemed the only constant." A shiver ran down Blue Feather's spine as she was reminded of the terror and slaughter during that period of their lives.

"Your father and uncles moved the family around so much. We struggled to swiftly reassemble our *wiikiwas* in each new campsite. You know what a difficult task it is, from helping your father repair our domed hut with fresh tree bark and dried grasses.

"Oh, I do, Nie-kea. Strapping the branches together to build the dome for our wiikiwa is so hard to do without causing the branches to bend too far and snap. It must have been so hard tearing our village wiikiwas down and rebuilding them on the run." Dancing Moon shook his head back and forth in contemplation of the speed at which his fellow villagers would have had to move.

"Indeed it was, son, we would find a safe spot away from the fighting when all too soon your father and uncles would march off to join Blue Jacket in another raid against the hairy mouths, who had crept deeper into our lands. The battles had many names, depending on who was speaking of them."

After hearing the names of several of the decisive battles, Dancing Moon asked his mother, "What did the palefaces call these battles, Nie-kea?"

Pausing a moment to recall what she had learned from a Presbyterian missionary's wife teaching at a wilderness trading post during their flight from the Miami valley, Blue Feather answered, "My speaking of the hairy mouth tongue is no very good, but some of the battles I remember were Dunmore's War, the Chickamauga Wars, and the Battle of Point Pleasant." She ticked each one off on her fingers, shaking her head unable to recall any other white devil names for the bloody battles. She summed up her short litany. "The white men lumped them all together, calling them the Northwest Indian Wars."

"When did the hairy mouths drive us from the Miami River, Nie-kea?" Dancing Moon asked his momma.

"That happened, my son, when our Chief Blue Jacket and Chief Little Turtle of the Miami tribes merged our warriors to fight the white men on the banks of the Maumee River. We were not prepared to take on their mighty warrior, Anthony Wayne, and his force, the Legion of the United States Army. We were beaten in what became known as the Battle of Fallen Timbers. It was after this defeat when Blue Jacket and many tribal elders gave our rights to the Miami Valley lands to the United States of America. Not all of us agreed with what the palefaces call the Treaty of Greenville. It was, and still, is a theft of our homeland."

"Several of us Shawnee moved here to where the white men call the Indiana Territory. We hope in the future to reclaim our Miami River lands and keep all these lands safe for our peoples. Our great warrior, Tecumseh, seeks even now to unite all our nations west of what the Lenape tribes call the Allegheny Mountains. Tecumseh prophesizes that as a united force, we will drive the white devils from of our lands."

"When do you think this will happen, Nie-kea?"

"I am not sure, Dancing Moon. Tecumseh has yet to unite the nations. In the meantime, your father has continued moving us farther and farther west, away from the smell of white men. Their expansion into our lands has grown worse, especially after they began building forts south of the Maumee River valley. Your father rightfully believes that our lives are in danger. We have no choice other than to flee ahead of the white man's approach. We are not strong enough as individual villages of warriors to defeat the white devils. Your grandfather, Drowning Bear, kept insisting that we should accept the white man's offer of peace. As a warrior, your father felt that protecting us was more important than any claims of peace by the palefaces. They have never been true to their words of peace."

Blue Feather took a deep breath and drew herself up. Dancing Moon watched her face go slack, and a sadness darken the sparkle of her eyes as his mother continued. "Three full seasons after the battle of Fallen Timbers, both your grandparents caught the white man's death. They died very quickly. The pain of losing them settled deep inside your father's soul. This was what drove your father to lead us, your uncles, and the rest of the village far away from the white men and their devastating diseases."

"So No'tha still misses his mother and father?" Dancing Moon looked at his mother with surprise written across his brow.

"Of course, he misses them. "Would you not miss us? Do not mention what I have told you to your father. Your no'tha is a very proud man and doesn't like to show emotion."

"I won't, Nie-kea. I know No'tha does not like to talk about grandmother and grandfather. What happened to your mother and father, Nei-kea?"

Blue feather adjusted to a more comfortable position and storied on. "We had stopped in so many temporary locations in our flight from the white man. Often I've lived in camps with only fur-skin tarps to shelter me, knowing that—all too soon—our group would need to pack up and move again. Your grandmother, Blue Sky, was very old when we fled the white man. My mother became very sick that first winter from the extreme cold in one of our camps. She died in just weeks. Your grandfather, Big Corn, swore it was the hairy mouth's disease. But I believe it was just the cold with such little protection. We had not had time to build anything, not even to put a single wiikiwa together. We were huddled under skins with worn-out fur-skin blankets wrapped around us against the wind and snow."

A tear ran down Blue Feather's cheek as she continued to reminisce about her departed parents. "Angry and determined to make the white devil pay for taking his wife, your grandfather was too old to fight but to stubborn not to. After your grandmother died, he insisted on going on the next raid with your father and uncles. A white devil's bullet found his heart, and he died instantly. I wept for my parents like your father did for his, but I had you and your older brother to worry about. You were about the size your little brother, Black Fish, is now. I had to be strong like your father and keep up with the constant moving we had to endure for many, many moons."

Blue Feather shifted sideways and scratched her rump for a moment before continuing. "Finally, your father found our home here in this quiet valley. Here you and your brother could grow up safe. This village is where your brother, Black Fish, was born. Right here in our wiikiwa. " Dancing Moon sat mesmerized by what all his mother had told him. He had many questions now. He had just opened his mouth to start a barrage of them when Blue Feather's youngest son's squeal like a wounded black crow interrupted her yarn to Dancing Moon.

They looked up to see Black Fish pointing like an arrow toward the neighboring cornfield. From the rows of corn emerged Black Wolf and Cornstalk, their eldest son, carrying a young doe tied on a pole between them. Black Fish took off at a dead run to greet his no'tha. Blue Feather waved at her two brave hunters, as they trundled their heavy burden closer to the family's wiikiwa.

"Black Fish, go and find your uncles!"

Caught up in the excitement of the suspended, swaying deer, Black Fish barely broke his stride as he raced up and clamped his little toddler fists onto his father's leather britches. "No'tha, No'tha, you killed a big deer today!"

"Don't pull on me, Little One. This deer is heavy to carry. We have traveled very far with it. Go and find your uncles, like your mother asked. "

"Okay, No'tha, I be back. No cut deer without me!" yelled Black Fish, scurrying away as fast as his tiny four-year old legs could carry him to find his uncles.

Blue Feather warmly greeted her returning provider with a generous smile and outstretched arms. "Welcome home, I see

Kuhkoomtheyna smiles favorably on her earth-bound grandchildren with a most successful hunt."

"Indeed she did, dear mate. We will have much meat with which to feast and a good strong hide to keep us warm this coming *paipoun'oui.*" Black Wolf beamed as he showered praise on his eldest son. "Cornstalk drove the beast directly into the path of my swift arrow. He is a true warrior among men. I am most honored to call him my son." Cornstalk blushed, lowering his head in response to his father's admiration. "Go, Cornstalk, gather the villagers that we may prepare this deer," Black Wolf commanded. Cornstalk bowed and went to round up the village. Together, the tribe would celebrate the good fortune of an excellent kill with plenty of meat to share.

A buzz of commotion filled the grove of trees beside the village, as the small community gathered to skin and butcher the deer. Laughing Fox and Lone Arrow, Black Wolf's brothers, arrived and began assisting their brother. First, blessings were offered to the fallen sister deer's spirit for providing sustenance to her brothers and sisters who would continue to survive thanks to her great sacrifice. The preparation and preservation of the slain deer consumed the entire day, involving special processes handed down through generations of Shawnee. When work was finished, no part of the deer would go unused.

A sumptuous feast was prepared to rejoice Kuhkoomtheyna's generosity. A blazing bonfire provided the backdrop to some joyous chanting and drum beating in celebration. Some of the youth regained their energy, dancing and frolicking around the fire. Laughter and story sharing filled the night air. Eventually, the families retired to their wiikiwas, exhausted, yet filled with a sense of purpose and renewed faith in life's bountiful blessings.

The next morning, Black Wolf sat by a small fire outside his wiikiwa, watching the sun rise on the October horizon. His thoughts were focused on the battle he felt brewing in the region. The white man presence had continued to grow. A scattering of forts had been built along the banks of the Wabash River. Where there were forts, shortly after, battles generally ensued. He dreaded the assault war would have on his little cluster of family and friends. They were already so small in numbers. War with the palefaces would dwindle their numbers further.

Somber, he stared at the twelve small bark covered wiikiwa nestled before him. He and his brethren remained in these dome-shaped branch-framed huts covered in bark and dried grasses. The easily transported homes afforded them the flexibility they might need to pack up and flee hairy mouths invading their territory. Near the base of the southern hill the tribe had built a large structure, which served as their community meeting place. The rear of the building, which functioned as the village's smokehouse, was now filled with the bounty of a good hunt and hard work by his village.

Feeling a bit nostalgic, Black Wolf took a moment to gaze about at the excellent spot he had chosen for his family and friends. Five generous natural springs formed a tiny brook winding down the village's center, supplying them with plenty of fresh water. In every direction he looked, Black Wolf could appreciate the surrounding forest. Next to their village locust groves provided ample firewood. Scattered around the hillsides were sturdy maple and locust trees, shading the village from the summer heat. A short distance beyond the trees grew thicker and denser into a forest filled with plentiful game to keep his tribe well fed. He hoped they would not be driven from this peaceful site he had found.

So far, no white settlers had invaded. Black Wolf knew it was only a matter of time before they poured into the area like a plague of summer locust. The white man swarm, once started, would spread en masse devouring all the land. He cringed at the impending doom headed their way. In anticipation of once again having to battle with the palefaces, Black Wolf's thoughts drifted to his fellow veteran of the Battle of Fallen Timbers, Tecumseh. The mighty Shawnee warrior Tecumseh led the many tribesmen, like Black Wolf, who had refused to sign the treacherous white man's Treaty of Greenville. Recognizing the need for a sizable force, Tecumseh had recently traveled to the southeast to attempt to build alliances with the so-called Five Civilized Tribes—the Choctaw, Chickasaw, Muscogee, Cherokee, Seminole, and Creek nations—to join him in the fight against the white man's expansion into what remained of tribal lands. If the white man continued to press westward into the Indiana Territory, where would the tribes hunt and grow their crops? White peoples did not share with native peoples. So fight they must for their very survival.

Tecumseh had made a promise to the Indiana Territories governor, William Henry Harrison. He had boldly sworn that he would seek a confederacy of Indian tribes to fight the white man's unjust theft of land at the 1809 signing of the Treaty of Fort Wayne. Tecumseh contended that the white man had—no right—to encroach upon tribal lands. Harrison, the future ninth president of the United States, countered that the land was owned by the Pottawatomie and Miami Indians; therefore, it was their land to cede, if they wished. The stalemate that ensued between the two rivals was quickly heating up to a full-blown confrontation. It was inevitable that scattered skirmishes would soon erupt—Tecumseh's war was on the horizon.

Black Wolf's reflections had now fully disgusted himself with the fight he knew would have to be waged. Rather than sit moping about it, he rose from the fire and began the day's work. The prospects that faced him and his fellow villagers were menacing.

* * *

A lone rider came galloping into the village at dusk, the beginning of the frost moon, November. Breathless, the brave sought to speak with Black Wolf. Rushing from his home, Black Wolf greeted the rider with familiar warmth.

"What brings you to our village, Running Bear?" Black Wolf asked with genuine alarm in his voice.

"Harrison marches north, dear brother!" Running Bear exclaimed in a burst of pent-up passion. "We must have you and your brothers' help to save Prophetstown. We are certain that is where he intends to attack."

"What proof do you have that he intends to attack?" Black Wolf countered in surprise at the claim.

"His men are all armed, and they carry banners of war. They left their Fort Knox last week. Marching an army from Vincennes takes no more than six days. They will arrive in Prophetstown tomorrow or the next day." Running Bear panted.

"This is serious, my brother, of course, we will fight by your side," Black Wolf assured him. "Let my warriors gather their weapons. We will make ready our village and depart at dawn. We can reach Prophetstown by early afternoon, tomorrow. You rest, and then ride on to warn others."

"I will rest briefly, brother," Running Bear gasped. "Time is a luxury we do not have, I fear!"

The entire village had heard Running Bear's warning of danger. The families had returned to their homes to begin the necessary preparations. With troops headed up the territory, Black Wolf could not leave the village defenseless against wild animal or two-legged beast attacks. He would take his oldest son, Cornstalk, with him into battle. Dancing Moon and two warriors would remain to protect the village against any threats.

The warriors slept fitfully, knowing they were about to face a most powerful and ruthless foe. In the morning, they painted war stripes on their faces and arms. They then gathered in a circle, while Black Wolf evoked blessings from Kuhkoomtheyna for success in battle. The warrior party rode north just as the sun peeked over the horizon, forty miles of hard ride lay ahead of them.

* * *

They arrived at Prophetstown late in the afternoon where a small dust cloud was swirling from the frenzied preparations of its inhabitants. Harrison and his army were just a few hours away from the frantic town.

Tenskwatawa, the Prophet, had been left in charge of Prophetstown by his brother, Tecumseh. Tenskwatawa's followers rightfully feared an imminent attack. Fortification of the town had begun, but the defenses were far from complete. Tenskwatawa was a spiritual leader—not a military man. He was immensely relieved, as Black Wolf and several other warriors from the surrounding area arrived. Black Wolf expertly gathered the warriors to plan strategies of action. The warriors trusted Black Wolf. He carried himself with purpose and spoke with decisive authority. His leadership was respected among the warriors in the nation, even Tecumseh held Black Wolf with well-earned esteem. The warriors and village were anxious having to confront this challenge without the strength of Tenskwatawa's brother, Tecumseh, leading them.

As Harrison's forces approached Prophetstown, late on November 7, they were met by one of Tenskwatawa's followers waving a white flag. He carried a message from Tenskwatawa requesting a meeting the next day, when the two sides could talk peacefully. Harrison agreed but was wary of Tenskwatawa's profession of peace. Believing that the negotiations would be futile, Harrison moved his army of about a thousand soldiers to a nearby hill overlooking the confluence of the Wabash and Tippecanoe Rivers. Harrison ordered his men to make camp in battle array then settled into a guarded night's rest.

During the evening, Tenskwatawa consulted with the spirits. From his divinations, the Prophet decided that sending a party to murder Harrison, in his tent, was the best way to avoid a battle. He assured his warriors safety and victory. He proceeded to cast spells that he promised would prevent them from being harmed. He boasted that confusion would envelope Harrison's army rendering them powerless.

Invigorated with confidence, the warriors moved out and swiftly surrounded Harrison's army. Harrison and his soldiers awoke to scattered gunshots. Discovering themselves encircled by Indian forces, the attack took the army by surprise. The Shawnee warriors shouted war calls and rushed the camp defenders, initially breaching the camp. After several bloody skirmishes, the soldiers regrouped, eventually repulsing the warriors. The Indian warriors retreated to Prophetstown where hysteria had led to a harried mass exodus from the relatively defenseless town.

The following day, November 8, Harrison sent a small group of men to inspect the red varmints' town. They found it deserted, except for one elderly woman too sick to flee. The rest of the defeated redskins had evacuated the village during the night. Harrison ordered his troops to confiscate everything of value then burn Prophetstown to the ground. In the center of town, the soldiers dug a mass grave, into which they unceremoniously dumped the bodies of the fallen savages. As the town burned around them, the soldiers built large fires over the mass grave in an attempt to conceal it from the Red Scourge, whom they feared might seek revenge.

Chapter 15

Shawnee Village of Black Wolf,
Twenty Miles Southwest of Sugar Creek
The Indiana Territories
Mid-November 1811

Black Wolf held his head lower and lower as he and his fellow warriors neared their home. Exhausted, bruised, and recovering from wounds, how was Black Wolf going to tell Lone Arrow's family that he had been killed in battle? Worse, he had been scalped by the evil white soldiers. Perhaps he would spare this detail. Lone Arrow's death would cause the entire village heartrending pain. He had been well-liked and treasured for his strength and gentle manner. It had been two long weeks, since the disaster at Prophetstown. He had sent Cornstalk home to the village to help protect the families there. He asked him not to reveal Lone Arrow's death. Instead, he instructed him to prepare the village for refugees who might wander in from the aftermath of the Prophetstown massacre.

As Laughing Fox and the rest of the warrior party entered the village, a somber air of mourning hung over the huddled wiikiwas. Blue Feather and his three sons came forward in greeting. Although overjoyed to see the warriors' safe return, a great sorrow was marred across their faces.

"No'tha, I did not tell anyone about Uncle Lone Arrow," Cornstalk declared. Black Wolf's countenance lowered further still as he realized the village knew of his brother's heinous death. He knew, now, they were all in mourning at the loss of their great friend and fellow warrior. He swung off his horse with a labored grunt and approached his family. He clutched his wife and youngest son, Black Fish, in a deep embrace. Ruffling the hair of Dancing Moon, he turned to Cornstalk and placed his rough large hand on the young warrior's shoulder.

"If not you, son, then, who did tell the village of Lone Arrow's death?" Black Wolf inquired softly of his trembling son.

"Some warriors from a village further south stopped for food and rest, No'tha," Cornstalk reported. "They spoke at length in the meeting house about much of the bloody battle, including Uncle's death and scalping at the hands of white men!"

"I understand, brave son. I should have known that you would not betray my trust. It is very good to see you well and protecting our village. I am very proud of you Cornstalk. You fought valiantly in the battle and have fulfilled my wishes here in the village with honor," Black Wolf praised his eldest son. He looked into his family's eyes and said, "I must go now and greet Whispering Quail. She must be devastated at the loss of Lone Arrow."

"She wailed for many nights mourning her husband, but as a mother, she must be strong and stand firm to raise and protect her children," Blue Feather spoke while tightly hugging her husband. "I will go with you to greet her."

Together, Black Wolf and Blue Feather approached a well-built wiikiwa on the far western edge of the village. Whispering Quail sat by a small cooking fire outside her home with her two small sons. Noticing the approach of Black Wolf, she leapt to her feet and ran toward him, shaking her fists in the air. She reached Black Wolf and began pounding on his strong broad chest with her frail fists. Deep wails and cries of agony erupted from her lungs.

"How could you have let him be killed?" she screamed. "He trusted you with his life!" We trusted you with his life! How could you fail us?" Great heaving sobs overcame Whispering Quail as she sank to her knees, cowering at Black Wolf's feet. Blue Feather bent and gathered the sobbing woman in her arms. She stroked her matted hair as she patted her back and held her tight.

Eventually, her sobbing slowed. Whispering Quail raised her swollen eyes to meet Black Wolf's stoic gaze. "I am so sorry, brother.

I know you loved Lone Arrow, and that you did everything you could to protect him. Forgive me please, for my sorrow and misspoken words. I am so very sad," Whispering Quail muttered from a deeply broken spirit.

"I share your great sorrow and loss, dear sister. Lone Arrow was more than a brother to me. He was my treasured friend. I cannot describe the anguish that fills my heart. I am destroyed at his passing. I pray only that he looks down on us from the Great Spirit world. I ache to find some way to continue on without him," Black Wolf spoke tenderly to his sister-in-law, before tilting his head back and roaring at the heavens. "Why did you take my brother? I need him! We need him, here, with us!" he shouted at the heavens, shaking his fist skyward in anger. The three adults clung to each other, wailing uncontrollably. Tears coursed down their cheeks in great rivulets; each mourner heaving their shoulders in agony, as gulped breaths filled their lungs for another round of harrowing moans and wails. The villagers gathered round the trio, and soon, the entire night was filled with the combined wails and skyward curses of a village mourning a cherished member of their tribe.

Eventually, the villagers wandered back to their own homes. The reunion of the returning warriors was bittersweet, given their shared loss of Lone Arrow. Laughing Fox and his wife, Raven's Egg, joined Whispering Quail and her children in their home for the night—not wanting to leave them alone after such a tender outpouring of emotion from the entire village. Black Wolf and his family reluctantly returned to their home. He promised a full accounting of all that had happened at Prophetstown the next day.

The next morning, Black Wolf gathered all of the villagers into the meetinghouse. The crowd was oppressively tight in the cramped quarters, not intended for the entire village. Black Wolf let the group settle then began by detailing the battle with Harrison's larger army. Black Wolf used expansive hand gestures to highlight the major points of the battle's ebbs and flows. His voice softened as he told them of the rallied efforts of the United States army to cause their strong warriors to retreat in desperation. Back at Prophetstown, the warriors found the town at a peak frenzy of panic. The women and elderly were gathering what they could carry, hustling their screaming children off into the woods.

In a reverent voice, Black Wolf recounted, "Several of our returning bloody and wounded warriors surrounded the Prophet, railing accusations of betrayal at him. They accused him of deceiving them. They even denounced him as actually being on the side of the white man, just like Black Hoof from down south. Tenskwatawa stubbornly denied such actions. He cowardly blamed his wife for desecrating his medicines; that being, he claimed the reason his protection and victory spells had failed. Disgusted, our warriors turned their backs on him and stormed off to join their fleeing families. Like a rabid dog, Tenskwatawa raced about the town, trying to convince warriors to allow him to invoke a new blessing to the spirits for another attack on Harrison's tired and weakened soldiers. His cries fell on deaf ears."

Taking a deep breath, Black Wolf explained further, "In a desperate effort to regain some level of confidence in his leadership, Tenskwatawa began ranting at the Winnebago tribal members who were slinking off into the woods in retreat. He accused them of instigating the initial attack on the soldiers' camp before the Prophet's incantations of blessings could be finished. It was their fault, he bellowed, for the resounding defeat and loss of so many of our brothers in battle. The Winnebago stopped, bent over, and blew gas in Tenskwatawa's direction, giving him the respect they felt he deserved for his betrayal. All our brethren frantically fled Prophetstown until the entire village was empty. While our peoples fled, Harrison's soldiers were busy fortifying their camp all afternoon. They paid little attention to our fleeing brethren."

Black Wolf paused a moment to collect his thoughts, giving time for the image of Prophetstown completely deserted to soak in. The villagers visibly shuddered as they reflected on the confusion and fear their fellow brethren had to have felt. As the crowd quieted, Black Wolf went on, "Myself, Laughing Fox, Cornstalk, and a few other warriors hid on a hillside overlooking Prophetstown and the army camp. Throughout the afternoon and evening, we heard the bloodcurdling screams of men being killed in the tall grasses and nearby woods. We knew it was our fellow brothers, but there was nothing our little band of survivors could do against the scores of white men. It was then, I ordered Cornstalk to make his way south to our village to warn you that stray soldiers might be a threat."

The crowd irrupted into shouts of gratitude for Cornstalk's bravery and warning. Black Wolf again waited for them to quiet and continued his tale. "In the early morning, we watched a company of hairy mouths leave their camp and make their way toward our abandoned wiikiwas of Prophetstown. The soldiers cautiously entered the town, searching for survivors of the battle. After they blew a signal on their horn, Harrison and a large contingent of his soldiers arrived, executing a further search of every wiikiwa in town. The sole resident they found was an elderly squaw, left behind, being unable to travel. Shouting and raising his sword in victory, Harrison ordered every building in the town burned to the ground. As the fires blazed, his soldiers began dragging the bodies of our fallen brothers into the burning village. They piled them into a heap at the center of the town, throwing burnable materials on top so that the bodies charred and burned down to bone bits and ashes."

Upon hearing this savagery, the gathered villagers erupted with shouts of outrage and curses spat at the hairy mouths. Their raging and beating of chests continued for some time. Eventually, Black Wolf raised his hand to quite the group. After a few more rants, they calmed and listened as he began the mournful story of Lone Arrow's death.

"Having burned Prophetstown to the ground, Harrison sent scouting troops out into the neighboring woods to search for any survivors. We watched them stomp through the brambles at the wood's edge. Scanning ahead of the soldiers' advance, we spotted Lone Arrow, crouched behind a patch of dense blackberry bushes. There was absolutely nothing we could do to save him. The troops had spotted him also. They had him surrounded. With bayonet's lunging, the soldiers hacked at Lone Arrow until he fell onto the ground, spurting blood. In silent horror, I watched as a savage soldier yanked my brother up by his long hair. Breathing in labored huffs, Lone Arrow looked skyward and loudly invoked *Mishe Moneto's* blessings on his family. With a wild scream, the savage holding up Lone Arrow's head plunged the hunting knife deep across the top of Lone Arrow's forehead. He viciously thrust the knife backwards along Lone Arrow's skull in a gruesome act of violence. The whole while, Lone Arrow bellowed in pain. As the savage yellow-eye proudly displayed his bloody prize, my brother's body quivered, and then, his bleeding head slumped. Lone Arrow's spirit escaped to the heavens with a final sigh of pain."

Whispering Quail unleashed a high-pitched animal scream and fainted. Many of the villagers began to wail anew at the gory description of Lone Arrow's final moments. Even Black Wolf had to pause his accounting. As a community, they wept and grieved aloud. For some time, the meetinghouse walls shook with the clamor of their sorrow.

Regaining his composure, Black Wolf told the assembled village, "Lone Arrow's death was the saddest moment in my life. To witness my own brother's disgraceful death at the hands of an uncaring and ruthless white man is a continuing punishment to my soul. Worst of all, there was nothing I could do. Lone Arrow was already dead. Giving up our location with a shout of protest would have sealed the fate of the Prophet, how we were obligated to protect."

Continuing his tale, Black Wolf recounted what transpired next. "We watched in morbid silence, as Lone Arrow's and other warriors' bodies were carelessly dragged into town and flung upon the bonfire of seething human carcasses. Shouts of triumph and joy erupted from Harrison and his troops, as they stood, watching the town burn completely to the ground. After a time, they returned to their camp, breaking it down for transport south to Vincennes.

"Finished with their treacherous work, Harrison's troops broke camp the next morning, marching south to Vincennes. An hour after Harrison's last troops faded over the horizon, we descended on the makeshift mass grave of our brethren. We offered prayers and blessings over the buried members of our tribes, beseeching their spirits to find peace and happiness in the great hunting grounds. We needed to get the Prophet to safety, so I devised a plan to journey westward to a village of our allies, the Kickapoo, on the Sangamon River. With practiced stealth, we traveled unmolested a safe distance behind the advancing army. After many days, we came to a never-before-seen structure on the highlands above the banks of the Wabash. The tiny French trading post of Terre Haute had been transformed into the beginning stages of a major fort.

"We crossed the Wabash River a mile or so north of the new fort. From there, we continued our trek westward to the Kickapoo village along the Sangamon River. On hearing of the tragedy that had befallen Prophetstown, the villagers vowed to see the Prophet safely south to a Hathawekela Shawnee village in Muscogee territory, near the white man's town of Cape Girardeau. Freed of the burden of protecting the Prophet, we anxiously began our return home."

Black Wolf humbly announced that the story had ended by walking out through the gathered villagers. The crowd stood and followed him out into the brisk sunshine of late November. As they pressed around him, Black Wolf raised his arms to the heavens. Looking up to the sky, he began a slow somber chant. He invoked Mishe Moneto and Kuhkoomtheyna to watch over his departed brother, asking that his spirit find peace and happiness in the great hunting ground of the sky. He implored Grandmother Earth to bless his friends and family—to keep them safe and free from harm. Bowing his head, he turned and walked toward his home, leaving the group to disperse.

Chapter 16

New Madrid Earthquake Zone
December 1811

When Tecumseh found out about the disaster at Prophetstown, he made great haste to meet his brother, the Prophet, at the Hathawekela Shawnee Village, near Cape Girardeau. From there, he called upon his favored warriors, scattered all across the Shawnee lands, to join him at the Cape. Black Wolf, his brother; Laughing Fox; and another village warrior, Smooth Rock, answered his call. It took them a week to ride the long distance.

By the time they arrived, Tecumseh had whipped the gathering warriors into a fury, seeking revenge for their fallen brothers. Tecumseh spouted vicious threats of what should be done to the heinous hairy mouths. Many at the gathering preached restraint, appealing to their brethren to consider both sides of the situation in a spirit of understanding. A number of the Shawnee, like Black Hoof, had already adopted white customs. Their hopes were that the yellow-eyes would allow the tribes to continue to live on the land if they adopted white customs. They were following the examples of the Five Great Nations: Cherokee, Chickasaw, Choctaw, Creek, and Seminole. These venerable tribes had, long since, adopted the white man's ways. In fact, they were admired as the civilized savages among the white men. Not that this civility ultimately rewarded them; they were, in fact, summarily expelled by force to western reservations with Andrew Jackson's signing of the Native American Removal Act.

The talk of adopting the white man's ways further enraged Tecumseh. He had spent months trying to convince his southern brothers to join him in the fight against the white man. To his dismay, the Five Great Nations simply responded that they had personally felt the superior weapons and power of the white man; as a result, they had adopted the white man's way of life. For them, it was a means of self-preservation in a world expanding daily to the flood of overflowing whiteness.

Now, members of his own tribe were trying to abate Tecumseh's efforts with similar inaction. No, he would not stand idle while the white man stole their native hunting grounds. He would not allow American soldiers more opportunity to rape their native sisters and pillage their vulnerable villages. The plague of encroaching white men must be stopped here and now at all costs.

The arguments for and against retaliation on the palefaces continued for days. The heated discussions often erupted into physical confrontations. Almost hourly, tribal members' opinions swayed back and forth. Above it all, Tecumseh's rants for revenge rang the loudest. Black Wolf and his fellow warriors had experienced the hatred and greed of the growlers just weeks earlier. They chose to align themselves with their friend and compatriot, Tecumseh. They would continue to support him in his warmongering against the spread of the evil white skins.

On December 16, long before the first rays of sunlight glimmered in the east, the encampment of warriors was jolted from slumber by a violent upheaval of the earth. They were camped a few hundred miles from the initial epicenter of an 8.1 magnitude earthquake along the New Madrid fault line, which ran directly beneath their prone bodies. Leaping to their feet, the warriors were shaken and thrown about like tall grass blowing in the wind. The noise filling the night was deafening. All around them, the darkness was punctuated by the screams of frightened warriors running to and fro. The cacophony intensified with the haunted cries of fowls and beasts. Violent cracks and pops of falling trees crescendoed with the deep roaring of the Mississippi River to create an audible nightmare. When the shaking stopped, the hysteria of man and beast stilled. The eerie silence was as unsettling as the confusion of the ground shaking.

At dawn, the warriors discovered that none had perished. Awestruck, they gawked at the fallen trees all around them. Many of the local tribe's buildings had collapsed. Peering down upon the river, they spied massive sections of the cliff side that had collapsed and fallen into the river, explaining the splashing noises heard in the darkness. The gathered warriors were just building fires and making food, when the earth began to shudder once more with equal intensity. Fire embers were violently thrown through the air, landing like small flaming arrows on the bedding lying about the camp.

Trees still standing swayed and snapped, crashing with great bouncing thuds to the trembling ground. The birds and animals, again, took flight and fled in all directions. More cliff bank avalanches slid thunderously into the river. A rumble, like mighty thunder, filled the hillside. Deep cracks split open in the ground in numerous spots. The whole while, the earth shook and shimmered back and forth like a child shifting sand in his open hands. Some sections of ground transformed into glutinous quicksand, engulfing people and animals in a sea of moving dirt. The river itself seemed to shift backwards, flowing north, before righting itself. Great waves sloshed out of the Mississippi's banks and spread out across the lowlands in a massive flowing flood, swallowing trees, shrubs, and any wildlife that could not escape. At the great bend in the river, below the Cape, waves crashed in all directions.

Eventually, a guarded calm returned, at which point, the warriors milled about checking on fellow campmates. Suddenly, a great cry pierced the sizzling hum of the camp. Tecumseh had climbed atop a fallen tree trunk, ranting at his highest level.

"The Great Spirits have sent a sign that our confederate resistance to the white man's expansion is favored. Who will join me in this sanctified quest to rid our sacred hunting grounds of the accursed yellow-eyes?"

Still in shock from the second release of nature's furious power, most of the warriors carried on, surveying the earthquake's damage. Tecumseh would not be ignored. He dashed about the gathered groups, imploring each of them to join him in his righteous quest.

Aftershocks continued to rattle the area. The anxious warriors had heard enough of Tecumseh's warmongering rants. As a group, the tribesmen gathered their skittish horses, packed up their belongings, and began the onerous journey back to their distant villages. Black Wolf and his fellow warriors were eager to get home as well. In unison with the departing tribes, they set off on a journey that would take them a week to navigate past the flooded lands and fallen trees strewn across their path.

* * *

The rumbling New Madrid fault had sent shock waves radiating outward toward Black Wolf's village several hundred miles away. Reaching the tiny village near simultaneously as it shattered the areas alongside the Mississippi, Black Wolf's village was jounced as if the mighty fist of Mishe Moneto had been slammed against the ground. Terror-stricken, the villagers leapt from their sleeping skins and ran into the night air. Several of the wiikiwas collapsed in the violent shaking. Birds screeched as they set flight into the night sky. Animals stampeded. The panicked screams of frightened women and children shattered the darkness. The muffled cries of those buried beneath collapsed bark and dried grasses were drowned out by the piercing clamor. As the bedlam calmed, the villagers gathered around three collapsed wiikiwas, pulling survivors from the wreckage.

After tending to the injured, the excitement began to assuage. Several of the warriors made torches to inspect the surrounding area. A surprise was revealed in the west, causing a collective shout from the gathered villagers. The open western valley, into which the brook used to flow, was now blocked by a jagged, fifteen-foot-high wall of dripping mud. From where had this monstrous natural wall sprung? The villagers stood, gaping at the barrier to their western fields. The brook, continuing to flow, had begun to pool at the base of the newly formed hill.

Warriors clutching torches scaled the original hill to the south, marveling at the perfectly formed swath of sloped grass on the western side of the new hill. It seemed their village was now in a valley surrounded by hills. Kuhkoomtheyna had blessed them with a generous outpouring of her benevolence, a gift they were powerless to return. Climbing back down to the village floor, the warriors gathered their weary families and headed toward their homes. There was little they could do in the limited visibility of the late hour. The entire event had been terrifying and exhausting. They would resume their investigations at first light.

In the daylight of dawn, the villagers could see toppled trees and damage on several of the still-standing homes. The animals had all returned, yet remained anxious. Now able to see the wall clearly, the villagers realized it looked exactly like what it was. A massive chunk of the earth yanked out of the ground by its roots. The wall side, facing the village, was raw earth with stones and other debris jutting out from its face. The oozing mud had hardened in frozen runnels down its face. The top of the wall was ringed with loose plant roots, dangling freely in the air like hair strands.

The villagers were astonished at a copse of locust trees flung in scattered heaps along the south hill. They were like discarded sticks left from a child's play. A mighty grove of oak trees, formerly shading the western edge of the village, had plummeted several yards away into the center of a nearby cornfield; their branches crushed into shards of timber. The ever-widening pool of water, collecting at the base of the new cliff, presented a great challenge. How were they going to divert the water around the wall?

Mishe Moneto gave them little time to ponder their new circumstances. A scant six hours after the first wave of shaking, the animals in unison hiked their tails and raced headlong across the surrounding land. Shortly after, birds took flight, unleashing haunting cries of terror. The animals were simply reacting to a force they felt on its way.

The residents of Black Wolf's village stood transfixed by the chaotic display of animals in flight, knowing it to be a sign of impending doom. The earth began to sway and rumble in undulating waves of motion. The villagers were knocked to the ground where they desperately sought something stable to cling to. Their collective gaze was captured by the dancing waters of the babbling brook. Its shallow waters were bouncing several feet into the air in a looping cycle. As they stared, mesmerized by the hypnotic ballet, a sinister force of water was speeding their way.

The spring-fed brook that the villagers had so enjoyed for several years was, unknown to them, fed by an underground aquifer lake. Their cluster of homes sat atop the shallow southwestern edge of the lake, which stretched some fifteen miles to the northeast away from the village. The depth of the underground lake sloping to thirty feet the further east it expanded.

In the second round of tremors to shatter the peace of that morning, the rocking wave motion of the captured lake waters was intensified from having been set in a sloshing, back-and-forth wave six hours earlier. The deluge of water rushed in a massive seiche wave toward the eastern limits of the lake. The firm bedrock above the lake's eastern shore held tight, as the powerful wave slammed against the lake's lid. The resulting backwash shoved an even larger surge coursing back toward the western shore. The much shallower western end of the lake was no match for the powerhouse wave that punched into its earthen cap.

Above ground, the unwary Shawnee were clambering upright from their tenuous positions scattered across the ground. Crying children clung to their mothers. Warriors embraced their families in their expansive arms. A geyser of water and earth erupted from the ground beneath their feet, shooting some seventy feet into the air. A massive wall of water and mud rained down on the village. It pulverized everything into unrecognizable bits of matter. The village and its inhabitants, simply, ceased to exist. There was no pain, no suffering. Their upward gaze at the fountain of death was met with a swift passing into darkness.

As the wall of water crashed back to earth, much of it—and the debris it had accumulated—drained back into the gaping hole that had moments before been the Shawnee village grounds. The massive wave had begun its churn back toward the eastern shore of the underground lake. A few more surges of water escaped the new yawning fissure as the entire underground lake undulated, trapped in its bedrock container. After the motion calmed, the surface water drained back into the buried lake. The churning mud and floating debris of bodies, bark, and fallen trees circled the opening, slowly clogging the water's egress. The swirling waters deposited a loose wall of mud and debris in its wake. Gradually, the chasm on either side of the western earthen wall that had risen from the ground in the first morning tremor was filled in between it and the flanking hills with sluiced mud and chunks of wreckage from the destroyed village. The resulting makeshift earthen dam stretched along the entire length of the newly formed wall. Each new deposit of rubbish solidified the dam, adding to its girth and height.

By nightfall, a new pond stood atop the area that the village had occupied. Sludge rapidly hardened on the newly formed dam's outer surface, plugging errant leaks. Within a few days the pond would masquerade as a random body of water nestled in a pasture of rolling hills. The skeletal dried stalks of corn in the western field would be the only evidence that any human life had visited this plot of wilderness.

Overhead, forty new spirits danced in the moonlight of the great hunting grounds of the heavens.

Chapter 17

Quaking Pond, Nestled in a Rolling Pasture
Twenty Miles Southwest of Sugar Creek
The Indiana Territories
December 1811

Black Wolf and his companions had ridden as hard as they could through the devastated countryside, making their way back to their village. The massive number of fallen trees and havoc they had encountered was proof that there would be clearing and repair work waiting for them. After a full week of hard riding, they neared the woods east of their village. The lack of fire smoke rising on the horizon alarmed them. They whipped their horses into a gallop for the final stretch.

Cresting the last hill, they abruptly reined their horses in unison. The men could not believe their eyes. In front of them, where their village should have been, sat a muddy pond filled with heavy floating debris swirling in its silt-laced waters. Where had their village disappeared?

Cautiously, the warriors guided their horses to the pond's edge. Perhaps the spirits were playing tricks on them for having taken a week to return. This was no trick. Their village should have been right there. Staring out over the pond, they identified several chunks of floating debris. Inconceivably, a severed arm floated past them. Laughing Fox screamed in horror. He recognized the delicate fingers of his wife attached to the severed limb. The men leapt from their horses and waded into the shallow waters to retrieve the floating limb. How could this be? How could their village be entirely gone?

A collective groan of agony burst into the afternoon silence. The three warriors stood motionless, as the sullied waters swirled about them. None of this made any sense. Dumbfounded, the warriors remained transfixed while broken shards of debris from the village floated by their knees. Incomprehensible as it was, they came to accept that the earth had swallowed up their village, leaving behind this murky pond in its place.

Jolted from their trance, the warriors marched out of the shallows and leapt on their horses. They frantically scouted the toppled woods, hoping to find family members safely huddled nearby. Their distraught search revealed nothing. Hysterical, the men collapsed in front of the leaking earthen dam. They saw further evidence of their village's destruction knitted in the woven debris of the dam's outer edges: planks, cooking utensils, cutting tools, and even body giblets. The warriors grudgingly conceded that their entire village—families and all—had been ripped from their lives.

"Arrrgh!" bellowed Black Wolf his eyes gazing skyward. "Oh Mishe Moneto, what have I done to bring your vengeful wrath upon me and my family?" He beat his chest with his fists and screamed at the skies until his voice could scream no more. Laughing Fox and Smooth Rock joined in Black Wolf's wailing. Their spirits racked with pain. The trio sat mourning as the sun vanished in the west. Everything was, gone. It was, as if, the entire village had drifted up to the heavens like a wisp of smoke.

Now, men without a home, the warriors returned to Cape Girardeau. They would follow Tecumseh wherever he might lead them. Black Wolf, Laughing Fox, and Smooth Stone fought valiantly alongside Tecumseh throughout the bloody battles waged over the next two years. Together, they all rode into the Battle of the Thames on October 5, 1813. This was to be the final battle of Tecumseh's War. None of the three warriors nor Tecumseh would survive this decisive victory by the Americans.

As the full hunter's moon rose over Quaking Pond that same late October, a small pack of roaming wolves found themselves joined by a floating mist-like apparition. A dark wolf formed in the swirling mists before their glowing amber eyes. Together, the spirit wolf and the pack raised their howls at the glowing orb in the night sky. Black Wolf smiled at his brother spirits as he visited his former home one last time before ascending to the heavens to join his waiting family.

Westward Ho

The United States Stretches Its Borders

On July 4, 1800, the Indiana Territory was chartered, establishing it as the westernmost defined area of the Northwest Territories. The availability of cheap land led to a rapid increase in the population of the territory with thousands of new settlers pouring into the region. Large settlements sprang up along the Great Lakes and navigable rivers of the area. For the next decade, most of the territory's interior was a ibes.

Indians Suppressed—White Man Flood Gates Burst Asunder

The Battle of Thames in 1812 heralded the end of Tecumseh's War. The victory opened up the central Indiana Territory to settlement, allowing pioneers to safely venture beyond its aquatic borders. The dam had burst. The ensuing flood of white blood into the territory fulfilled Tecumseh's greatest fear. In short order, the population reached the status of statehood. Indiana became the nineteenth state in December 1816.

Chapter 18

Miller Farm, Resident Home of Quaking Pond
Twenty Miles Southwest of Sugar Creek
Montgomery County, Indiana
June 3, 1:35 p.m., CST

The Miller family finished up a great outdoor picnic lunch. The Miller male trio hated putting their smelly, muck-crusted boots and gear back on, but the attraction of exploration was just too strong. Joe and his sons returned to the pond where they strode in unison over to the slime-covered Corvair frame. They gave the old Chevy Corvair one last look over to see if there was anything inside the glove box or trunk. It had sat, draining ooze, ever since they had hauled it up from its perch on the south side of the pond. Even though Joe knew it was beyond salvaging, it would be fun for him and the boys to scavenge over it. No telling what they might find.

The body, having been painted a rather bland shade of beige, added to its camouflage appearance. The pond detritus laced across it in random, clinging strands completed the look of a vehicle attempting to hide in the shadows like a crouching predator.

From atop the hill, the Miller trio could look out over the entire remains of the pond below. Joe pondered the pile of logs that had been dumped on the east end, near the railroad tracks. They obviously had been part of some structure in the past. The notches in the individual log ends and left over caulking material on the log edges indicated that they had been previously interlocked. Joe knew that logs submerged under water lasted for years; it was no telling how old they were. He should contact someone from the historical society to come check them out. He might even look up old man Hunt from whose family Joe and Kris had bought the farm. They were among the first settlers in the area. Granted it was two centuries ago, but Willie Hunt might know some history of the original family. After he got this dam fixed, he might have time to pursue some local history and lore. Right now, he had more pressing matters.

Joe's vantage spot offered him an unhindered view of what looked suspiciously like human bones over on the northwest side of pond bed. He had specifically steered the boys toward the south and east directions of the pond floor. As he had hoped, they had not noticed the bones yet. Right now, they were too engrossed in opening the trunk of the Corvair to notice anything else.

Chapter 19

Wilderness Road Trail
Western Virginia through Central Kentucky
Ohio River Crossing into Northwest Indiana Territories
1815

Ezekiel Johnson was a determined man. He and his kin had endured the wealthy landowners in his home state of Virginia, directing the fates of the poor for decades. Among this elite group of landowners were family names such as: Culpeper, Jefferson, Madison, Pendleton, Reade, Warner, Wythe, and even Washington as in President George. They had dictated where and how a man could live for far too long. Many of them were now leaders in the US government, giving them an even broader group of subjects to dictate how their lives would be lived.

Several of the Johnson's neighbors and friends had slipped through the Cumberland Gap in search of a new beginning, further west, from the oppressive crowding and regulations of the eastern coast. In many regards, the average man had simply traded one over-lord for another. Whether it was a king or a congress, it seemed there was always some wealthy group of people telling the poor folk what to do.

His friends had not returned along the Wilderness Road, lead-ing Ezekiel to believe that they had found the freedom and happiness they were seeking. Zek, as his friends called him, was resolved to carry his young bride over the pass into a better life for them in the

Northwest Territories. After all the hubbub with the British a few years ago, the entire nation had settled into a period of relative peace and anxious exploration. It seemed the savage natives had quieted down. Now, while he could swing an axe and plow a good-sized field all by himself was when Zek needed to get him and Phoebe out of Cedar Bluff, Virginia.

He and Phoebe didn't have enough money to buy a Conestoga wagon. Not only was the wagon expensive, but the heavy old boat required eight or more oxen to pull it. There was no way they could muster the gold for that. Besides, toll fees were charged along some of the wilderness roads. The more they carried, the more they would have to pay. Instead, the couple had purchased a sturdy two-wheel cart that would hold the tools and supplies they would need to get started. Zek would build whatever else they needed. Neither of them was accustomed to fancy things. Essentials were all that mattered to them. Their little wilderness party would consist of a strong ox to pull their cart, a horse Zek would ride, and a spare mule to help pull the cart on occasion. Their goal was to get as far away from other folks as possible. They packed up their meager belongings. They were staged and set to begin their step off the precipice of the known as soon as the last snow melted. In late March, the Johnson party was primed to answer the beckoning call of the western wilds.

Zek turned in his saddle and asked his bride of six months, "You ready to head out, my beautiful wife?"

"Now seems as good a time as any, my sugar cream pie!" Phoebe replied, alertly perched atop the cart. She was as anxious as Zek to begin their new phase of life. There was so much promise in store for them. "You say when, love of my life, and I will follow."

"Westward Ho!" Zek bellowed as he swept his outstretched arm in an ascending arc to start their quest.

The desire to move west was a burning passion for the settlers, as their journey was no joyride. Zek's mount, the mule, the ox, and the wheels of the oxcart constantly slipped back and forth across the slick mud track that served as a road in the early 1800s. Phoebe had to be on constant lookout for large rocks that littered about, which might cause a wheel to bend or break. They had two spare wooden wheels, once those were exhausted, so too might their journey be.

Neither she nor Zek wanted their new home decided by a busted cart.

The spring rains had made the narrow trails a treacherous muddy soup; nevertheless, their first day got them some nine miles from Cedar Bluff. They were quite pleased with their progress.

"We got a lot further than I thought we would today, my little buttercup." Zek grinned broadly at his wife. On their first night on the road, they nestled contently before a roaring fire. They were both grateful the rains had kept away throughout the day. "We might make better time than expected," Zek interrupted the silence, once again.

"I wouldn't count my chickens before their hatched, husband," Phoebe chided. "We have a long way to wherever we are goin' to end up. A lot can happen travelin' that far."

"True enough, I am just grateful for a grand beginnin' to our search fer a better home." Zek beamed. "I love you so much. I want us and our future children to have more than our parents ever did."

"I agree," Phoebe said, bobbing her head up and down. "That is why I was willing to come out into the scary wilderness, away from everyone we know. I have faith in your vision, Zek. I know we will be much better off with our own farm, far away from the rich folks tellin' us what we can and cannot do." They speculated a bit longer about what they might find out west, falling asleep quickly.

Zek and Phoebe rose when the eastern sky had barely blushed pink. Their robust breakfast and rested start were not to be repeated for several weeks. Late in the afternoon, it began pouring rain. The Johnsons managed to find shelter underneath a small rock cleft overlooking a rapidly swelling creek. Progress, they now realized, was not going to be easy. They and the animals huddled beneath the outcropping, trying to dry out beside a sputtering fire made with water-soaked branches.

Not well rested, the next day proved a mighty challenge, as the rain-drenched trails were now trenches of wheel-sucking sludge, refusing to release neither hoof nor wagon wheel without strenuous effort. Rain-swollen rivers and creeks were life threatening to ford. Exhausted, the pair stopped in a grove of trees to make camp. They propped a leather skin over the edge of the cart to provide slight relief from the relentless downpour. Too wet for a fire, the pair snuggled beneath a wet bearskin blanket, which was scarcely warmer than the air outside. The animals were resolved to sleep, standing up, with their backsides to the blowing wind and rain.

The reality for the next several days for the Johnson party consisted of a well-rehearsed execution of freeing the cart. Zek would dismount his horse. Coax her to lift her trapped hooves out of the thick mire up onto more stable ground. Next, to free the immobile cart, he would gather nearby branches, lining them into a trail of broken limbs for the cart's wheels to ride over the deep mud. Each step he made in the mud sank his boot deep into the grasp of the gripping quagmire. The branch bridge in place, Zek would pull the ox forward by his reins then let the strong ox shift backward, gingerly producing a wobbling back-and-forth rhythm. Eventually this would generate enough momentum to free the cart. Freed, he and Phoebe would guide the ox and cart over the makeshift bridge of branches. At times, prodding the ox's backside as necessary. This time-consuming activity was repeated several times a day, as the trails were endlessly filled with quicksand gullies of mud and mire.

The traveling Johnson party spent hours of being drenched. They would barely dry out, before the next onslaught of rain descended upon them. They felt fortunate to rarely chance upon other pioneers. Those encounters usually entailed backbreaking efforts to help fellow travelers dislodge their wagons from the mire. There were multiple occasions when the ungrateful pioneers would free themselves then ride off. Exhausted Zek and Phoebe were left to cross through the mud pit on their own, having to free themselves. The rare dry nights when they were able to build a fire became a favored treat on the journey. They and the animals would scoot in as close to the roaring blaze as possible in an effort to warm their weary, drenched hides. The promise of their own land, with no one around, drove them onward despite the many hardships.

Traffic on the Wilderness Road was heavy enough to negate any predatory animal dangers for the Johnsons. Phoebe and Zek were both excellent shots. Other than killing an occasional rabbit for meat, their skills went unused. The threat of Indian attacks seemed nonexistent. The few natives they came across were dwelling in bark-covered cabins similar to those back in Virginia. They seemed disinterested in the pair's march across their lands, going peacefully about their daily business. Zek concluded that either the fight had been taken out of them, or they were part of the tribes who had chosen to live peacefully. Regardless, the Johnson's journey proceeded unimpeded by gunfights with hostile red varmints. The weather and barely passable trails were their greatest concerns.

After several weeks of exhausting journey, they came upon the mighty Ohio River. Much too wide and deep to cross, they began a lengthy trek along the shore, looking for a ferry to safely transport them to the Northwest Territories on the northern shore. They headed west, avoiding the likelihood of greater numbers of settlers closer to civilization in the east.

They happened upon a cluster of settled pioneers who had built their cabins on bluffs overlooking the falls near what would become Louisville, Kentucky. From advice given by these friendly folks, the Johnsons made their way west to a tow-and-ferry line operated by the Mauck family. The Maucks ferried settlers into the Northwest Territories at a crossing named Mauckport just south of the tiny cluster of cabins called Corydon. The Johnsons were no strangers to rivers, having lived on Cedar Bluff above the Clinch River in Virginia. The Ohio River dwarfed any river they had ever seen. Its massive flow was heightened by spring rains; as a result, the Johnson's huddled away from the ferry's sides from fear of falling in and being drowned in the expanse of water.

Arriving safely on the very southern border of the Northwest Territories, Zek and Phoebe set about prepping their animals and cart for an even more strenuous venture. From this point forward, uncharted wilderness stood between them and their eventual destination. There simply were no roads to speak of in the Northwest Territories, especially this far west, in what was being called the Indiana Territories. To the Johnsons, the obvious lack of human presence was exactly the people-free space they had sought. Reaffirmed in their convictions, they began a cautious northward ramble. They fled the areas near crossings or sizable rivers, reckoning it would soon fill with throngs of eager settlers. It was their intention to avoid such a pitfall. Crowds led to someone lording over the masses. The Johnsons were committed to self-rule.

Travel without a defined roadway was slower. The pioneer couple had to squeeze around trees and make their way through thick brush and brambles. The tall grasses tickled the bellies of their animals, releasing a constant plume of airborne pollen, causing human and animal alike to sneeze constantly. The party was fortunate that the rains had finally dried, offering a more pleasant passage on dry ground.

The pair smiled at each other, as their journey suddenly took on a true feeling of accomplishment. They had escaped to the wilderness. They were certain their home awaited them in the near future. For several days, they wound their way northwest. Wherever they found a cluster of cabins, whether natives or fellow colonists, they continued on further north. They did not want another human within several days ride of where they would build their home.

Their wanderings brought them past endless hills, pastures, and lush forest glades. On a couple occasions, they came across rivers. Despite the heavy rains earlier, none was beyond fording. The rivers were teeming with fish. The wildlife was so abundant one could hardly look in any direction without seeing a creature. They were resolved that they had made the right choice to travel to this distant land. The weather continued to warm, heralding bugs of every sort, swarming about the cart in search of meals. Bees were everywhere, buzzing in clouds of yellow and black, as they danced among the blossoming rainbow of peony, wild rose, clove currant, and lilac flowers.

It was heady and romantic, as they slowly traipsed through the tall grass fields. The fragrant smells and their elated joy of success fueled several nights of heated passion. Zek and Phoebe were deeply and passionately in love, quite giddy over their safe migration.

Spilling out of a dense thicket of trees and brambles, Ezekiel and Phoebe chanced upon a beautiful pond situated in the midst of gently rolling hills. A young grove of sapling trees fringed its shores. To the north, stood an established forest of maple trees filled with deer and pheasants.

"Oh, Zek, this is the perfect spot for our home!" Phoebe exclaimed. "Do you not agree?"

"It is as beautiful as you are, my cherished bride. Best of all, there is not another soul around for several days ride in any direction," Zek encouraged. "I think this might be the spot for us, dear Phoebe!"

"Oh, let's settle here, Zek," she implored. "I am weary of traveling. It has everything we wanted. I can see our cabin on the east shore of this pond. That way, the evening light will gently fade over the horizon before us every day of our lives."

"Phoebe, how could a man argue with that?" Ezekiel smiled. "Let's unhitch the cart over there on that little rise above the pond. That grove of maple trees beyond will supply us with plenty of logs to build our cabin. I love you, dear wife. I agree, let's make this our new home."

The pair carefully secured their worthy beasts of burden up to nearby trees so they could graze in peace. Later in the day, they hung dried animal skins between two saplings to form a makeshift dwelling. Its meager protection would keep them dry until Zek could build their cabin. They knew the next several months would be filled with frantic labor. They had to get a cabin built and some provisions laid in before the winter snows came.

For Zek, the rest of the summer involved felling trees and hewing the trunks into measured logs. Phoebe spent her time hunting deer, rabbit, and other game. The laborious task of lumbering transformed Zek's muscular frame into a godlike state of toned, chiseled muscles. His ripped chest, glistening in the campfire light, inevitably led to serious romps of lovemaking. By midsummer, Phoebe discovered she was with child. They both rejoiced at the revelation—their family was about to start.

Their backbreaking efforts paid off. By late summer, Zek had prepared a collection of twelve- and fifteen-foot logs hewn with foot-long notches at their ends, sufficient to build their cabin. Stacking and fitting the logs in place, Zek finished off the structure with a corbelled roof covered with wood shingles, chopped from the tree bark of the maples. With the main structure finally complete, Zek and Phoebe began dredging mud and moss from the pond, wedging it in the cracks between logs and shingles. Dried, the natural caulking would keep some of the harsh winter wind from invading their cabin. With winter nipping at their heels, Zek and Phoebe quickly stacked rocks and mortared them in place with pond mud. Their finished fireplace was far from attractive, but the draft drew smoke safely up the flue. They would have a way to warm themselves and cook inside for the winter.

Winter descended quickly with cold northern winds and snow flurries gusting about the meager cabin. Phoebe and Zek daily applied fresh mud caulking over cracks that seemed to let in the worst winter fury. They would never call themselves warm in their drafty cabin; regardless, it was much better protection than huddled beneath a skin out in the open. At night, they bundled under a pile of animal hides and curled up next to their woefully inadequate fireplace. A family transplanted to a spot of freedom in the new nation. They were happy and satisfied with their achievements.

Chapter 20

Quaking Pond, Cabin Site of the Johnsons
Twenty Miles Southwest of Sugar Creek
Montgomery County, Indiana
1816

Spring arrived to the relief of all. The animals frolicked in the greening pastures, chomping eagerly at the fresh growing grass. They spent hours grazing each day to fill out their winter-withered frames. The mornings were filled with the chatter of returning birds. The pond ice slowly melted away, giving way to gently lapping waves blown by warm southern breezes. Life was good in the central Indiana Territories. Phoebe was about to give birth; her swollen body was difficult to maneuver. Over the winter, Zek had lovingly fashioned together a cradle for the arrival of their new baby.

Ezekiel was extremely anxious about the birth. He knew very little about midwifery, a task womenfolk attended to. His limited delivery knowledge gained from birthing calves and lambs back in Virginia. He guessed it must be a similar process—surely they would be fine. People had been having babies since the beginning of time. If he and Phoebe could travel this far into the wilderness, then surely they could birth their new child successfully. Couldn't they? That reasoning served only to raise Ezekiel's anxiety.

Phoebe's water broke on the morning of April 17. Zek immediately began boiling some water and gathering what cloth they possessed. Panicked, he began pacing back and forth in front of Phoebe, who sprawled on a deer hide inside the cabin. Her contractions came swift and frequent. After a few yelps, labor began in earnest for her. Unlike many women, her first baby flew into the world with minimal pushing. It was a relief to both parents when their new son came flooding out in a soppy bundle. Following a quick snip of the child's cord, Zek held his infant son aloft; whereupon, the little Johnson began to wail with the full force of his tiny lungs.

Neither parent could believe how effortless and easy the process had been. Phoebe, back in Virginia, had sat with birthing mothers for agonizing hours. Her little Zachariah had popped out, filling their hearts with joy in mere moments. The parents wrapped the babe in cloth and skins to keep him warm. They knew the specter of death was a serious threat to their new son. Here in the middle of nowhere, they would be helpless should something befall their cherished bundle of happiness.

Phoebe fashioned a makeshift baby sling from one of Zek's old shirts, tying the sleeves together in a knot to wear draped over her neck and shoulder. With baby Zack securely fastened against her chest, Phoebe was able to commence making meals and light duties about the cabin. Zek tilled heartily in the abandoned western cornfield. The Johnsons basked in the satisfaction of having attained their vision.

Chapter 21

Quaking Pond, Cabin Site of the Johnsons
Twenty Miles Southwest of Sugar Creek
Montgomery County, Indiana
Winter 1818–19

Zachariah and his parents had survived the previous two winters that mirrored the Johnson's first winter in the central part of the Indiana Territories. At nearly three, Zachariah was stumbling about under his own power. His mother constantly chased after him to keep him corralled within the confines of the cabin's front. She and Zek had added additional mud and moss caulking over the past two years to make their cabin more secure. The serious leaks in the roof had been caulked. A lean-to windbreak off the south side of the cabin had been transformed into a substantial animal shelter with bark walls and stretched-skin roofing. This coming summer, Zek intended to build a proper barn for the animals, in which, they could store hay and perhaps even some corn from the ever-burgeoning field. Over the past seasons, they had collected enough fur pelts to purchase a much-needed milk cow and a few hens. The milk and eggs produced a constant supply of food for their growing needs.

It was good the preparations had been made on the cabin and makeshift animal shelter. The signs for the fall season indicated a wickedly cold winter approaching. The wooly-bear caterpillars had been nearly solid black in the fall, as they inched their way into winter hiding spots to cocoon for their spring transformations. For as long as Zek could remember, the color scheme of the little caterpillars had been used to predict winter weather. Wider bands of their orange centers meant mild winters. Whereas a narrow or, as in the current season, nonexistent orange center band meant winter was going to be frigid. Anticipating a brutal winter, the Johnsons had stockpiled as much corn and dried meat as they could into the cabin. Zek had chopped and chopped firewood, which he stacked to great heights between trees surrounding the cabin. They were as ready as they could be. This winter season, they were fortunate to have a few heavy wool blankets to cuddle themselves and their toddler in against the cold.

Winter blasted the area with sideways blowing snow in mid-November, drifts threatening to bury the cabin. The roof bowed under the weight of snow atop it. Cold air found its way in through remaining chinks in the caulking. At times, the winds were so strong they blew out the fire. The animals bellowed in pain and discomfort as they scrunched together, desperately trying to stay warm through collective body heat. By February, the pond was a frozen mass with snow blowing across its frozen surface. Despite the solid appearing surface, the pond depth kept the lower waters just at freezing; as a result, the ice depth was shallow.

Baby Zack and his parents found the confines of the cabin restricting and depressing. All of them were suffering from cabin fever and colds. The snow and winds continued week after week without subsiding. Zek would sneak outside to bring in firewood. Every other day, he would go searching for game. The harsh winter had driven most of the wildlife into hiding. Zek was forced to search longer and farther to find game, often he returned empty handed.

Near the end of February, the sun broke through the clouds, reflecting a bright crystal glare across the frozen sea of white dunes outside the cabin. Zek struck out early in search of game. Phoebe let young Zack outside, for the first time in days, to romp a bit in the freshly fallen snow. She could hear her son gleefully throwing snow into the air then giggling as it cascaded back down on his face. A typical toddler, the need to explore quickly enticed Zack to begin wandering down the slope outside their cabin.

The animated toddler continued walking at a hurried pace with the downhill motion adding to his gait. His steps onto the frozen pond registered no difference to Zack than the snow-covered ground he had already been scampering across. He continued his adventure, escaping ever farther from the cabin. He had wandered far out onto the pond's center, giggling with joy, before turning to discover just how far he had meandered. Fear shook him, as he gazed across the great distance separating him from his mommy. His eyes stinging with tears, he began to wail, bouncing up and down with all his might. Fists balled tightly, he defiantly anticipated his mother's immediate arrival to his bawling. He was confident she would race to scoop him up for a piggyback ride to the warmth of the fireplace.

Phoebe had been busy by the fireside mixing up some cornmeal when she heard Zack wailing. He sounded so far away. *Where could the little scamp have wandered off to?* She had just let him out the door moments earlier. "That little demon is a fast one." She laughed aloud as she got up to see what trouble her son had gotten into this time. Clearing the doorway, Phoebe's heart skipped a beat. There stood her son, far out on the frozen pond, throwing a royal temper-tantrum.

"Stand still, Zack. Momma's coming!" she yelled. With her thoughts focused on retrieving him, Phoebe never considered the stability of the pond ice before stepping onto the frozen surface. She heard faint crackles, as she advanced a couple of feet. The pond ice held, so onward she rushed.

As she neared Zack, the cracking noises became loud pops like an echoing musket shot. Zack continued to jump up and down in a full-blown rage. Phoebe was within feet of him when spider-web-bing cracks emerged from Zack's direction. As they widened, a puff of snow danced from the ice-covered surface in announcement of a broadening rip in the polar cap. Before her, Zack came plummeting down from his most recent leap. He didn't stop as his feet struck the ice; instead, he plunged beneath the ice and snow, as a fissure of shattered ice chunks swallowed him whole. A wave of water splashing over the ice surface was all that marked where her son had stood. After what seemed like hours, Zack bobbed back up from the icy depths. Upon surfacing, a rattling wail erupted from his opened mouth. Phoebe dove forward to grab her son's outstretched arm.

She had just clamped her hand around his fragile little wrist when the ice crumbled beneath her body. She and Zack slipped into the freezing pond water at an angle. Phoebe's natural buoyancy launched her back to the surface. She gulped in a lung full of air then raised her arm to clear Zack above the water. The frigid water sapped the energy from her in waves.

With her teeth chattering and her entire system going into shock, Phoebe desperately thrashed about the floating chunks of ice, seeking purchase to pull herself free of the chilling water. Each handhold of ice she gripped broke loose, sending her and Zack back under the surface. Through relentless repetition, the pair endured the brutal submersions. When above the surface, Zack frantically wailed and sputtered, as Phoebe clutched his languishing body in the crook of her arm. Panic rattled Phoebe as she grappled with their situation. Holding onto Zack, she couldn't maneuver quickly enough to swim to more stable ice where she might pull them free. If she let go of him, he would disappear to the depths of the pond. Neither option held much hope for their survival. With energy quickly ebbing from her, Phoebe resolved their fate was destined. Clutching her suddenly still son tightly to her, she heard a shout in the distance.

Zek had returned to the cabin. He saw his wife and toddler son slip beneath the surface of the icy pond. Yelling for them to hang on, he struck out across the pond's ice. The integrity of the ice cap was completely compromised, it would never hold up against his weight. Regardless, Zek charged forward, desperate to save his family from certain death.

A few feet from his family, a hunk of ice calved loose, and without constraint, dumped Zek into the black pond waters. The trajectory speed and angle sent him deep into the pond's water, propelling him several feet beyond his struggling family. He broke the surface, initially trapped beneath ice. Gulping a quick breath from an air bubble trapped under the ice cap, Zek dove and swam back toward his family.

He surfaced, just in time, to clutch his wife's waist, narrowly preventing her from sinking. Determined to save his wife, Ezekiel treaded water frantically to keep her body floating above the surface. Both of them sputtered and spat water from their mouths. Shivering, they gasped for air to fill their lungs. They were desperately dog paddling to stay above the surface, when Phoebe realized little Zack was no longer in her grasp.

"Our baby! Where is HE?" she screamed, frantically casting about to locate her son. Zek, realizing he had to be below the surface, dived under once more. He could just make out the flaccid body of his son, sinking rapidly. He swam downward, trying to grasp him. At last, he nabbed the boy's hair. Zek's powerful legs propelled him and his limp son's torso toward the surface. Emerging in an impressive geyser of spray, he found Phoebe with frozen tears crackling down her blue cheeks. She couldn't catch her breath. His wife was desperately struggling to stay afloat, her frozen limbs refused to move. With his son's body grasped in one arm, Zek struggled to pull his wife's spiraling body toward the surface. Zek's adrenaline charged muscles were withering in the freezing water; even so, he managed to maneuver him and his family over to the closest edge of ice.

Loose chunks of sharp broken ice banged against him, slicing his skin. Exhausted, he let the lifeless body of his son float free. He had to have a free hand to grasp the ice, if he and Phoebe had any hope of pulling themselves free of the freezing waters. He grasped the ice and pulled his shoulder up above the surface of the pond water.

I might just get us out of this, Zek thought as his body cleared the water's surface. Hope filled him, as the ice held. Zek struggled to get his elbow solidly wedged against the surface of the ice. He planned to use it as a fulcrum to pull himself out of the water.

A deafening clap reverberated across the pond, followed instantaneously by the entire ice surface suddenly calving, pitching him downward into the water. Zek and Phoebe were driven several feet below the surface by a log-sized wedge of ice. Zek's grip on Phoebe failed, and their bodies began a downward spiral. Bubbles streamed from their noses, as the cold consumed the last of their energy.

After some time, their spent bodies floated back to the surface, face down. Their body cavities teased the sunshine with their backsides. In hours, the ice reformed on the pond, cementing their bodies on the surface. Blowing snow quickly covered the ridges of their upturned backs. The first white settlers in the area were no more.

The folks back in Cedar Bluff never heard from the Johnsons. Everyone assumed that they, like others before them, had found the tranquility they sought. In reality, the Johnsons never returned or sent word back through the Cumberland Gap because they, like many of the early pioneers, were victims of one tragedy or another without another living soul around to witness or report their demise.

Chapter 22

A Quaker Journey from Philadelphia to Indiana
1824

After both sets of their parents died from diseases directly related to the stagnant swamps surrounding Philadelphia, the Hunts decided to flee west. They were determined to find land in a more arid region where they were less likely to suffer death from some water-borne killer. Filled with conviction, they merged their loaded Conestoga wagon with a wagon train of several Quaker families. The sizable congregation was intent on settlement in the new State of Indiana.

The former territory had been a state for seven years. Settlers had been pouring in with the defeat of both the natives and the British that had plagued the area. Cities were popping up along the shores of the lakes to the north and the river trade routes to the south. The Hunts hoped to find a choice piece of land on the western side of the new state where a distant cousin, William Offield, had recently staked a claim in the newly formed Montgomery County of Indiana.

Jonathon and Molly Hunt and their fellow pioneer travelers endured, and for the most part survived, the typical hardships of travel across the primitive roads chiseled from animal paths scattered through the nation's vast forestlands. The Quaker brethren chose to depart over the National Road running from Cumberland, Maryland right through the center of Ohio to Indiana. It was difficult but much better than hazarding through raw uncharted territory. Although safer than other routes, the trip had not been without its tragedies.

Abraham Williams had been crushed beneath his heavy Conestoga wagon. He had safely removed a busted wheel. Midway of slipping a new wheel onto the axle tip, a bump from one of the oxen had caused the entire wagon to topple over, crushing him beneath its weight. His wife, Helen, was inconsolable in her grief. Wailing and flaying about, it had taken hours to calm her. The group of Quaker men prepared a proper roadside grave for Abraham. After which they offered a moving service of tribute to their cherished brother. The tight-knit group of friends, both in terms of religion and longevity together, finally convinced Helen to continue on their journey to a better land. They assured her that she and her daughter, Mary, would be well cared for by the group. At last, she had relented, figuring that it was her and Mary's duty to fulfill the family's destiny.

The road was surprisingly crowded with a multitude of pioneers pacing westward for various reasons. Their journey was marked periodically by the tollbooths they passed on the young nation's federal turnpike. They arrived just after sunset at the border crossing to the State of Indiana. A guard emerged from the toll shack.

Peering beyond the faint glow of his oil lantern, he announced, in a distinct Southern drawl, "Who's there?" To the Pennsylvanians, it sounded like a mumbled mouthful of "Hoosier?" From this comical border greeting, the residents of Indiana soon became known by their eastern neighbors as the Hoosiers.

The National Road ran some thirty miles south of Montgomery County, Indiana. As they neared the trail that led off north toward the newly established settlement of Greencastle, the group knew they were within days of their destination. The friends were familiar with Greencastle. It had been founded on a land grant just a couple years earlier by Ephraim Dukes, a cousin to one of the brethren. He had named the settlement for his hometown—Greencastle, Pennsylvania.

They stopped by to visit with Ephraim. He informed them of several choice locations for a thriving settlement community. Rested and anxious to stake their claim, the group ventured north in search of a perfect spot. Ephraim had been honest; the area was an endless stretch of excellent farmland with lush, game-filled forests. Healthy streams and babbling brooks spilled across the landscape in all directions, providing an ample supply of fresh water, unfettered by stagnant swamps. The group decided to continue further north, to where cousin Offield had settled.

The brethren group emerged out of a thick forest of fine maple and fruit trees into a broad expanse of rolling grassland. They had traveled for two and a half days, covering a little over twenty miles. By all reckoning, they had to be near where their cousin had settled. In front of them appeared a moderate-sized pond nestled amidst rolling hills.

"This looks like a perfect spot to build our new lives!" Jonathon Hunt exclaimed, turning to his wife on the wagon bench beside him. "There is even a starter cabin already built for us."

"It's enough to make a stuffed bird laugh, if you think I will let you build our cabin on top of this stand of water, Jonathon Hunt." Molly crossed her arms in defiance. "I do not care beans for it, whatsoever. That jumble of logs was obviously abandoned. This bilge before us probably killed the souls who built it."

John's wife was opinionated about where they would live. Molly Hunt refused to have her home built beside any standing body of water. She asserted that they had not traveled hundreds of miles from the festering swamps of Philadelphia to settle alongside any harbinger of summertime death. Both of her parents had died of typhoid. John's parents had been stricken with yellow fever, which was passed on by malicious mosquitoes. Philadelphia, in the summer, was a seething cesspool of death. The poorly drained Philly shores along the Delaware River basin teemed with all sorts of diseases. Stifling heat annually whipped it into a frothing, stagnant haze of the Grim Reaper.

John patiently shrugged his shoulders in defeated agreement, guiding the oxen onward toward a rise further north. As the wagon crested the next hill, a vista of rolling farmland, intersected with tree-lined streams filled their view. "Now, this looks like a place to build a cabin. Don't you think, John?" Molly gloated as she surveyed the vision of bounty before her.

"I can't argue with that, my dear," John said, shaking his head. "This is definitely our future home site, Molly."

John leapt from his wagon and announced that he and Molly had found their spot. Laughing, the others agreed that it was a choice hilltop, indeed. The entire hillside was ringed in mighty maple trees just leafing out. They would provide excellent raw materials and shade.

Another of the friends, Thomas and Beulah Elkins, announced that they intended to build on an adjoining hill deeply ensconced by its own grove of maples. Andrew Dukes hollered out that his family would claim a spot southeast of the pond. Molly wished them well, doubting their success in building a cabin next to that cauldron of death. Helen Williams claimed a hilltop spot, for her and Mary, near where they had emerged from the forest edge onto the grasslands.

Having chosen their favored spots of land, the four families of friends needed to secure a land patent for their individual properties. Indiana, like the other states of the Northwest Territory, was a federal land state where unclaimed public land was surveyed then granted or sold by the government through federal and state land offices. The first sale of a piece of land from the government was called a land patent and the first owner of the land was called a patentee. Later, when the land was sold or mortgaged by private owners, the document was called a deed. The transactions were recorded at the office of the county register of deeds. For the friends, this was a five-mile ride into the newly established county seat of Crawfordsville. Here they obtained a patent for their proposed farms in Union Township, Montgomery County, Indiana. As part of the stipulation of a land patent, the patentee agreed to till at least an acre of ground and build a home on the patented land.

The Quaker brethren eagerly began working their surveyed properties. Jonathon tried to get Molly to let him use some of the hewn logs from the abandoned cabin by the pond to start their cabin. She would have none of it. The cabin had clearly been abandoned for a reason. Molly could not be convinced that the previous owners had not died of some horrible disease. She feared most likely associated with the pond it sat beside. Jonathon gave up and began felling trees to build their cabin. Each of the neighbors helped one another build their cabins, as was the way among the tightly knit group of brethren.

In rapid succession, the cluster of homes was ready for the coming winter. Each family's large Conestoga wagon had carried enough provisions to amply prepare them for the challenges of starting out in the new land. A wise and thrifty congregation of brethren, they had the forethought to cart along a healthy collection of livestock and chickens. Their larder of plenty kept the group well fed during their initial months of settlement. The settled group of friends was fully primed to expand on their lands in the coming seasons. Established, they would witness the burgeoning assemblage of settlers that populated the area over the next few years. Several of the newcomers chose to worship with the friends in their meetinghouse built their second year in Indiana. Health and prosperity shined upon the brethren, as they kept strict moral values keenly focused in their lives.

* * *

Growth in the new states of Ohio, Indiana, and Illinois was explosive over the next several decades. Bountiful populations of migrating pioneers created an urgent demand for swifter transportation between lake and river trading ports and the agricultural production powerhouses in the core of the territory states. A little over a decade after establishing their small community, Jonathon and Molly found themselves grateful for the railroads that began crisscrossing the new American nation. The power of steam-driven engines eliminated their isolation from the manufacturing mills and supplies in the east. Even their remote location on the western edge of Indiana was destined to be joined to the rest of the country by the promise of iron rails. The Monon Railroad was born from the need to connect Lake Michigan to trading ports on the Ohio River. The Michigan City to New Albany line opened in 1853.

During its construction, the line passed through Montgomery County, Indiana. About five miles south of the town of Crawfordsville, the tracks were spiked in a straight line bisecting the property between Jonathon and Molly Hunt and their eastern neighbors, the Elkins. The progress of the tracks brought it just east of Quaking Pond—as it would be christened some one hundred and fifty years later. The abandoned Ezekiel Johnson cabin sat directly in the path ordained by inflexible railroad engineers. Vacant and ignored for several decades, the structure barely stood by its own volition. The railroad crews toppled the old pile of logs off into the pond to clear the path for the rails. The scuttled, weathered logs represented the last vestiges of the first white settlers in that part of the Indiana Territories.

The Ultimate Dodge

A *draft dodger* is "one who avoids military service" regardless of how it was done. Marrying and/or fathering children, if the military in question will grant deferments to spouses and/or parents.

—"Draft Dodger,"
Webster's Unabridged Dictionary. 1968.

Chapter 23

Miller Farm, Resident Home of Quaking Pond
Twenty Miles Southwest of Sugar Creek
Montgomery County, Indiana
June 4, 7:35 a.m., CST

The Miller boys were disappointed when they discovered they were not going to continue exploring the pond for the next couple of days.

"I know it sucks, but we do have chores around this farm," Joe remonstrated to his sons. "Mikey, today, I want you to help your mother pull weeds and gather vegetables in the garden."

Aww, Dad. I hate pullin' weeds," Mikey complained. "And I don't like vegetables, neither!"

"That doesn't matter, because your mom needs your help. So you are going to help," Joe commanded. "You're not old enough to drive a tractor, yet. When you are, we'll find someone else to pull weeds," Joe added with a smile. Turning to Joseph, Joe informed him, "And you will be helping me repair a fence back by the woods. We should finish that up by lunchtime. After that, I will take Mikey on the tractor with me, and you and I will mow up the back hay field. It's not supposed to rain for a few days. That'll give it time to dry before we rake it up and bale it."

"While you're handing out duties, Mr. Boss Man, what am I supposed to do?" Kris joked with a big smile on her face.

"How 'bout you keep looking beautiful and make us some lunch," Joe teased. "Okay, everybody got their assignments? Let's move out boys!"

Kris and Mikey picked the beans and a large basket of tomatoes. Kris hoed around the potatoes while Mikey groused at having to pull weeds out of the rows of onions and beets. After a while, Kris left Mikey to his weed extraction. She hurried off to the kitchen to prepare lunch.

Joe and Joseph skidded to a dust-trailed stop on their ATVs, having raced all the way back from the woods. "We're starved, hon. Whatcha got cookin'?" Joe announced as he entered the kitchen. Behind him, the back screen slammed twice, as both sons trundled into the kitchen.

"What did I say about slamming that door?" Kris reprimanded them for the umpteenth time. She knew it was not likely to soak in, but there was always hope. "Oh, I've got us a delicious lunch prepared. How's grilled ham sandwiches, fried potatoes, and macaroni salad sound?" she answered Joe. "You all finish washing up, and we can eat. Mikey, can you set the plates, please? And Joseph, would you please bring the jar of sun tea in off the porch?"

"Yes, Mom," both boys responded as they headed toward the washroom to clean up.

"Those fried taters sure smell good, hon," Joe said, wrapping his strong arm around his wife's waist, planting a kiss on her cheek.

"Don't think that is gonna get you an extra helping, mister." Kris giggled.

Lunch, as always, was a delicious feast prepared by Joe's culinary-blessed wife. As they sat around recounting the morning's activities, Joe spoke up.

"Oh, I don't think I told you. Bob Dvorak is bringing a flatbed tow truck out here tomorrow to haul away that Corvair heap. He wants to try to restore it."

Kris started laughing. "You think it will take him twenty years to finish, like that model-T Ford he finally restored? That thing sat in his big old barn of a garage until I thought his wife was going to crown him over the head." Kris chuckled at the image.

"She was madder than a wet hen over that contraption taking up room," Joe agreed. "I bet the same thing will happen with this old heap of junk. The boys and I looked through the trunk and glove box the other day and found nothing, not even any ID. There were a few bone bits on the floorboard, nothing identifiable though. I pitched them back into the muck."

"Well, I am just glad someone wants to haul that thing off. It saves us a little money from having to dispose of the junker," Kris announced, breathing a sigh of relief.

"Oh, I haven't told you the best part, Bob is giving us five hundred bucks for the thing," Joe added with a grin. "That'll go toward the damn dam rebuilding fund."

"Joe, watch your language in front of the boys!" Kris scolded.

"Not the first time they've heard that, dear," Joe countered. Looking up at his wife's disapproving glare, he quickly added, "You are right, hon. I shouldn't swear at all." He sheepishly dipped his head and scooped up a mouthful of potatoes to avoid any further chastisement.

Mikey had been busily inhaling his food while his parents bantered. Without warning, he unleashed a healthy belch. Quickly he responded with, "Excuse me, I'm a disgusting pig."

"You got that right, you and your father both are being disgusting pigs today!" Kris harrumphed. An unsettled silence descended over the family, as they migrated from the table to begin their respective afternoon chores.

Chapter 24

Reflections at the Pasture Site of Quaking Pond
Twenty Miles Southwest of Sugar Creek
Union Township of Montgomery County, Indiana
June 18, 1963

Gene Bennett sat staring at the glowing colors reflecting off the pond's surface, as the sun sank slowly in the west. He had driven over to his friend Ryan Hunt's farm, knowing he was away with family on vacation. Ironically, Ryan was a doctor, but he would not be saving Gene tonight.

"How have I gotten myself to this point?" Gene mumbled toward the deserted pond. Here he was on the brink of taking his own life, and frankly, he was too chicken-shit to even do that properly. His recently ex-wife, Connie, had berated him regularly, calling him a yellow-bellied asshole. Maybe she was right about the yellow-bellied part at least. He had always been afraid. As a young child, he was terrified of the dark. Even now, he had to sleep with a night-light shining in the hallway.

In school, he was always the last chosen. He perpetually petrified to stand up and be recognized. Shyness was not really his issue, rather a stark fear of everything. He was afraid of girls all through his teens. It was only at the persistence of his mother, seeking out a respectable girl, that he had ever met Connie. His lovemaking was always below par, constantly panic-stricken that he would not do it right. That again, was one of Connie's continual complaints. "You have the passion of a dead fish, you limp noodle."

There was one fear she didn't know about though. He had only married her to ensure that he had a child to get himself out of the draft. Going to Vietnam was his greatest fear. One that consumed nearly all of his waking thoughts. Initially, he had dodged the draft by applying to ministry school.

He was far from religious by nature; however, a 2-D deferment for study in preparation for the ministry kept him out of the service. At least for a year it did until his rotten grades got him kicked out. Man, what a pitiful dope he was. He couldn't even hack Bible studies. He had literally flunked out. His parents could not believe it were possible. How difficult was it to fill in multiple choice answers about biblical facts. He hadn't even been taking theory or philosophy classes, all his first year classes had been basic requirements. His folks knew Gene was not the sharpest crayon in the box; still, his grades in high school had at least been passable. In his college freshman year, he flunked out of English, for God's sake.

He had been home for about a month when his mother's friend introduced him to her niece. He jumped at the chance to change his status with a wife and potential family. The government had been notified of his change of status qualifications for 2-D. They would be sending him recruitment papers in no time. Connie was from a large family with abusive parents. She had desperately wanted to get away from home. They both needed each other for very personal reasons, mutual love and concern for each other not being either of those. After an extremely short courtship, the couple was married. Gene hit the jackpot, getting Connie pregnant a month or two before they got married.

Now he could defer enlistment based on a 3-A status—registrant with a child or children. Life was grand. He was safe from the service. That alone, was worth putting up with the continual complaints and nagging from his new bride. It seemed that nothing made her happy. She found fault in everything he did. How he ate, how he chewed his gum, how he snored at night, how he laughed, how he popped his fingers, how he groomed himself, even how he stood or pointed his finger. It took nothing to set her off on a tirade. None of that mattered to him, though. He was not going to Vietnam. That was what mattered most.

His daddy had been afraid of the service, too. He bought a farm just to prove his intent. He had avoided the service under the hardship on dependents and agricultural occupation deferments. In fact, Gene's fears were probably inherited from his father. That man was afraid of his shadow. His coping mechanism was being the meanest son of a bitch in the county. Gene's old man raged at him and his mother to deflect attention away from his own basic fears. It was no wonder that Gene had ended up the way he was. Funny thing was that his three uncles all served honorably in the service—Army, Navy, and Marines. They loved to sit around family gatherings, telling stories of their adventures in both theaters of World War II. His dad would slink off into another room, embarrassed by his lack of participation, pissed off at himself for being such a coward. Maybe, all of this was his old man's fault. Growing morose and more than a little angry, Gene turned pensive about his marriage.

Gene had found a good job at a local bottle cap manufacturing plant. The work was extremely repetitive and boring, but it was relatively safe. His job was to bulk package printed and stamped bottle caps for shipment to various beverage companies, which used their bottle caps to seal the tops of glass bottles. A steady paycheck had kept him and his new bride well supplied with the necessities of life. His parents had helped him buy a Chevy Corvair for graduation from high school. Thanks to his steady job, he was able to keep up the payments. The couple rented a nice little house in Ladoga, and they were as well-off as others their age. Connie, of course, wanted more; however, she was just gonna have to be content with what Gene could provide.

Even though it was early in her pregnancy, Connie had started buying things for the nursery the first month they were married. Gene hadn't been sure how he was going to afford the baby and all the things Connie would inevitably just have to have. The baby was keeping him out of the service, so he would have to find a way to provide for his family. He simply could not be carted off to the war in Vietnam.

Gene knew several guys who had fled to Canada to escape the draft. Gene would have joined them; for him, though, the fear of the unknown on the other side of the border had been too great. With his luck, the government would have sent agents seeking him. He knew, even now, he would never have survived up in Canada trying to avoid the authorities—a situation that would definitely have been beyond his abilities. None of that had mattered after he had gotten Connie pregnant. In a way, his prayers of freedom from service had been answered. Well, kind of, he still had to put up with her yammering away at him all the time.

It had been so bad that he had dreaded the time he had to spend in the house with her. To avoid home his first few months of marriage, he had stopped by a local dive bar in Ladoga where he had slammed down a few ounces of courage to face the buzzing pest at home. It wasn't long until the smell of beer on his breath and smoke on his clothes became new complaints to be lodged at him.

He just hadn't been able to win with that woman. Her cruelty and complaining had intensified as her pregnancy had progressed. As her stomach had swelled, so too had her level of discontent. Fits of rage had been accompanied by thrown dishware and glasses. Each time as Gene had stooped to clean up the mess, Connie had raged at him for having driven her to behave so badly. Right, as if she had needed any encouragement from him to act like a raving lunatic.

During her pregnancy, rubbing her swollen feet had been the only physical contact he had with Connie. She had refused to have sex with the baby growing inside of her. Adding a barbed insult, she had told him sex wasn't worth the effort with him. Dejected, Gene should have sought a lover on the side. Once again, his insistent fears had kept him chaste despite his burning desires.

Their baby son had finally arrived, amid a lengthy labor, which had been filled with a continuous litany of curses flung at him by Connie. He still remembered his gratitude when the doctors had finally put her out after the birth. He really hadn't thought he could have taken much more; truth be told, the medical staff couldn't have either.

He had been unexpectedly thrilled to have a newborn son. He had become overwhelmed by the parental instinct that kicked in upon his arrival. Up until the birth, he had looked at the expected child as his escape route from service. Tenderly cradling his newborn child, he had gazed into the face of his cooing son, Andrew, and had bonded inseparably with him.

The pride of fatherhood had sadly been short-lived, as the demand from Connie for more and more things immediately intensified. Her desires had had no limits—all of which she had claimed were a necessity for the baby. As justification, she had frequently bellowed, "Why can't you realize that we simply cannot let our son grow up in a house without blah…blah…blah?" Gene had gladly taken on overtime shifts to avoid being around her. He wasn't being drafted, but was his life really worth it? Working long hours to come home to a house plagued with a wicked, greedy wife hardly seemed a happy alternative to fighting in the trenches of Vietnam.

Several of the local boys had been returned to their families in flag-draped coffins. The pain and devastation of loss had been and still was etched on the faces of each and every family member. Compared to this, Gene reflected, his life hadn't been so bad. Having realized the benefits of his situation, Gene had bucked up to face his demon at home. It sure as hell beat the alternative, being shipped off to Vietnam.

One particularly somber moment, Gene had entertained a possible solution: Maybe, he could kill Connie. He could still avoid the service with a dependent child. His dark thoughts had had him almost convinced to start figuring out a way to rid the world of Connie. In the end, he had been too fearful to consider the options. As Gene sat reflecting, he conceded that Connie was right—he was a chicken-shit.

Unhappy, but free from the service, Gene's life had continued in a monotonous routine. His baby boy had grown so quickly and sooner than anticipated begun trundling everywhere. During his terrible twos, Connie and Gene had spent endless hours chasing after the little scoot. He sure could move awfully fast on two tiny legs. In the end, it was that speed that had led Gene to sitting where he was now.

On a warm September afternoon, Connie had ran into the house to answer the ringing phone. She had left little Andy on the porch for just a second. In those brief moments, the little scamp had clambered down the steps, chasing after his rolling multicolored ball. The ball bounced and had come to rest in the middle of the street.

Andy had darted out from between two parked cars, right into the path of an elderly couple, coming home from a visit with their sick mother. They couldn't possibly have stopped in time to avoid crushing the life out of Andy. The poor couple was destroyed for the rest of their lives, having taken the life of a small child. There were not enough drugs or therapy on the planet to alleviate their guilt.

Connie had been beyond grief. In reality, they both were; they had grown extremely attached to their young son. As one might have expected, Connie had blamed Gene for the tragedy. She had claimed that if he had made enough for a nanny, then someone would have been watching Andy. They both had known that was complete fabricated bullshit; yet, it had offered Connie an opportunity to vent her anger onto Gene to mask her own shortcomings. Their marriage had quickly spiraled out of control after the death of Andy. Connie couldn't stand herself, readily taking it out on Gene. Being the chicken-shit that he had been and still was, he hadn't been able to summon the courage to seek professional help for her. Nor had he put forth the effort to sit her down and possibly help her rationally deal with the situation.

Gene had been and remained devastated beyond imagination. His 3-A status was in complete jeopardy. With no kid, he was eligible for the draft once more. His crippling grief at the loss of Andy had been clouded by an overwhelming fear of having to enter the service. It had been years since he and Connie had been intimate. The likelihood of getting her pregnant was zero. Dispirited, he now faced compulsory enlistment with no recourse. His greatest fear loomed on the horizon.

Connie had become a nonissue in his life three months ago. Still in a state of guilt-induced shock from the loss of their son, Connie had filed for divorce from—according to her—that useless, yellow-bellied, chicken-shit, life-support system for a penis. The divorce had become final a week ago. The process had flown through the courts.

With the divorce, Gene now had no remaining deferment options to avoid the draft. Essentially, life was over for him. And that, he knew, was what had brought him to sitting here in his Corvair, staring at the sunset on a hill above this old country pond. He was certain no one would miss him. Most would think he had finally run off to Canada to escape going to Vietnam. Had he not been such a wuss, he might have done just that. Instead, his wimpy ass sat in his car, building up the courage to end it all.

Gazing at the setting sun's reflection, he remembered a quote from high school history class. General George Patton had said, "If we take the generally accepted definition of bravery as a quality which knows no fear, I have never seen a brave man. All men are frightened. The more intelligent they are, the more they are frightened."

I must be pretty damn intelligent, Gene brooded, because he certainly was damn frightened. How was he going to do this? Well, it shouldn't be that difficult. If he shifted the car into neutral, it would roll down the hill and splash right into the pond. The fact that he couldn't swim should bring the end quickly for him. He knew he better do this fast before he lost what little courage he had mustered.

No one would even know he had been here. He had driven up the drive slowly to avoid tracks. By the time Ryan returned from vacation, the growing grass would have covered any trace of his plunge into the pond. He figured the car would float to the bottom of the pond, never to be seen again.

"All right then, best get this over with." Gene depressed the clutch and shifted the car into neutral. He had made sure that nothing was in the car, both trunk and glove box empty. He said a quick prayer, one he had learned in Bible College, then let his foot off the brake. He had left the ignition turned on so he could listen to the radio as he descended to his demise. Bob Dylan's mellow lyrics wafted in the wind, as the Corvair began its gentle roll down the hill.

Gene sat back and rolled the window down to speed the water's rush into the car's interior. He closed his eyes, as the front grill plunged into the pond waters. The downward momentum was just enough to float the car out a few feet from shore. Shortly, the heavy rear-mounted engine pulled the car down backwards. The rear bumper came to rest about ten feet below the pond's surface on the south side of the pond. The rest of the car drifted down with a gentle plunk, coming to rest at an angle on the pond's bottom.

Inside, Gene panicked at the volume of water pouring in around him. It figured, now faced with eminent death, he gained the courage to fight for his life. Perhaps he could drag himself out of the car; his body would naturally float to the surface. He couldn't be that far from shore. The inward rush of water was too hard to paddle against. His attempts to escape served only to shift him further into the interior of the car. He found himself floating with his head just above the water level near the car's roof. He desperately gulped in air from the tiny air pockets, which still bubbled at the crest of the roof. As the water filled the inner cavity of the car, a final air bubble began shifting toward the open window. It moved as one giant undulating bubble, drifting ever closer to the only escape route it had.

Gene floated with the air bubble, trying to suck in as much air as he could. At last, the bubble slipped past the edge of the roof above the open window. In a swift surge, it gurgled out of the car and hurtled toward the surface. The last trace of Gene was a massive air-burp erupting out onto the pond's surface. A few random air bubbles continued to rise from various pockets of trapped air. In the end, Gene found he did have some courage, but it ended up just blowing in the wind as escaped puffs of air.

Fearful Choices

Whenever a man knowingly has sex with a woman against her will—that is rape.

—Tony McNulty

Short of homicide, rape is the ultimate violation of self.

—Byron R. White

Chapter 25

Miller Farm, Resident Home of Quaking Pond
Twenty Miles Southwest of Sugar Creek
Montgomery County, Indiana
June 15, 9:05 A.M., CST

It took a little over a week to finish up the chores that just had to be completed around the farm. Joe and Joseph had gotten all the hay mown. After a few days of drying in the hot summer sun, Joe and Joseph had raked it into tight rows for baling. Baling hay had only taken a couple of days.

Now that haymaking was over for a couple of months, the Millers were gathered around the breakfast table, each of them anxious to know the day's agenda. To their great surprise, the boys were elated to learn they could return to their exploration of the pond bottom for a day or two.

"Really, Daddy! No more chores?" Mikey exclaimed gleefully.

"Oh there will be more chores, little squirt, but not today," Joe assured him. "We can explore this afternoon. Let's see what we turn up. We need to finish up our explorations soon. We have to get this pond dammed back up so it can start filling up with water."

"Awh, Dad!" both boys complained.

"We barely got to dig up anything," Joseph grumbled.

"Yeah, Daddy, I bet there is a whole bunch of treasure buried under that guck," Mikey added.

"You seriously think so, boys? We haven't found any real treasures so far," Joe reminded them. "I don't think there is a whole lot left to discover. Today, we'll take a look at the north end of the pond, see what it holds."

"All right, Dad, at least, we get to look a little longer," Joseph spoke forlornly, holding his head down in a sad puppy dog stance.

"Joseph, you know that look isn't going to change your dad's mind," Kris chimed in. "Your dad is right, we need to get on with rebuilding the dam. Besides, I think you three have played in the mud long enough. I am tired of having to wash your filthy clothes, every night." Kris finished off with an understanding grin on her face, as her head bobbed up and down, giving the trio the obvious sign that the matter was closed for discussion.

"Let's get to it, boys, see what we can dredge out of that old pond while we still can." Joe enthusiastically rallied his boys.

Joe had put off examining the pile of bones in the northwest corner of the pond, as long as, he could. Their lingering presence in the pond demanded an investigation. Of course, facing the northwest corner, the boys immediately saw the bones and wanted to traipse right over there.

"We can work our way over there, boys," Joe suggested. "Let's start here and move that way. When we get to the bones, we will have covered most of the pond." Begrudgingly, the boys began to comb the immediate area, gyrating on a course headed toward the pile of bones.

It wasn't long before Mikey dislodged a claw-hook hammer from its muddy grave. "Look, Daddy, I found a hammer!"

"That's been in there a while, Mikey, but I think we may be able to clean that up and put it to good use." Joe beamed at his youngest son.

"Dad, you are not going to believe it," Joseph shouted. "I found some more of those brass buttons. There are, at least, three of them here!"

"You and the shiny stuff, Joseph, are like magnets to each other." Joe laughed. "You know, it's said that a Taurus, like you, are attracted to shiny things. Guess it must be true."

"Daddy, why is Joe-Joe a terrorist?" Mikey queried with a look of fear on his face.

"Not, terrorist, Mikey. He is a Taurus," Joe informed. "Your brother was born in late April, which is the sign of Taurus the Bull."

"Oh, what am I, Daddy?" Mikey asked quickly.

"You're a ram, Mikey. You were born in early April."

"What's a ram, Daddy?"

"It's a stupid goat," yelled Joseph, laughing.

Mikey gave his brother a pouty glare, as Joe intervened and explained, "The ram is a mighty beast with curved horns. As a ram, you are the first sign of all twelve zodiac signs." Hearing he was first, Mikey turned to Joseph and stuck his tongue out at his older brother.

"Hey, Dad, isn't your birthday the end of June?" Joseph queried.

"Yep, it is Joseph."

"Well, we know what you got for your birthday, at least twice!" Joseph snickered.

Completely red in the face, Joe responded to his eldest son, "Well, aren't you just a little too big for your britches, mister. Guess you're proud of yourself for figuring that out, all by yourself." With a big grin on his face, Joe winked at his bright son.

Mikey fortunately became engrossed by a new find, helping Joe avoid having to explain what Joseph was talking about. "Dad, what is this big ol' thing?" Mikey exclaimed, as he pulled on a muck-covered piece of cloth. As he was inquiring, his grip on the new discovery slipped, and he fell backward in a gooey splash.

"Way to go, mighty ram!" Joseph chortled.

"You all right, little one?" Joe asked as he helped his son dislodge himself from the grip of the slimy muck.

"Yeah, I'm fine, Daddy," Mikey responded, eager to return to his salvage of the material trapped in the mire.

Joe clamped onto the cloth with Mikey, and together they pulled until the huge piece of cloth yanked free with a splatter of mud spray arcing in Joseph's direction.

"Great, get me covered in muck too, why don't ya!" Joseph snapped. "Now we're all going to need a good hosing off." Joseph shook his arms to fling the worst of the mud off then wiped his chin off on his shirt sleeve.

"Your mom is going to have a fit if she sees us before we get washed up boys." Joe laughed. He looked down at the muck-covered, odd-shaped mess he and Mikey had pulled free. Already filthy, he and Mikey rolled the thing out, pulling it apart where the mud had bunched it together. When they were finished, they discovered a trapezoid-shaped cut of cloth about five feet at the bottom, tapered to just two feet or so at the top, both sides about four feet long. It was some kind of woolen material. Brushing some of the caked-on goo off of it, Joe uncovered a curly-tailed poodle design descending along the right side. Instantly, Joe realized what they had found.

"Boys, this is an old poodle skirt!" Joe exclaimed. "The kind of dress they wore back in the fifties. Man, I can't believe this old thing is still recognizable. Wait till your mom sees this, she won't think everything in here is just junk."

"Dad, it's not like you can clean it up and wear it," Joseph said, rolling his eyes.

"I know that, Joseph, but an old-time skirt is, finally, something your mom will find interesting. Unlike the guy things, we have dragged up to the house, so far," Joe retorted. "She will think, this is cool. She may even try to clean it up."

"Doubt that, Daddy," Mikey said. "She'll probably make us throw it back in the pond, saying it's too filthy to mess with."

"Yeah, you're probably right, the both of you," Joe responded. "Let's dig around and see what else we find. This may be our last day here in the pond."

Chapter 26

Dr. Ryan Hunt Farm, Resident Home of Quaking Pond
Twenty Miles Southwest of Sugar Creek
Montgomery County, Indiana
Early Summer Day of 1956

Susan Marie Connors sat, staring at her reflection in Dr. Hunt's waiting space window. The sun had set about an hour earlier. Dr. Hunt performed these special procedures at his home office. It was a nice home. It sat atop a maple-tree-covered hill, probably why, the signpost at the end of his driveway read "Maple Hill Farm." The house was a large two-story design with a long glass-enclosed side porch facing east. The multipaned windows allowed sunlight to flood into the enclosure, bursting with hanging baskets and floor pots filled with all sorts of blooming flowers and plants. Susan would have enjoyed the fragrant display had she not been there for an ominous reason.

Instead, she sat nervously staring at herself in the window glass. She looked forlorn and extremely weary. She had cried all the way as her friend, Mitsy, had driven her out to the doctor's. The skin around her eyes remained puffy and swollen. Mitsy was someone she felt she could trust. She was a freshman in nursing school at Purdue University. Fortunately for Susie, Mitsy had been home for summer break. The minute Susie told her what had happened with Randy, Mitsy suggested the option that she was now pursuing, despite the moral dilemmas associated with it.

Susie was terrified, yet determined, to go through with her decision. She knew her parents would be devastated if they ever found out. Taking the life of an unborn innocent was a sin. Her strict Presbyterian family would condemn her to an eternity in hell for what she was about to do. Their biased views would not sway her from ridding herself of the evil growing inside her. They could judge her, but they would never understand the pain, trauma, and degradation she had endured. She had to have this abomination wrenched from her body. She could barely stand herself knowing it was festering inside of her. She felt filthy and used continually. How could that vile bastard have violated her innocence with such blatant disregard?

Susie sat, waiting like a proper young lady, for Dr. Hunt to return. She had worn her beige poodle skirt and a cream blouse. It was a little dressy, but she felt she needed to be dressed up as if she was going to church. She reasoned, if she were dressed for Sunday church, God might favorably forgive her for what she was doing. She did hope he would forgive her. Either way, she had to get this demon out of her belly.

Her errant thoughts wandered back to the terrifying moment it happened. She could recount every heart-pounding detail with singular clarity. She had been ripped from sleep nearly every night since the violation by gut-wrenching nightmares of chilling horror. She still didn't understand how a boy, who seemed so nice and polite, could turn into such a threatening mauler.

Where is that doctor? He said he would just be a moment preparing the room and some equipment for the procedure. That seemed like hours ago. Frightened and deeply depressed, Susie slunk back into the waiting chair and continued her reverie of exactly what she had told Mitsy and Dr. Hunt.

Susie was sadly aware that the whole mess had started by her own initiation. She had started her story on both occasions by stating that she had herself to blame, she guessed. With that admission, her story started with what she felt was the root cause of her situation.

* * *

You see, I have inherited my mother's ample bosom, so naturally the boys are prone to staring at my chest. Not all sixteen-year-olds are as well developed as I am. But sadly, I have inherited my father's nose and somewhat awkward features. They looked fine on him but have left me a bit on the comely side. Thanks to that and my freakishly large hands to boot, I have suffered rather disappointing potential suitors. Lots of boys are eager to ask out the girl with the big bazombas. Sadly, most of them are just plain ugly, both in looks and personalities.

I had been sweet on Randy Overstreet pretty much since classes began in the fall. Over the summer, he had shot up several inches. The hard labor of summer work on the farm had filled out his muscles quite pleasingly. He still remained shy and a bit awkward, but that seemed to add to his charm. It appeared that he was never going to ask me or any of the girls out, despite our frequent flirting with him.

The annual Sadie Hawkins dance changed dates every year in our school. This year, the role reversal dance, where the girls ask the boys out, was being held in early May. I finally summoned up the courage and asked Randy to accompany me to the dance. It would be the first dance I had ever attended. Up till then, I had turned down the unsightly boys who had had the courage to request my hand at a dance. Randy had turned bright red. Then to my great relief, in a soft voice, had agreed to accompany me. I should have known then he was trouble, when he never looked me in the eye the whole conversation. His vision had been narrowed in on my chest the entire time.

On the night of the dance, I had worn my favorite light-blue poodle skirt with a gorgeous white poodle stitched into the hemline, detailed by a lengthy white leash curling upward in loop-de-loops all along the side nearly up to my waist. Being my first real date, I had wanted to look spectacular. To compliment my skirt, I had dressed in a finely weaved white wool sweater with delicate pearl-shaped buttons. My petite earlobes, thankfully inherited from my mother, had been adorned with small pearl earrings. An ivory clutch that matched my ivory-and-cream loafers had completed my dazzling ensemble.

Randy had pulled up in his dad's 1947 Cadillac convertible. I had hardly believed my eyes as I had peered out the living room curtains. I was going on my first date ever in a convertible. A convertible! Like a true gentleman, Randy had bounded up the porch steps and rung the front doorbell. When my father answered, Randy had politely asked if it were all right with my dad to take his daughter to the dance. Impressed by the young man's manners, my father had readily agreed. Turning, he had given Mom an approving wink about the young suitor on our doorstep. Randy and I had had to endure the usual parental fuss of repeated warnings about being back by my ten o'clock curfew. A final parting admonishment to Randy—no funny stuff young man. My father should have warned him about that, a few weeks later, with a baseball bat in his hand.

The dance had been a typical gymnasium dance—over chaperoned and moderately interesting. Randy and I had danced to a few of the more lively songs. During the entire night, he had ogled my chest, completely mesmerized by my bust; yet, never once, had he made any inappropriate comments. At promptly nine-thirty, he had escorted me to the car, driven me home, and pulled up to the curb outside my house.

His shy demeanor had then taken on a more aggressive approach, as he had made a grab for my breast. At the time, I had easily deflected his advance by pointing out my mother peering through the front door curtains. That had stopped him cold. I had jumped out of the car and hustled onto the porch, clutching my purse.

The next Monday, Randy had run into me in the hallway. He had apologized for his poor behavior when dropping me off the previous Saturday evening.

"I would love to take you to get a milkshake, if you can forgive me, Susie," Randy had intoned. I forgave him. At the time, I had been surprised at what a gentleman he could be, when he chose to be. We had ended up having a pleasant time. We had repeated milkshakes after-school dates before school let out for the summer—the end of May. At that time, I couldn't believe that a third-string football player and member of the wrestling team had been interested in me. I had felt woefully inadequate.

My inadequacy certainly disappeared a few weeks after our last milkshake together. Randy had stopped by my house unannounced. He had surprised me by asking me to go to the drive-in. I had agreed immediately. I had told my parents. Randy and I were going for dinner and a drive. Thus began a series of spoken lies and hidden secrets shared with my parents. Maybe, if I had been more honest with them, none of this would have happened. But it had, and now I had to fix it.

Randy had shown up with the top down on the Cadillac, and off we had gone to the local drive-in. He had left me in the car while he bought popcorn and sodas. A light breeze had been blowing. I had begun to rub my arms to fight off the slight chill in the air. Randy immediately noticed other telltale signs of the chilling breeze, and soon, had become aroused. I had quickly crossed my arms over my chest when I had noticed his persistent stare.

The movie had been about to start. Randy had suggested we put the top up to stay warmer. He had claimed that if we didn't right then, the other patrons would be upset by lifting the roof and blocking the view later. I had agreed. It might be more comfortable with the top up. After having raised the roof, Randy had slithered across the bench seat next to me. He, then, had reached over and had turned the volume on the hanging window speaker up extremely loud.

"Don't you think that is a little loud, Randy?" I had inquired politely.

"Doesn't matter, does it? We're not here to watch this dumb old movie, are we, Susie?" Randy had grinned, slinging his arm over my shoulders. I instinctively had retreated closer toward the passenger door. Randy had then proceeded to clutch my shoulders and pull me closer to him. "Now, where're you going, clear over there?"

"Randy Overstreet, I don't think that shows proper manners at all!" I had declared, shaking at the intensity of his embrace. "I came here to watch a movie with you and nothing else."

"Come on, Susie. I saw you sticking your chest out, all pointy in the breeze!" Randy had accused. "That is a sure sign you are looking to put out tonight!"

I had tried to pull away from his grip. "You have no right to say such things, Randy!"

"You know you want me, Susie. Let's not play games all night. I have to get you home by ten. That only gives us a couple of hours. And I plan on filling them to the max," Randy had spouted off while grinning at me like a starved wolf.

171

Now frightened, I had reached for the car door handle. Randy had instantly grasped my wrist in his tight grip and had pulled me toward him. I had tried to push myself back toward the door. Randy had then launched completely across the seat, pinning me against the passenger door. With his free hand, he had triumphantly punched down the door lock.

Gazing lustfully at my chest, he had growled, "Now, let's see what those puppies look like outside your blouse!" He had kept me pinned against the door with his hips. He had used his left hand to wrench ever tighter on my wrist. With his right hand, he had ripped my blouse open, popping all the buttons off in one fell swoop. Eagerly, he had plunged his chin between my breasts, licking ravenously. His chin had remained at a constant pressure against the tension of my bra while his mouth had worked feverishly on each breast. With a flop, my bra had slipped under my breasts, lifting them plopped out for full viewing. This had served to excite Randy beyond reason. I had then been able to feel his hard manhood pressing against my thigh.

"Nobody can hear you scream, bitch!" Randy had taunted. "You might as well lay back and enjoy this till I'm finished." He had mercilessly continued slobbering on my exposed breasts while fidgeting to pull my skirt down. With his full weight of powerful muscles pressing down on me, there had been no way for me to wiggle free. I had slapped at Randy's face with my free hand, with little effect other than angering him. My pleas for him to stop had gone unheeded. My screams had been deafened by the speaker's blare. His yanking on my skirt had popped the waist button loose. Freed, he had quickly pushed it down my hips. The waistband had been ripped; he had used that slit to shuck my skirt off completely. Tears had been streaming down my face, as I had repeatedly begged Randy to stop.

He had let go of my wrist to fondle my breasts with both hands. Suddenly realizing I now had both hands free, I had clawed at Randy's face. He had reared back, raised his fist in the air, and slapped me hard across the face.

"Do that again, and I am going to kill you, bitch!" he had bellowed. I had known by the crazed glow in his eyes that he meant it. Resigned to my fate, I had leaned back against the door and braced myself for the violation I was about to suffer.

Having freed his throbbing member, Randy had thrust himself deep inside me. The pain had been excruciating, as though my insides were being torn in half. Randy had grunted and repeatedly slammed into me, all the while panting heavily. Spittle had sprayed from his moaning, open mouth all over my tear-streaked face. Fortunately for me, Randy had inherited his father's miniscule stamina, erupting quickly with a heaving sigh. Momentarily satisfied, he had pulled his shriveled self from my swollen, bleeding crotch.

"Damn, that was great!" Randy had crowed. "I had no idea you would put out like that, you slut! Stop your crying. You know you just had the best you'll ever have."

Traumatized, I had doubled over and clutched my midsection, weeping into the floorboard. Randy knew he needed to get me out of the drive-in. He had quickly turned the volume down on the speaker and pitched it out the window. With the lights off, he had pulled forward and crept slowly between the rows of parked patrons.

As we had neared the entrance, I had let out a deep guttural scream. It was a primordial howl I had no idea I could make. Randy had gunned the car and had sped out the entrance, flipping on his lights as he hit the street at a run. He had sped along for a couple of blocks. Seeing no lights, he had violently pulled to a stop along a stretch of road with no houses.

"Get out, you whore! I don't want you stinkin' up my daddy's car with your used up hole!" he had barked at me.

Terrified at what else he might do to me, I had pulled up the door lock, yanked the door open, and fled the car. I had then stood, bleeding. My clothes were ripped and torn, hanging from my bruised and aching body. Randy had menacingly yelled something unintelligible then screeched away, pelting me with a kicked-up spray of road-side gravel. Shaking uncontrollably, I had been frightened beyond imagination. Sobbing, I had staggered home. Silently, I crept into my bedroom through an upstairs window. I had smothered my violent sobbing into my pillow all night long. I had dared not cry out, for fear of waking my parents. If they had found out what had happened, they would have blamed me for having gone to a drive-in movie. I had had no one to share my ghastly experience with. The next day, I had secretly burned my clothes in a burning barrel behind our house. I had watched the flames leap from the barrel, carrying away the evidence of my violation. As I had stood there sobbing, I had prayed that I would find a similar way to purge the horrifying memories from my brain.

I had kept the entire thing hidden from everyone. Being summer break, I hadn't had to see any of my classmates. I had explained the bruises on my face as a nasty fall down the back porch steps. Each night since the attack, I had been and continue to be hurtled from my sleep by nightmares, through which I relive the entire attack over and over.

Barely able to get up each day, I have found it harder and harder to suppress my nervous shakes, which randomly overtake me. The situation exploded a few days ago, when I had skipped my period.

"My God, I am pregnant with that asshole's child! No! No! This can't be happening to me! What have I done Lord to deserve this?" I had pled aloud, all alone, in the upstairs bathroom.

*   *   *

Shaking from the memories of the events leading up to her seeking advice from Mitsy, Susie shivered in her chair as though it were winter. She knew for certain she couldn't have confided in her parents or sought their advice. In desperation, she had gambled that Mitsy, a nursing student, would know what could be done. Terrified and uncertain where else to turn, she sought help from Mitsy. And sure enough, Mitsy had not only listened and known what to do, but had actually acted to help me with her problem. Susie grew less morose as she thought about how Mitsy had held her tightly while she had revealed the details of her attack. For the first time since Randy's cruelties, she felt safe. Having finished recounting the horrid story, she remembered collapsing and sobbing into Mitsy's arms. It had been so good to tell someone, about the horrible violation she had suffered.

A tear slipped down Susie's cheek as she reflected on how grateful she felt when Mitsy had taken her to Dr. Hunt's office in Crawfordsville—where it meant revealing the entire story, once again. Dr. Hunt had had a troubled look on his face as he had nodded his head in empathy. All of that had led her to sitting right here in this chair. Shivering once more, Susie recalled the entire conversation word for word with Dr. Hunt at his office.

He had said, "I think I can help rid you of this problem, Susie. I can perform a procedure at my home office, just south of town. But I must tell you, it is against the law here in Indiana. In medical terms, Susie, we call it an abortion. I would remove the newly formed embryo from you. You will be a little sore, but after some rest, you should be just fine. Now, considering your age, we should have a word with your parents."

"Oh no, Dr. Hunt, they must never know anything about this!" She had blurted while reaching out and grasping hold of his lab coat. She remembered tears coursing down her face as she pleaded with him to help and to keep it all a secret.

Dr. Hunt didn't say it to her, but Susie suspected he had preferred secrecy anyway. What he was doing was clearly beyond the letter of the law. He had been performing the removal of unwanted babies at his home office for years. The women of the community knew where to go.

After a brief pause, he said to her, "All right, Susie, I will keep this between you, me, and Mitsy." Dr. Hunt had gone on to confide in us girls. "You both must promise that you will never breathe a word of what we are doing. We could all go to jail. I won't charge you a fee, given the nature of your pregnancy. I wish there was something I could do to relieve the mental pain you are in, too. I'm afraid time is the only thing that will ease that. Since I am not charging you, I must have your word that you will keep this a secret forever."

"Most certainly, Dr. Hunt, I will keep this secret to my dying day. I don't want anyone knowing about it any more than you do. I had no idea how I was going to pay you," Susie had gushed.

"I will keep it quiet, too, Doctor. I certainly don't want to jeopardize my nursing degree," Mitsy had affirmed.

* * *

Lost deep in her memories, Susie hadn't noticed Dr. Hunt standing beside her.

"Susie!" Dr. Hunt repeated. "Do you hear me? Susie?"

"Oh, sorry, Dr. Hunt," Susie responded after being startled from her musings. She straightened her skirt and wiped the tears from her face.

"I am ready for you now, Susie. Are you ready to begin?"

"Oh yes, please, Doctor. Let's hurry and get this over with." Standing up, Susie followed the doctor down the glass-enclosed corridor to his office. Doctor Hunt didn't comment, but he thought Susie was a tad overdressed.

The procedure was completed in under a half hour. Susie was dressed in her patient gown and resting comfortably with mild discomfort on a cot in the doctor's office. She lie there with her eyes closed, praying for God's forgiveness, while Dr. Hunt went about cleaning his equipment. They were both surprised to see headlights appear in the driveway.

Mitsy must have come back early, Susie reckoned.

Doc Hunt continued staring out the window. He excused himself, stepping out of the office into the porch reception area. Susie heard pounding on the side door of the porch. The melee was intensified by a deep voice booming complaints. Susie was too sore to sit up, so she just listened carefully.

Dr. Hunt opened the door to a puckered wall of a man on the wrong side of forty. Doc recognized Wallace Overstreet, the Exalted Cyclops of the local Ku Klux Klan, choking the doorway with his menacing frame. He pushed his way in against the doctor's protest.

"Ryan, don't you go gettin' all uppity with me!" Overstreet blared. "You think 'cause you is a doctor, you is better than me. I am the Exalted Cyclops of this har region! Now show me some respect." Dr. Hunt acquiesced not because he was a fellow Klan member, but because he rightfully feared the damage a maniac like Overstreet could inflict.

Barreling his way further in, Overstreet turned to the doctor and demanded, "Whar is that whore who is carryin' my boy's child?"

"Now, Wallace, there is no need for such language in my house," Dr. Hunt countered. "You need to control your temper and tell me what you're after."

"You know what I'm after, Ryan!" Overstreet howled. "I watched that floozy scurry off with some whore friend of hers this afternoon. I figured she was sneakin' out here to see you for your special services.

I suspect that no-count slut got herself pregnant. If she is here, then she is tryin' to git rid of it. I ain't about to let that happen. You had better not has done nothin' to my future grandchild, Hunt!"

"Calm down, Wallace. Susie is here." Dr. Hunt soothed.

"Well, whar is she?"

"She is in my office, resting..." Dr. Hunt trailed off, as Overstreet slapped him hard across the face.

"You done plucked my grandbaby out of 'er, ain't ya? Ya snivelin' donkey's ass!" Overstreet exploded. "I'm gonna kill 'er, Doc. No one kills my grandbaby and lives another second. Your sorry ass is gonna help me dump 'er in the pond out back."

He continued after seeing the skeptical look in doc's eyes. "Yeah, I know you got a pond. Not the first time, I've been on this farm. My daddy and me was here back in '26, takin' care of some no-count bootleggers. Their hell-bound bones is already settled in your pond."

Wallace stampeded his way toward the office door, toppling plants and throwing pots as he raged forward. He pounded the office door open with such force that the window shattered as it banged against the wall, scattering shards of glass across the floor. Overstreet crunched broken glass chunks beneath his boots, stomped over to the cot, and yanked Susie up.

Overstreet slapped her across the face, busting her lip and chipping a tooth in her mouth. He cut himself on the chipped tooth, enraging him further. He bellowed right into Susie's face, "You Jezebel bitch! You seduced m' boy, gettin' him all upset. An' now, you done killed my grandbaby! You are gonna hurt for that, you whore."

Overstreet yanked Susie to her feet and swung her around in his powerful grip. Her weak body twirled like a spinning top across the shard-covered floor. Knife-like pieces of glass slashed at her bare feet. Halfway across the office, her feet stumbled over some equipment littering the floor. Susie fell in a jumble amid the broken glass peppered across the linoleum.

Overstreet stormed towards Susie's slumped form. His clodhoppers slipped on the glass bits, tumbling him forward. Overstreet's head slammed down on the pointed knives of broken glass protruding from the bottom of the office door windowpane. A ten-inch sliver penetrated his left temple, pinning him to the door. Blood gushed down the door, as the Exalted Cyclops's limbs quivered. The weight of his body pulled him downward, snapping the glass sliver free. His head smacked the floor, burying the glass shard deep inside his skull, splashing blood droplets everywhere.

Susie sat shivering on the office floor, as Doc Hunt checked for a pulse in Overstreet's limp heap. Finding none, he gathered Susie in his protective arms and rocked her gently in an effort to calm her trauma.

"It was a horrible accident, Susie. You had nothing to do with what happened." He soothed. "Let's get you cleaned up. I'm so sorry you had to endure such a wicked scene."

"Serves that evil bastard right. If only his son had suffered the same slash to his skull!" Susie dripped tears and trembled involuntarily as Doc Hunt cleaned and bandaged her cuts. Susie stared blankly ahead in a silent state of shock until her eyes spied her favorite poodle skirt hanging on a hook behind the shattered door drenched in blood. "Oh my god! My beautiful skirt. What am I going to tell my parents about that?"

To Susie's relief, Doc Hunt had some clothes her size belonging to his nieces kept at the house for when they visited. Reluctantly, Susie agreed it was best to dispose of her treasured skirt. A small penance for her transgression against life.

"Susie, I think it best we keep this accident to ourselves," Doc began. "I will take care of Overstreet's body after you leave."

Mitsy arrived a little after ten, pulling up behind the Chevy pickup she assumed to be Doc Hunt's. Susie scrambled into Mitsy's car with the apprehension of escaping something horrible. On the drive home, Mitsy's inquiry about the procedure were met with silence as Susie shook her head and stared out the passenger window at the sullen darkness of the country roadside. Susie had a scarf over her head, hiding her facial injuries. She lamented over the tragic loss of her favorite poodle skirt. As Susie wearily withdrew from Mitsy's car, Mitsy offered that Susie could relax now and move forward with her life. Susie assured her that she felt the worst was over now.

According to her upbringing, Susie was a murderer now. She would have to find some way to live with that. Tonight, she needed to curl up in her bed and will the nightmares to finally end. The next morning, Susie appeared at the breakfast nook alert and prepared for her parents with a story about slipping in the bathroom and hitting her jaw against the sink as explanation for her bruising and missing tooth.

Randy Overstreet never approached Susie again. When school started in the fall, she learned that he had left town to live with relatives in another county. For Susie, the nightmares gradually receded until they faded to plaguing her only on rare distraught evenings. Doc Hunt had been correct—time slowly eased her anguish.

Doc Hunt's time in the military and his years of composed medical practice helped him rationally approach the unexpected catastrophe of having to dispose of Overstreet's body and hide his Chevy Apache pickup. He had faced much worse in the Pacific during the final days of the war. He decided Wallace's idea of using the pond was a good idea. He had to make sure that no evidence was found. Blood on his office floor was easily explained. A floating dead body was not. He had the necessary surgeon's implements, so he spent the night sawing Wallace's body into small, less recognizable chunks. It was time-consuming, but well worth the effort. By morning's light, he carried several bucket loads of the chunks and Susie's ruined skirt out to a waiting farm tractor and trailer just outside his backdoor. He drove the trailer around the perimeter of the pond, flinging parts randomly into the still waters. Trusting nature and the pond's healthy bale of turtles to render the evidence, Doc Hunt returned to the barn and washed down the trailer and buckets. There were great advantages to living in the country with no one around for miles to witness whatever one might want to keep hidden.

The task of hiding the truck was resolved by removing the license plates and all materials in the cab then burning them. Doc Hunt set the truck ablaze in a nearby field and then towed the charred frame into a side shed on the backside of his barn. As he pulled the barn door shut on it, he also closed the memory of Wallace Overstreet forever.

Wallace was notorious for his violent temper and itch for a rowdy brawl. When he didn't return home the next morning, it was assumed he'd gotten himself beaten up. After hours turned into days, the family feared he'd been the victim of a power grab for his position in the Klan, a frequent enough occurrence in the region. Under which circumstances, it was best to keep one's head down and not make inquiries. The local sheriff, a Klanner himself, knew better than to stir up a hornet's nest searching for the cantankerous old cuss. Overstreet, like many Klanners, had chosen to live by the sword. He ended his days at the end of a glass blade.

Manifest Secrets

For nothing is secret, that shall not be
made manifest; neither anything hid, that
shall not be known and come abroad.

—Luke 8:17, KJV

Exploiter

Someone who uses other people or things for his or
her own profit or advantage

Cambridge Advanced Learner's Dictionary & Thesaurus

Copyright © 2014 Cambridge University Press

Chapter 27

Miller Farm, Resident Home of Quaking Pond
Twenty Miles Southwest of Sugar Creek
Montgomery County, Indiana
June 15, 9:28 a.m., CST

The Miller men left the poodle skirt where it was, splayed out atop the mud. Joe's boys had made it plain that their mom would want nothing to do with the mud-sopped cloth. Joe agreed. Besides, he had a much bigger concern staring him in the face.

With a ghoulish lure, the pile of bones clustered a few feet away beckoned them. The bones were covered in muck like everything else on the pond's bottom. The corrosive pond waters had turned them a milky, yellowish tinge. As the trio came abreast of the pile, Joe could see that it was a nearly intact human skeleton. Joe wasn't sure, if they should even touch the remains before calling the police. It was no telling how old they were. The pond water had surely washed away any discernible markings left on the picked-clean bones.

"Jeez, Dad, is that a real skeleton?" Joseph queried.

"It sure looks that way, Joseph," Joe replied. "I think we need to call the police before we touch it, boys. See that hole in the top of the skull? I'm afraid this body may not have landed here by accident."

"You think somebody was murdered, Daddy?" Mikey exclaimed, anxiously hovering over the pile of bones.

"I'm not sure, Mikey. Step back from those bones. I don't want you breaking any evidence, if it was a murder," Joe commanded, looking at both his sons.

Disappointed, both boys took a step back, and the trio marched their way through the muck to return to the house. As Joe came through the back screen door, followed closely by the freshly hosed-down boys, Kris looked around the kitchen doorway with a spoon in her hand.

"You boys called off the exploration early. What's up?" she asked, concerned by the serious look on all three of their faces.

"We took a look at those bones I told you I had seen on the north end of the pond," Joe replied. "I am going to have to call the sheriff, looks like there is a big hole in the cap of the skull. It may have been foul play."

"Joe, that's some serious stuff, you think it's a murdered body?" Kris was worried.

"Don't know for sure, but it sure looks like someone bludgeoned that skull with something," Joe said as he picked up the phone. "Best call the sheriff in to take a look at it. Just to be on the safe side. If it was a murder, they could have been looking for the body for a long time."

The family sat quietly, staring at Joe as he spoke into the telephone. "Yes, sheriff, we will not touch anything around the body. You say, they'll be out here in an hour or so. Okay, we'll take you out to the pond. They better bring some mud gear. It is mighty messy out there." Joe hung up, and looked up to see three sets of eyeballs glued on him. "Sheriff is sending some detectives out to take a look at the bones. We're not supposed to touch anything out there until they arrive. Looks like our pond exploration may be coming to an end."

The boys let out a collective sigh, both looking crestfallen. They had enjoyed the unusual adventure, digging about in the muck and mire of the pond. "Hey, Dad, we should show Mom the skirt we found," Joseph announced.

"Oh yeah, I forgot about that. We didn't bring it in from the pond. Punkin, we found an old poodle skirt buried in the mud, thought you might want to take a look at it."

"Now, why would I want to look at any filthy, no doubt stinking to high heavens, old strip of cloth? That is just disgusting!" Kris huffed.

"Told you she wouldn't be interested, Daddy." Mikey gloated.

"You were right, little one." Joe smiled at his youngest son. "We'll leave it out in the pond, hon," he responded to Kris.

The Millers deliberated the mystery of the bone pile for the next hour or so until the detectives arrived. The family had imagined their way through a whole series of possible scenarios of how the body had gotten into their pond. None of them guessing even close to the reality.

The detectives had wader boots and rubber gloves to protect themselves against the mud. They were lucky the worst of the stench had dissipated, as they hadn't brought filtering masks with them. The detectives mumbled quietly and then set about marking off sections of the pond with yellow crime scene tape.

After a while, they informed the Millers that the entire pond was now a crime scene. They should not enter until told it was clear to do so. The detectives returned to their vehicle to retrieve a couple of heavy bags, which looked suspiciously like large garbage bags. They carefully placed all the bones and skull into the bags then hefted the filled bags into a plastic tub for transport. The Millers were informed that the remains would be tested in a lab.

The Miller family was assured that they would let them know when they could return to the pond. It was understood that the Millers needed to get the pond repaired but that would have to wait until their investigation was completed. The Millers should expect it to take several days, maybe even weeks. The caved-in skull indicated some sort of blunt force. The detectives suspected foul play was involved. The pair hoped to get some ID on the body through dental records, as most of the other potential evidence had eroded away. They concluded the bones would have to have been a man since the body was over six feet in length and the bones were extremely dense and heavy.

"Well, that puts us in a pickle," Joe complained after the detectives left. "How am I supposed to get the pond fixed if it is tied up in a crime scene investigation?"

"The detectives didn't seem to think it would take that long, Joe." Kris soothed.

"True, but every day is a day longer I'm delayed from plugging this dam back up," Joe grumped. "Well, boys, looks like we can focus on chores around here fulltime." The boys groaned in unison, whining their complaints.

Pond exploration was at a standstill on the Miller farm.

Chapter 28

Vermillion and Vigo Counties
West-Central Indiana
1970s

Ellen Styles was a reliable worker. She had been on the line at the Terre Haute Clabber Girl Bakery for going on three years now, ever since she had graduated from high school. She wasn't the prettiest girl on the block, but her tight-fitting clothes emphasized her fit, toned body. Mousy-blonde hair curled tightly against her round face that was always punctuated by what appeared to be a slanted smile, which resulted from her penchant for mouth breathing. She looked a little like a compact pug with its mouth open. Ellen was even prone to similar panting sounds.

Ellie, Ellen's preferred nickname, was praised by her bosses frequently for her energetic approach to work. Speed was Ellie's primary talent. She exhibited signs of mild ADHD. It was not brought on by chemical imbalance in her system; rather, it had developed from years of avoiding the beatings her drunken father had liberally doled out. She and her siblings were hyperactive, tense you might say, always ready to move. And move she did, Ellie could get more done in an hour than most took days to accomplish. Eager that she was, she couldn't focus or concentrate worth a darn. Her work reviews consistently noted this flaw. Her supervisors complained that she required constant instruction and redirection to keep her active pace headed the right direction.

Growing up, Ellie had not had the luxury of stopping long enough to concentrate on anything. She was the oldest of eight siblings—seven brothers and herself. It was her job to watch them. She had to ensure that they were fed, bathed, and ready for school each day. The pace she sat for herself was breakneck like a hen running around a barnyard, scratching for worms. The reality was, she had taken on too much of an adult role way too early in life. Her momma was sickly most of her childhood. She passed away shortly before Ellie graduated high school. Her daddy had three primary talents: drinking heavily, getting fired frequently from his manual labor jobs, and getting his wife pregnant.

A caustic old cuss, Jerry Styles was crotchety from the day he was born. His abuse of alcohol and tobacco had served to cement a permanent scowl on his face. He groused about everything in a gravelly voice. If Jerry were awake, then he was angrily propped up somewhere, bellyaching about some perceived injustice in his life. Any living being within his swinging range was fair game for a pummeling to satisfy his sadistic need to damage others as much as he felt ruined.

His wife and kids bore the marks of frequent beatings. They lived their lives cowering out of the asshole's sight and reach. He was so mean that once he kicked a pregnant dog down the basement steps, because he thought it was whimpering too much. The miserable beast was starving, having to subsist on a meager helping of table scraps. With a poor family of ten and a regularly unemployed provider, anything that was edible in the house was consumed by the humans first.

Ellie's siblings adored her. She was the only one of the bunch brave enough to stand up to her father. Oh, she got her fair share of beatings but that never deterred her spirit of defiance. She would yell right back at her derelict father, threatening to harm him if he hurt her or any of the family. Despite his merciless beatings, she would brazenly threaten that she would kill him one day. Jerry backed off; he could see by the determination in her eyes, and Ellie meant it. There wasn't much old Jerry Styles was afraid of, but his oldest daughter was one of them.

After graduation, in May 1971, Ellie had struck out to find a job. She was tired of the beatings at home, and even more tired of being—literally—dirt poor. Their family lived in a three-room shack with actual dirt floors. People wouldn't believe her when she said it, but it was true. The brick foundation the house sat on had no flooring. The family had strewn old carpets over the dirt to keep the dust down when it was dry. Every time it rained, the edges of the carpet would get wet, and mud would creep in.

They weren't alone in their poverty; many of the folks living in tiny hamlets along the Wabash River weren't called river rats for nothing. Just about everybody in her wretched hometown lived in dirt floor shacks. The buildings were so small they daren't be called houses. They were shacks, plain and simple. To add insult, each of them had outhouses, leaning sideways out back. Her roost was a cluster of about six shacks scattered around a grain elevator that sat alongside the railroad tracks. A few miles from the Wabash River, the group of shacks was well within the frequent flooding range of the muddy river. Sandbags cost too much money; consequently, water swirling about the foundations and seeping into the houses were a yearly occurrence. Ellie had no intention of staying impoverished. She was willing to do whatever she had to do to climb up out of the bottom of the barrel.

Clabber Girl Bakery was a hiring mecca for the region. They paid decent wages and had good benefits. Ellie had an old beat-up sedan. With the help of her mechanically inclined brothers, they kept it running well enough to carry Ellie the forty-five mile trip to work in Terre Haute and back. Ellie spent most of her earnings on buying necessities for her siblings. Still, she managed to save a little of each paycheck toward her moving out of the dirt floor shack fund.

Due to her comely appearance, Ellie didn't have many dating prospects. Most of the men who approached her were of the same caliber as her father. Her possibilities headed toward a positive new direction with the arrival of a new well-built man hired onto the loading dock. Ellie liked his strong physique, olive skin, and pale gray eyes. Her workstation was the perfect vantage point to allow her frequent glimpses of the bulging muscles of Dale Greene, as he maneuvered loaded carts through the factory. Her location gave Dale a clear view of Ellie's firm butt poured into her work uniform. In between stolen glances, Dale finally asked Ellie out. A short dating romance led to marriage a few months later.

With their combined salaries, the couple could afford an apartment in Terre Haute. Ellie had finally escaped from the dirt floor of her childhood home. Her daddy had injured himself really bad on one of the rare occasions when he was actually working. He ended up on Social Security disability. Although he still drank like a fish, he was unable to stand without assistance. This put his remaining family well outside his range of swinging fists. Her siblings still had to endure his abusive griping, but the steady disability income was greater than any wages he had ever brought home. Overall, life improved for them all. Ellie was relieved that her siblings were relatively well cared for. She could now move forward with building her own life. Her brothers each registered for the army as soon as they were old enough. They knew that would free them of their toxic old man, and better yet, it would give them career skills.

Over the next six years, Ellie and Dale popped out three daughters—Candace (Candy), Constance (Connie) and Christen (Chrissy). In general, life was good for Ellie and the girls. They all had a warm dry place to live. Their wages provided them with most of the necessities. Perhaps it provided too well. There was enough money for Dale to start drinking. It started as an occasional night out with the shift boys on Friday paydays. In no time, it escalated to every night or so. As Dale drank, like her father, Dale became physically and verbally abusive. His rages were mild compared to her father's. Having grown up with it, Ellie was not inclined to relive those nightmares as an adult. Plucky, she began fighting back. Although short, Ellie was a compact powerhouse. Her punches, honed fighting her father and siblings, could inflict serious damage. Dale and she established a détente of sorts.

He would stay out of the house until he sobered up. In turn, Ellie would not clobber him. Their marriage was not joyous, but it was mutually beneficial. They both adored their darling daughters. To Dale's credit, he never laid a hand on his young children. The altercations, initiated by Dale, continued to lead to physical brawls between the adults. Ellie was considering a divorce. Something she had confided only to her brothers. Her only hesitation was that without Dale's income, she would be hard pressed to support the girls.

During one of their more raucous fights, Dale blurted out, "You treat me like the masters used to treat my great-grand mammy down in Mississippi." Ellie stopped fighting and stared at him in incredulous awe.

"Are you saying you are black?" she demanded.

"My great-grandmother was a slave, not that that should matter," Dale replied.

"Why didn't you ever tell me before?"

"I guess I just never thought about it," Dale answered. "I never met her. My momma used to tell me stories about her slaving on a plantation down in Jackson."

The fight ended, both of them retreating to their own thoughts for the rest of the evening.

I am married to a Negro. Ellie sat, mulling the ramifications of that newly revealed fact over in her mind. Her redneck family would go ballistic if they found out she had introduced a darkie to their bloodline. Man, what was she going to do? And to top it off, their marriage was on the skids.

Ellie confided what she had discovered about her husband to her oldest brother, Jeremy.

"That's messed up, sis." Jeremy shook his head in disgust.

"I know, Jeremy, but what am I gonna do?" Connie cried.

"How about me and our brothers scare him off?" Jeremy offered.

"All right, but don't do anything stupid," Ellie warned.

Stupid was what Jeremy and his brothers did best. They had plenty of brawn but scarcely a brain cell between the seven of them. They decided they would hijack Dale after work then drag him up north of their shack. There, they would beat the living crap out of him. They would tell him to get his black ass out of the region or they would break it—permanently. They didn't inform their sister of their intentions; that way, Dale couldn't say she was involved. They adored Ellie and would do anything to protect her.

Their plan went off without a hitch. They snuck up behind Dale as he was getting into his truck. They threw a dark gunnysack over his head and manhandled him into the back of Jeremy's pickup. Several brothers piled into the cab while the rest surrounded Dale in the truck bed. Each time he uttered a protest, one of the brothers would plant a fist in his face still covered by the sack. It wasn't long until blood soaked through the sack. Exhausted from the blows to the face, Dale fell silent and stopped struggling.

The boys drove to a cliff that overhung the Wabash River. They dumped Dale out onto the ground, beating him all over with baseball bats. The whole while, they yelled racially charged slurs at him. They berated him, telling him he wasn't worthy of their big sister. Dale lay motionless after the beatings, barely breathing.

"Get up, you lousy nigger, and get the heck outta here!" Jeremy shouted. Dale didn't move. Jeremy and some of his brothers began kicking him with their steel-toed boots. Dale didn't fight back or protest their assault; in fact, he didn't move at all. Not even his chest was moving. The boys realized he was no longer breathing. Panicked, they checked for a pulse. Sure enough, they had gone too far. Their intended beating to scare Dale had ended his life.

Spring rains had swollen the Wabash River beyond its banks. The boys decided to pitch Dale's lifeless body into the swift-flowing waters. They were certain the raging river would flush him all the way out to the Mississippi—probably down to the Gulf. Ellie needn't ever know what they had done to protect her honor.

When Dale didn't return home that night, Ellie became alarmed. His boss called, asking why he hadn't shown up for work. Deeply concerned now, Ellie called the police to report Dale missing. For weeks, her husband was presumed to have run off.

A little over a month passed when the mystery of Dale's sudden disappearance became clear. His bloated carcass was found floating in an eddy along the Wabash River some twelve miles south of Terre Haute. The sheriff suspected foul play, but Dale's body was so decomposed they could not determine whether the bruising and abrasions had been from his treacherous drifting along the swollen banks of the Wabash or inflicted injuries.

Ellie could not say that she was heartbroken at the disappearance of her Negro husband. She would miss his salary. Suddenly single, she would have to care for their daughters on her own. She didn't know that her brothers had beaten the crap out of Dale Greene. She never imagined that her brother Jeremy would hatch a murderous plot to rid the family of its colored blemish. She wouldn't have told him of her husband's heritage if she had known what Jeremy and her brothers would do.

The brothers panicked when the body was first found but relaxed quickly as its battered condition was dismissed as an accidental drowning. The Styles boys were ecstatic that they had rid the family of an unwanted colored stain, and at the same time brightened the future of their sister with the new prospects of finding a respectable white husband.

Chapter 29

West-Central Indiana
1980s

A new decade started a new chapter in Ellie's life. Her first husband gone under mysterious circumstances. Ellie was now a widowed, single mother of three little girls under the age of six. She, again in her life, had a tremendous burden riding on her ample shoulders. Her energetic, hard-working approach to life was about to get a full-press test. Her late husband hadn't had any life insurance. With nothing to speak of in savings, Ellie faced a serious financial crisis.

She found her and the girls a cheaper place to rent. With the small Social Security pension she received from her dead husband, her salary at Clabber Girl, and some occasional food stamp assistance, Ellie was able to provide for her fledgling family. There was not a thing left over at the end of each month. The girls wore hand-me-down clothes and got new shoes only when the old ones completely wore out.

All in all, Ellie considered her life fortunate. She no longer lived in a drafty old shack with dirt floors. By most standards, she was getting by comfortably. Ellie had no social life outside of conversations at work. She didn't mind, though. She adored her daughters and gladly spent every hour she could with them. Ellie was concerned about what she was going to do when her oldest, Candy, started school in the fall. She wouldn't have a way home from half-day kindergarten classes. She had to find a solution to that dilemma, soon.

The solution came breezing into her life in the spring of 1980. Her coworker, Alice Davis, encouraged her to go out on a date with her cousin, Harland, who had served two tours of duty in Vietnam. Although her cousin was shy and reserved after he returned from the war, Alice was certain Ellie's bubbly personality would bring him out of his shell. Best of all, she knew Ellie was feisty enough to keep him in check during some of his mood swings.

"You know, he gets a little touchy sometimes when he dwells on what all he saw in the swamps over in Nam," Alice whispered to Ellie. "I am sure you and my cousin would hit it off. Besides, you need a father for those young'uns of yours, Ellie!"

"All right Alice, I will at least meet Harland, see if there are any sparks," Ellie conceded. *Can't hurt to meet the man*, she thought to herself. She hadn't had sex in over a year and a half. She was achin' for some shakin'.

Harland Davis turned out to be a big guy, six-foot three-inches tall, and two hundred and thirty-five pounds of muscle, shifting—rather rapidly—to blubber. He was no movie star to stare at, but Ellie recognized, neither was she. He arrived at her house clean and smelling halfway decent. His curly dark hair was slicked back like a biker from the fifties. His dark leather jacket, white t-shirt, and swagger reminded her of a character from a 1950s musical. Ellie kind of liked the thought of a tough guy to match her somewhat aggressive and, according to some, abrasive mannerisms. *All right*, she thought, *I'll give this gumba a chance.*

Ellie had inherited her old man's sex drive. She needed it rough, and she needed it often. After several months of abstinence, she was jonesing for a romp in the hay. She had already fried out two dildos. Harland looked like he could give her a good ride. As it turned out, their passion and proclivities burned equally. Night after night of thunderous sex led to moving in together after only a few short weeks. Harland was well medicated by the VA. There seemed to be little residue of the war plaguing him.

He became maudlin after Christmas, dwelling on all of his fellow platoon members who never made it home. Depressed, Harland refused to take any of his meds, claiming they made him forget too much. As the medicine's effect dwindled, his mood worsened. A side previously suppressed pharmaceutically reared its ugly head. His passion for rough sex, Ellie discovered, was rooted in an underlying streak of violence. In no time at all, the man she had ridden to blissfulness turned into a raging bull whose full destructive force was backed up by his size and stature.

Harland mumbled and grumbled about the house when home from work, taking random swats at Ellie and the girls. To Harland, the swings were harmless little taps. To the recipients of taps from a powerful man like Harland, the taps translated into a bludgeoning. It was fair to say, Harland didn't know his own strength. Unmedicated, he wasn't aware of the damage he inflicted.

The tension grew in the house until Harland's mirrored behavior at work met with a violent confrontation with his boss. Danny Thompson owned the garage where Harland worked. He, like Harland, was a veteran soldier. He had been among the last to leave Vietnam in '75. He could tell Harland was off his meds. He slapped the galoot around for a while, exchanging blows and barbs about the cowardice of dropping his meds. He gave Harland only two options: either let him take Harland to the VA to get his meds or get fired. With blood dripping from his busted lip, Harland reluctantly agreed to go with Danny.

Medicated, peace returned to Harland and Ellie's relationship. Ellie had come from a big family and hoped to have one of her own. She was well on her way with three kids already. The way she and the Harland went at it, like rabbits, she should have been pregnant by now. After months together and still no bun in the oven, Harland decided to get checked out. They both knew, with Ellie already having three daughters, the problem couldn't be with her.

Harland's results came back with a deflating revelation. His exposure to Agent Orange in the war had rendered him sterile. He left the clinic dejected, feeling less than a man. His anger came out when he got home through rants at Ellie and the girls. He immediately stopped his meds again. He saw no point in living if he couldn't father a child. Once more, in less than a year, he was spiraling out of control. The violence and abuse escalated at home and on the job. It took another intervention from Danny to turn him around. This time, his medication potency was increased. The new meds mellowed him into his old self; however, they had the side effect of diminishing his sex drive.

Happy to have a peaceful giant functioning in her house once more, Ellie's joy was dampened by the rapid drop in their lovemaking. She confronted Harland with the accusation that he didn't want any children. Harland had been too embarrassed to tell her of his sterility, believing it made him less of a man. Ellie's misinformed belief was met by Harland's weak response, "It ain't that I don't want children, El. It's these meds messin' with me."

"Well, why didn't you say something? I thought you was tired of me," Ellie huffed.

"Nothin' of the sort, I still loves ya a whole bunch," Harland offered.

The sex stayed erratic and less imaginative between them. Over time, the household caught its energetic routine. Life remained calm for a year or so. Ellie's sex drive never waned. Unfulfilled at home, she started sneaking stolen bouts of passionate trysts from willing coworkers. She reckoned, what Harland didn't know wouldn't hurt him. He seemed content and coping on his medications. Ellie's extracurricular antics kept her libido sated.

The happy-go-lucky façade of her boyfriend masked a dark secret he kept contained in their home. For months, he had been sneaking into Candy's room while Ellie was at work. It started as inappropriate touching and patting of the young girl before she went to bed. As his erotic enjoyment of the contact increased, his desire to fondle the nubile flesh of a young child multiplied. He figured his fondling was harmless enough. He had threatened her to keep quiet, preventing revelation of his actions.

The level of molestation continued to escalate week after week. Candy dared not reveal what her stepfather was doing for fear that he would honor his threats to harm either her mother or her siblings. Fortunately for Candy, her stepfather's diminished sex drive limited the frequency of his visits. Harland understood the limitations of what he could get away with; his perversion never ventured beyond excessive fondling. It was an evil, dark secret that he and Candy carried in silence.

Shortly after Harland and Ellie celebrated their fifth anniversary together, Ellie announced some terrific news. She was pregnant. Ellie was jubilant at the prospect of a fourth child. For Harland, it was a revelation of unimaginable disappointment. The only way Ellie could be with child was her sleeping with someone else. Harland instantly spiraled into a tailspin. Jealousy chewed through his insides like a drain cleaner dislodging a clogged sink. Rather than the joyous celebration Ellie had anticipated, Harland began stampeding through the house, breaking everything he came across.

Horrified, Ellie began screaming at him, "What the hell, are you doing?"

"We both know that's not my baby growing inside you!" Harland exclaimed as he threw another knickknack against the living room wall.

"How can you say that, Harland? That's so cruel!" Ellie cried.

"I can't make children. The war ruined me for life!" Harland shouted, tilting back his head, releasing a monstrous roar.

"You must be wrong, hon. How else, could I be pregnant?" Ellie demanded, weeping into her cupped hands.

"I don't know! Perhaps you can tell me how you got pregnant," Harland said in disgust and stormed out of the house.

After he left, Ellie sat on the living room davenport, sobbing hysterically. Her joyous mood completely devastated. Her girls surrounded her, patting her on the head and shoulders, giving her hugs. Together all four of them cried and cried. Amid sobs, Candy asked her mother, "What's wrong, Mommy? Why are you so upset?"

"I can't tell you precious one, it's a secret," Ellie sniffed a reply.

"Mama, I have a secret. I will tell you mine, if you tell me yours," Candy countered.

"What's your secret, my dear little darling?" Ellie coaxed her daughter.

Candy revealed what Harland had been doing to her. The horrifying exposé by her weeping daughter was overwhelming to Ellie. She was so distraught that she passed out and fell to the floor. She awoke to the frantic pleas of her children to get up, as they gently slapped her cheeks. She pulled herself back onto the sofa and embraced her three daughters in a giant bear hug. Tears streaming down her cheeks, she set her chin in resolve to actions she needed to take next.

She reached for the phone and dialed her brother Jeremy. He would know how to deal with Harland's betrayal. Within a couple of hours, all seven of her brothers had arrived at her house. She explained in detail what had happened, including her own promiscuity.

"What am I going to do now, Jeremy?" she asked her brother.

"Well, this ain't the first time we've helped you out with trouble, big sister," Jeremy replied.

"Yes, it is. I've never asked you for help before," Ellie corrected him.

"You remember Dale's busted-up, bloated body they found?" Jeremy asked.

"Of course, I remember them finding my dead husband in the Wabash River," Ellie responded, rolling her eyes as she exhaled heavily.

"Well, me and the boys are the ones who threw his dead carcass into the river," Jeremy proclaimed with pride.

Ellie gaped at it him with a look of sheer dread. "Are you telling me you killed Dale?" she probed, shaking her head in disbelief.

"I guess we should've told you a long time ago, but we figured you didn't need to know," Jeremy continued, joined by his brothers in a chorus of nodding heads. "Looks like you need us to take care of another situation!"

"I can't ask you to kill Harland!" Ellie screeched, grasping her cheeks in despair.

"Who said anything about asking? We'll just take care of it, like we did with Dale," Jeremy calmly stated his intentions.

"No, you won't! I want to hurt this bastard myself. I can't believe what he has done to my precious little girl. He is going to pay," Ellie ranted in a fit of fury while reaching down to pick up a broken chair leg from the floor. She was patting the heavy, club-shaped foreleg in her palm when in stormed Harland.

"What are all those trucks doing in the drive?" Harland barked. Ellie's brothers circled around the big man, forming a protective barrier between him and their beloved sister. "Oh, I see. You're having an idiot convention in our living room," Harland scoffed as he looked defiantly at Ellie's siblings.

"No, we were having a family discussion on what should be done with a man who would molest an eleven-year-old girl in her own home!" Ellie roared.

"What did you and your bunch of inbreeds come up with?" Harland taunted.

"We decided…we should…beat…the…stuffing…out of you!" Ellie shouted. "And I think, now, is as good a time as any, you disgusting pig of a messed-up waste of human flesh!" The brothers clamped onto each of Harland's arms, simultaneously gripping him around his chest, holding him in place.

"We don't want any bigger mess to clean up in here, brothers. The asshole has already wrecked enough. Let's take this piece of shit outside so he doesn't stink up the place!" Ellie spat in a full-on rage.

As her brothers wrestled Harland out onto the front lawn, Ellie turned to her three little angels, ordering them to their rooms where they were to stay until she came for them. Without argument, the terrified youngsters fled to their rooms as fast as their little legs could carry them.

Outside, the brothers had already begun tenderizing Harland with several well-placed blows to his face and torso. Harland managed to get in a few bone-cracking swings himself before the brothers flung him to the ground and began a fourteen-footed pummeling from all angles to his body. Blood was gushing from Harland's split lips and bashed-up face, as Ellie swaggered into his view.

"Pick that perverted lowlife up and hold 'im on his knees," Ellie demanded.

The brothers hefted Harland's battered body into a kneeling stance. They held him steady, as he wobbled like a fish fresh out of water. Ellie sauntered up to Harland, smacking the chair leg loudly against the flat of her palm. Harland looked up into her face and spat, "You think you can hurt me worse than the Viet Cong did? Not even close." Spent, he let his head flop back down.

"Oh, I am going to do, what they shoulda done. I am going to beat the holy stuffing out of you. No man who molests one of my children deserves to breathe another lungful of air," Ellie ranted. She raised the oak chair leg into a homerun, outta-the-park swinging position. Growing up with seven brothers had given her plenty of experience on how to handle a bat. With her shoulders squared and her body contorted into a perfect stance, she powered through a walloping swing nearly, thwacking Harland's head loose from his neck. The impact site on his skull imploded, leaving a deep indentation of shattered-bone fragments imbedded in mashed brain tissue. Harland's body shuddered. His system released fluid simultaneously from every orifice. It was as though Ellie had struck some macabre jackpot where out flushed bodily fluids in place of winning coins. The gathered siblings reflexively stepped back from the oozing corpse, as an overwhelming stench of coppery blood and expelled excrement wafted over them.

Ellie, in a stupefied state of shock, stood, laughing idiotically. The bloodied chair leg dangled in her arm like a clock pendulum, back and forth. "Guess I put an end to that bad seed, huh, brothers," she chirped. The seven siblings nodded their heads, grunting yips and sentiments of agreement.

Jeremy stepped up to his big sister and informed her, "I got a friend, Bobby, up in Montgomery County that has an old pond out back of the farmhouse he's renting. I've been up there a few times, shootin' the breeze with him. I thinks it might be a good spot to dump this piece of trash. Don't want this body reappearing like the last husband we had to dispose of."

"We need to talk about what you did to Dale. Right now, I guess we need to get this mess cleaned up. We'll talk about Dale, later, okay?" Ellie chastised her brother.

"Tommy and I can dispose of Harland's body," Jeremy volunteered, looking at his brother Tommy. "You and the other boys can clean up this here mess. You sure did swing that bat out of the park, sis. It's a wonder you didn't knock his head clean off," Jeremy crowed.

"Yea, yea!" Ellie barked. "Let's get a move on, and get this show on the road. I have to get the girls tucked in for the night." Pausing to watch her brothers scramble, Ellie whooped, "Looks like I am calling in sick to work tomorrow. My boyfriend has just gone missing." A wide grin spread across her face, as she strode off to tuck in her cherubs. The brothers hosed down the blood and waste in the yard then parked Harland's truck over the spot where he died. They decided that leaving the house torn up would provide a better alibi for Harland's disappearance.

The next day, Ellie reported Harland missing. She informed the officers who responded to her call that Harland had gone on a rampage during the night and then stormed out of the house. He hadn't been back since. The police were not surprised about his not returning. Domestic disturbances often involved a cooling off period. They assured Ellie that he would likely return in a few days.

She knew that was not going to happen. Her nerves were a wreck. What if they saw some blood that hadn't been cleaned up? Or worse, someone discovered the body? Her deep anxiety expressed itself the next morning. Ellie awoke to a pool of blood on her sheets.

"Oh no, no, no, this can't have happened. My baby, my precious little baby is gone!" She screamed, shaking her fist in the air. Hysterical, she beckoned her brothers to her side once again for comfort.

The police followed up a week or so later to discover Harland had not returned. Ellie put on a good show as a frantically concerned woman with no idea where her angry man had fled. She recanted news of her stress-induced miscarriage to the officers, who expressed their sincere apologies for her misfortunes. After a few more weeks passed, the cops concluded that Harland must have run off for good. They advised Ellie to consider moving on with her life.

Another one had bitten the dust, Ellie mused while humming some familiar old tunes that seemed appropriate, given her disappearing lover track record. Neither of them had left her any better off than what she had done for herself. If it weren't for the sex, she would have sworn off men. They seemed more trouble than they were worth. She and Harland had never married, so there would be no death benefits coming her way. Besides, she and her brothers were the only ones who knew that he was dead, not just missing.

Jeremy informed her that he and Tommy had dumped Harland's body without a hitch. They had told his buddy, Bobby, they wanted to do some fishing in the pond. Bobby didn't care as long as they didn't tear up anything. After his former girlfriend's son and his freakish buddies had ignited the old barn behind the house, Bobby was lucky to still be living there. He told them that he was glad the selfish ol' bitch had moved on.

The Styles boys dumped the body while Bobby was at work. They didn't have the good sense to weight the body down. Lucky for the nimrods, Harland's mass settled swiftly. The various pond scavengers made short work of his flesh, leaving only the bones and picked-over bits to liter the pond's bottom. By fall, all traces of Harland were gone.

Ellie had been at Clabber Girl for nearly twenty years, working the production line. She felt it was time for a fresh start with new possibilities. Factory jobs were not plentiful in the region. She didn't want to drive all the way to Indianapolis. Living expenses over there were much higher than they were in the rural areas. She decided to apply at the large regional employer, R.R. Donnelley & Sons. It was a commercial book printing facility about fifty miles from her current house. It would be a bit of a drive, but the wage advantage would offset the expense of driving.

Chapter 30

Parke and Montgomery Counties
West-Central Indiana
1990s

Donnelley's was always in need of reliable production line workers, especially someone with a long track record of favorable reviews. Ellie was hired on the spot. She quickly made daycare arrangements for the girls. Staring at the old heap of metal she had been driving, she decided to buy a more reliable car. She barely qualified for the payment plan on a used late-model Plymouth. The payments themselves were going to stretch her meager budget to its limit. Ellie was confident her new job was going to open better opportunities, so she took the risk. She harbored hopes that her new job would offer her improved dating potential. Perhaps she might find someone who didn't beat her or abuse her children.

After a brief orientation, Ellie was placed on a gathering-machine line at the plant. This involved lifting small bales of lightly bound printed pages then dropping them into a slotted feeding mechanism. The repetitive constant process appealed to Ellie's need to stay active. Her speediness shined in this new job. Her shift supervisor, Rick Chalmers, took quick notice of her determined effort and stamina. She rapidly became one of the fastest and most reliable members of his team. Ellie found it easy to charm Rick with her beguiling smirk.

They engaged in long conversations at their lunch breaks, initiated initially by Rick's impression of Ellie's work. Over the coming weeks, discussions evolved to their personal lives. Ellie discovered that Rick had become a widower a year or so earlier. His marriage had been a disheartening, thirty-five year nightmare. Together, the pair found solace in shared stories of abuse, acknowledging that they were not alone in their mutual suffering. Over the ensuing months, Ellie and Rick found themselves drawn closer to each other. The bond of kindred wounded spirits was just too hard to resist.

Ellie was not the type of woman Rick would have even looked at in the past. She had a tight compact little body with an ample rear end; however, that was the extent of his physical attraction to her. Overall, her features were quite plain. Rick doubted that she cleaned up well. His first wife had been a real looker. Her buxom chest eclipsed the itty-bitty A-cups on Ellie's chest. Despite his reluctance at her looks, Rick continually found himself stealing appreciative glances at Ellie. Their souls seemed to cry out for affection from each other. Rick eventually asked Ellie out to see where things might lead.

Their first date ended in an exhaustive evening of affection-starved passion. The sex was intense, leaving them both spent and drenched in sweat. It was considerably more than either of them had expected. Rick being twenty years Ellie's senior; she assumed he would have the stamina of a worn-out old man. Boy, had she been wrong. Heaving page bales for years had kept the old man in remarkably good shape. They felt well matched. From their first date, their trysts escalated to three or four times a week.

Rick was in the process of residing and weatherproofing his farmhouse in the northeast corner of Parke County. It was nothing fancy, but he owned it and the hundred acres farm outright. Rick knew Ellie rented a cramped little place closer to Terre Haute. Realizing he was falling in love with her, he suggested that Ellie move in with him. Whoa, Ellie had hit the jackpot with this guy. Not only did they share a mutual kindred understanding of each other, they were great in the sack together. To top it all off, he was the richest man she had ever been around. He owned a damn farm. A farm, not just an acre or so, but a whole farm with a warm comfortable house. A situation better than anything she had ever experienced. How could she refuse an offer like that? They both agreed that neither was anxious to marry again, perhaps never. Living together suited them just fine.

Ellie couldn't have been happier. Her daughters were extremely well cared for. Her new lover seemed genuinely kind and gentle by nature. He doted on her daughters, getting along with her family when they visited. Rick was happy too. It thrilled him to have the house filled with laughter and excitement. The gratitude each of the girls expressed made gifting them even more special. His sons were grown; they had been gone from the house for years. They had had a disturbed childhood, putting up with the violent fights between him and their crazed mother. He really didn't fault them for avoiding the farm where unpleasant memories lingered. Rick could now make some pleasant memories with a woman who seemed to love him, almost to the point of worshipping him.

The nightly passion between Ellie and he was so unexpected that he feared the exertion might lead to a heart attack, if he were not careful. His dad's side of the family were prone to bad hearts, having all died before sixty-five. His regular checkups showed a strong healthy heart. His doctor assured him that he had little to worry about, other than a spreading middle-age tummy.

When Rick turned sixty-two, he opted for early retirement. He had worked backbreaking factory work for over forty odd years. It was time to enjoy the fruits of his labors. Ellie certainly could keep working, if she chose. He could save them some money in daycare by watching the girls himself. Sharing the idea with Ellie, he was surprised at her mixed reaction.

"I didn't know I was living with a retiree," Ellie huffed at him.

"I would still be getting a monthly income. My pension would kick in early. We would still be able to afford things like we do now." Rick mewled, completely confused at Ellie's resistance.

"I just don't want to be hangin' with an old man. What does that make me?" Ellie barked in a snit.

"Well, I guess it would make you my cradle-robbed lover, just like you are now," Rick teased with a big smile on his face.

"Oh, silly, I guess you're right. I don't know why I am getting upset. I just don't like the thought of getting older. If you are retiring, it scares me that I am nearing that age," Ellie explained in a more calm approach. "Sorry I got myself all worked up over nothing."

"Hon, you are a long way from retirement. Remember, you're a lot younger than me. Relax, you have many years before you have to worry about being old." Rick soothed.

Grinning at last, Ellie responded, "Thanks, I guess I just needed that reassurance. It would be nice having you home with the girls while I am at work. Can I expect to come home to a warm cooked meal?" She finished with a wink.

"Don't get too smart for your britches, young lady, or I am going to have to give you a spanking," Rick joked.

"Oh, please, Daddy. I've been such a bad girl," Ellie jibed. "'Oops, I better hush in front of the girls."

Their lives together settled into a harmonious routine. Rick enjoyed the time he spent with the girls, watching them grow up in a safe, happy environment. He pointed out to Ellie one day that it might be good for the girls to have some grounding in faith. That way, they could make informed decisions about what they wanted to pursue later in life. Ellie agreed it might be nice to provide the girls with a spiritual base. Even more important to her, it would offer an opportunity for socializing. The minister of the local church was not a fire-and-brimstone preacher. Rick and Ellie came away each Sunday refreshed by the uplifting revelations of Bible passages. In short order, they became respectable church-going members of the community.

There was one thing that sat sideways with the congregation of faith—Rick and Ellie were living in sin. The minister broached the subject with them; he made the suggestion that it would be a better example for the girls if they were married. Neither of them was thrilled about tying the knot again with anyone. The minister's persistence finally convinced them marriage would not dramatically change their current lives. It would, however, calm the nervous gossip of the overtly strict and prejudiced community in which they lived. They reluctantly agreed to a very simple elopement with only Ellie's brothers and her daughters in attendance. Rick didn't tell his sons he was getting married; for him, it was a nonevent.

Married life made an undetectable impact on their lives. Rick and Ellie continued on as before. They discovered the social outlet of the church community livened up their lives. Rick found himself as content as a bug in a rug. Ellie, on the other hand, was suffering intense boredom. She needed more action and excitement. Even sex was getting boring for her. Rick had slowed his pace considerably after retiring. Many a night, he begged off lovemaking entirely. She had heard men's sex drive diminished as they grew older. This was not working for her. She needed a partner who could romp at her preferred reckless pace. She was married now, so she reckoned she was stuck. Or was she? The itty-bitty wheels in her alleged mind began to turn, generating a newly hatched scheme to independent wealth. Being a former widow, Ellie knew that widows inherited their spouse's pensions, Social Security benefits, and possessions. Gleefully, she calculated her windfall of potential inheritance. With Rick out of the picture, she would also be free to pick up a much younger lover. Looked like man number three was gonna have to go. This time though, she needed to keep the body around. She couldn't collect on her winnings if they couldn't confirm that her husband had passed on.

Ellie's miniscule intelligence exhausted itself trying to conceive a plan. Her feeble brain was simply not able to formulate a plan by itself. As usual, she called her brother's soliciting help. For Ellie to claim her widow's share, they had to make the death look accidental while also keeping the body around. Their usual "smash 'em up and pitch 'em into a body of water" routine would never work. Devising a workable plan proved perplexing for the eight siblings. Together, their combined brainpower was comparable to the intelligence of a field mouse.

After hours of slow deliberation, Ellie remembered Rick's family coronary history. She suggested they devise a scheme involving a heart attack. As none of them had any medical knowledge, the planning screeched to a halt almost before it got started. Staring at each other like the idiots they were, Jeremy suddenly slapped his forehead and blurted out, "There's this nurse I know pretty well. I could ask her how to induce a heart attack." Always the resourceful one, Jeremy had proven his worth once more. Excellent plan, they all agreed. They would figure out how to pull it off, after Jeremy came back with the medical know-how.

Jeremy got the family together a few days later and explained, "We will need to inject Rick in his sleep with some drug—something that started out Anrthra, something or other."

"Anthrax?" Tommy cried out.

"No, you git, Tommy. Not anthrax. That's a poison they use in letter bombs," Jeremy derided his younger brother. "Gawd, you're a dumb-ass! Doesn't matter the name. I think I can get that nurse to get me a needle and some of the drug. She likes what I've got to give her," he explained, grabbing and yanking on his crotch with a goofy-grin on his face.

"Oh please, Jeremy. She must be really hard up," Ellie teased her brother. "So you can get what we need?"

"Sure I can!" Jeremy responded with confidence. "That nurse said it would be best to give it to him after some physical exertion to make it look more real."

"You told her what you wanted it for? Yur' dummer 'n dirt!" Ellie yelled at him.

"Nah, nah. It's safe. I told you, she really likes what I give her." Jeremy grinned. "I know how you can exert ol' Rick and then plunge him full of Anthra…somethin' or other," he yawped, winking profusely.

They all agreed there was no time like the present. Jeremy said he could get the drug to Ellie by early next week. They egged Ellie on by saying that she could do the deed on hump day. The brothers got a knee-slapping roar out of that one. Their plan was set. It was relatively simple. Rick has a heart attack, dies, then Ellie gets a farm, a well-maintained house, and money for life. Not a bad turn of events. Afterwards, she could find a willing stud to shack-up with, satisfying her overactive libido.

The next Wednesday, Ellie exhausted Rick in bed. He fell asleep after their prolonged session. Perfect, just what she needed him to do. She had never used a needle before. She struggled for some time before finally figuring out how to withdraw the fluid from the vial. With the needle full, she decided to inject it into Rick's butt cheek; that way, no one would immediately find a puncture mark. She thrust the needle into Rick's buttock like a dart thrown at a dart-board, depressing the plunger in one deft move. Rick bolted up at the stinging bite to his backside. Ellie pitched the needle on the floor and slapped him hard on the butt.

"What the hell?" Rick bellowed, confused. He was anxiously rubbing his burning rear end.

"You didn't think we were done, did you? You had your nap, now it's time for round two," Ellie announced coyly. She sat back on her feet, giving him a seductive curl of her pouty mouth.

Suddenly, Rick clutched his chest, croaking in pain. "My God, I think I'm having a heart attack!" he spat out between waves of muscle spasms.

"Let me call an ambulance, just lay back." Ellie soothed. She dialed an ambulance. She announced to the dispatcher what was happening to her husband, as she sobbed and carried on like a woman in despair. She turned to Rick and wiped his sweating brow. She held Rick, smiling like a Cheshire cat.

This shouldn't take long. I am about to get a farm.

The responding EMTs feverishly struggled to stabilize Rick. He was definitely in the throes of a heart attack. "Does he have any allergies?" they asked.

"None that I'm aware of," Ellie lied.

The paramedics quickly loaded Rick into the ambulance, hurtling away with Ellie and the girls in fast pursuit. At the hospital, joined by her brothers, Ellie delivered an award-winning performance—the distraught wife about to lose her husband. To Ellie's unexpected delight, Rick had an allergic reaction to the blood thinners the paramedics had administered. His entire body began swelling, distended similar to a serious bee sting reaction. Moaning and in excruciating pain, the medical team gave him a sedative to minimize some of his discomfort. The counter agent they used to combat the allergic reaction caused the swelling to intensify with pustules popping up all over his body.

In addition to battling the crippling effect of a cardiac event, the medical team scrambled to flush his system of the allergy-inducing drugs while simultaneously pumping him with life-saving medications to counter the cardiac episode. With his system fighting affronts from all directions, Rick fell into a semi-comatose condition. His body desperately fought to equalize its chemical imbalance. Different medications were tried with minimal effect, other than to require further medicines to counter their damage. Weak and wracked with pain, it was a blessing that Rick remained unconscious. After their arrival, Rick's sons held vigil beside their father's bed. Just outside, the entire Styles clan filled the small waiting room. Ellie wailed like a banshee out in the hallway, nervously rubbing her arms in frantic, excessive movements.

By late afternoon the next day, Rick's condition digressed with no signs of improvement. His damaged heart deteriorated by the hour, soon other organs began failing. Rick never regained consciousness. He slowly worsened until his heart finally gave out. His sons left the hospital crestfallen; they were now orphaned adults. Ellie shrieked dramatically down the hospital corridors, as her brothers physically transported her convulsing body into a waiting car. In the parking lot, she whispered to her brothers on either side of her, "Was that a good show or what?" Jubilant at her perfectly executed display of crippling anguish, she chattered animatedly all the way back home—her home.

Ellie continued her charade of the grief-stricken widow throughout the funeral and burial process. She demurely deferred to her stepsons to handle the arrangements, including the settlement of the estate. Inwardly, the widow leapt for joy at the wave of good fortune about to wash over her. Ellie remained awestruck by the fortuitous series of events that evolved from Rick's simple shot in the butt. His agonizing cardiac episode had effectively negated any suspicions of wrongdoing lodged at her.

Dancing around like a fool, Ellie cleaned the house in preparation for the attorney visiting with her stepsons later that afternoon. She couldn't seem to get a joyful theme song out of her head, humming it subconsciously—only she had altered it to "I'm in the money."

Her animated celebration was abruptly brought to an end, as the attorney explained that without a will, the estate property would be split in thirds, between her and Rick's two sons.

"What!" Ellie blurted. "I don't inherit everything as his wife?"

"Not according to Indiana State law," informed the attorney. "You and Rick's biological children are entitled to share ownership of the estate, but you do not own anything outright by yourself."

"Does that mean I have to move out of the house? Where will my daughters and I live?" she asked in a panic. She had never had the forethought to investigate the state laws of spousal inheritance—a shining example of her dim-witted self.

"By state law, you are entitled to live in the home, but so too are his sons," the lawyer intoned. "Together, you would share ownership of the property."

"You mean I have to let my stepsons and their families move in with me?" Ellie stammered; her face flushed with shock.

"That is entirely up to the three of you to decide. You all have a say in what happens to the property, as the surviving spouse you have a right to remain in the dwelling," the attorney persisted. "Perhaps you should all talk this over. I can counsel you on some of your decisions after you have had some time to think things out."

Thinking was not something Ellie excelled at, as she frequently demonstrated. She was going to have to consult with her brothers. What had Jeremy gotten her into? Damn, she might not even have a place to live. Well, at least the pension and life insurance money would be hers, a sizable sum she speculated.

All the parties separated to discuss their options among themselves. Ellie's moronic brothers were useless at developing a viable solution for her predicament. The entire octuplet of siblings had exhausted their cleverness devising the shot in the butt scenario. Since none of them had any money to pay attorney fees, they were reluctant to present their concerns to a lawyer. With no clue for their next recourse, the group sat staring at each other, occasionally scratching at themselves. Ellie paced like a caged lioness, anxious to bolt toward any proposal that kept her impending fortune within her eager grasp.

Converse to Ellie's circumstance, Rick's sons did have the funds for consultation. They were not about to be tied to that ditz-brained, river-rat whore their father had married. Their discussions with an attorney resulted in several alternatives, each optimizing their severance of any ties to the Styles clan.

They suspected foul play involved in their father's tragic end, especially given his recent doctor's report praising his healthy heart. Something seemed fishy about his death from a heart attack, just weeks later. The boys were informed by their stepmother, and later confirmed by medical staff, that their dad had just finished up a romping sex session with their stepmother right before he had his attack. The thought of the two of them pounding away was nauseating. Repulsed, they hadn't had the stomach to investigate the matter further. They just wanted the whole nightmare to be over.

In the end, the farmland was sold. The combined sale funds of the sons were pooled to exercise their best option at ridding themselves of Ellie and her ilk. After all the estate expenses were accounted for, they bought out their stepmother's interest in the farm, awarding her the house free and clear. When it all finally settled, the boys were ecstatic. They would never have to see that woman or her white-trash family again. Losing their childhood home was a small pittance to gain their complete freedom from the vile woman and her inbred relatives.

Ellie was euphoric over her acquisition of a wonderful home, free and clear. No payment, nothing—it was hers. Having lived a life with few possessions, she was beyond thrilled. She finally had something to call her very own. Her short-lived, fragile joy came abruptly to an end, as it all came crumbling down about her.

Greedily contacting the insurance claims representative, she discovered—to her horror—that Rick had never changed the beneficiary of his life insurance from his sons. She was not entitled to any insurance money. Worse, she knew—given the disdain her stepsons felt toward her—they would not be sharing any of that. She got yet another blow when she found out that Rick's pension plan had never been updated. His first wife was still listed as his spouse. With her dead, the pension simply reverted back to the company fund.

Government stipends proved another devastating punch to her deflating spirit. As the girls were not Rick's, they were not entitled to surviving children's Social Security benefits. At her young age, years away from retirement, Ellie did not qualify for spousal benefits.

No matter where she turned, she could not wrap her claws around any source of cash. Her ill-conceived plan had completely blown apart. Ellie found herself a withering virus casting about for a new host. She had no income, no babysitter, and taxes to pay on her newly acquired house. Figures, she lamented without a trace of remorse, three men down and she was just barely better off than where she had started out in life.

"At least I own this house," Ellie gloated to her brothers gathered around her dining table. She thanked them for helping her out of another jam. And this one, they didn't have to worry about someone finding the body. Rick was legitimately dead.

Chapter 31

Parke and Montgomery Counties
West-Central Indiana
September 8, 10:05 a.m., CST

Ellie and her most recent young stud were startled out of their rhythm by a sharp pounding at the front door. Ellie pulled on a robe and peeked out the bedroom window to see a sheriff's car parked in her drive.

Oh no, what have those idjit brothers of mine done now, she thought as she hurried to the door.

"Mrs. Chalmers?" the sheriff inquired.

"Yes. Is there a problem, sheriff?" Ellie responded. She couldn't believe the sheriff was standing at her front door. This must be some serious shit. "Would you like to come in?" she asked politely.

"Well, yes, we would like to talk with you, Mrs. Chalmers," the sheriff stated as he and his deputy entered the living room.

"Please sit down, gentlemen," Ellie offered. "Now, how on earth can I help you?" Ellie glided into a chair, facing them.

"We have had some developments that we felt we should bring to your attention, ma'am. There have been some discoveries you may find of particular interest, given your relationship to the parties involved," the sheriff explained in a calm steady tone.

"Relationship...to parties? What has happened?" Ellie asked, completely confused.

"If our records are correct, you were involved with a Mr. Harland Overstreet several years back. Is that right?" the sheriff queried, his eyes never leaving Ellie's.

"Well, yes, Harland and I lived together for about six years, back in the eighties. He ran off, and I've never heard from him since." Ellie finished.

"We have found him. We believe we have an explanation for his silence." The sheriff led Ellie along.

"You found him? Where has he been living all these years?" Ellie asked.

"It seems he's been feeding the fishes in a pond up in Montgomery County," the sheriff calmly continued.

"He's what? A fisherman, you say, here in Indiana? What would he fish for, here in Indiana?" Ellie challenged.

"No, ma'am, he's not been a fisherman. He has been feeding the fish in a pond. We found his body a few weeks ago. Seems he had his skull caved in then was dumped into the pond. We were finally able to identify his body through some dental records at the Veterans Administration. Otherwise, we might never have known who he was," the sheriff apprised Ellie, watching for any reaction to the information.

"Oh my, that's terrible!" Ellie exclaimed. *Oh my, good God, they found the body of that asshole. I am in deep crap.* Ellie inwardly screamed.

"You wouldn't know anything about his unfortunate encounter with a blunt object would you, Mrs. Chalmers?" the Sheriff inquired coyly.

"Heavens no! What are you saying, Sheriff? Am I suspected of something?" Ellie blurted in obvious alarm.

"We just wanted to have a chat with you, Mrs. Chalmers. Thought you may know of someone who might have wanted to do Mr. Overstreet harm," the sheriff politely explained.

"I am sure there were plenty of people who disliked that caustic drunk. I can't say I know of anyone in particular." Ellie sighed. Calm returned, as she realized, she was not suspected.

"We can appreciate that, Mrs. Chalmers. We felt it might be a long shot that you would know his potential murderer. I do have to tell you though…" the sheriff deliberately trailed off.

"Yes?" Ellie anxiously quipped.

"It does seem odd," the sheriff built up slowly to what he hoped would be a punch in the gut, "that the men in your life seem to disappear with frequency. If memory serves me correct, your first husband, a Mr. Greene, was found bloated and battered floating in the Wabash River. Then you have Mr. Overstreet here, fertilizing the bottom of a pond. I understand your late husband, Mr. Chalmers, passed away of a heart attack about ten years ago. Just seems a little odd that all these things keep happening to the men you have lived with. You know, just saying."

"What are you saying, Sheriff? Are you saying I had anything to do with their deaths? Isn't it bad enough, I have had such lousy luck with my past lovers? I don't need to have the police harassing me over my misfortune!" Ellie gulped and burst into a fit of tears.

"Please calm down, Mrs. Chalmers. I didn't mean to upset you." The sheriff soothed.

"Well, you did. Coming in here, flinging accusations at me," Ellie snarled.

"Nobody is accusing you of anything, Mrs. Chalmers. We just thought you might like to know what happened to your old boyfriend," the sheriff stated patiently. He stood up, and his deputy jumped up at the same time. "Sorry to have disturbed you, ma'am. My deputy and I will see ourselves out," the sheriff said as he turned toward the door. When his hand clasped on the doorknob, he suddenly whirled around. "Oh, I almost forgot to tell you. Your stepsons have asked us to exhume the body of your deceased husband. They feel an autopsy should have been conducted at his death." The sheriff pulled the door open. "You have a good day, Mrs. Chalmers. Again, sorry to have upset you."

"Sorry to have upset you!" Ellie ranted in mimicked repetition after the sheriff left. "Upset me? That man just ruined my life!" she blurted out in a shower of spittle. "What am I supposed to do now?" she asked, not expecting any answer. Her current lover started to say something. She cut him short with a wave of her hand. "I think it best you go home. I need to be alone." Ellie snipped.

After her lover departed, she sat on the sofa with her face cupped between her hands, sobbing in great shuddering heaves. Ellie turned on the disk player to drown out her melancholy. A distinctive bass voice filled the house with his prison house lyrics. She and Rick had loved his mournful melodies. His folksy music was helping to calm her frayed nerves. Right now, she felt she needed the comfort of a higher power. She yanked a rarely used Bible free from a bookcase. Reading a few of the Lord's passages would surely settle her anxiousness.

She decided to open the Good Book, intending to read the first passage her eyes fell upon. She haltingly traced her finger across the opened page, voicing aloud the words of Jesus, beginning at Luke 8:17. Of all the random passages she could have chosen, God's will brought this one to light.

"For nothing is secret that shall not be made manifest; neither anything hid, that shall not be known and come abroad."

She was doomed! Ellie began to shake uncontrollably, feeling the full weight of her guilt press down on her. As she sat trembling, Ellie bore witness that more than ponds quake in Indiana.

About the Author

The author is a liberal arts educated Hoosier. Formerly a management executive for *The Seattle Times,* he now focuses his energies on writing, teaching English to immigrant adults, and managing personal business enterprises. He enjoys spending time with his family in the greater Seattle area of the Pacific Northwest.

CPSIA information can be obtained at www.ICGtesting.com
Printed in the USA
BVOW05s0520160316

440535BV00007B/189/P